Candy Apple Kisses

OTHER BOOKS BY AMY CLIPSTON

CONTEMPORARY ROMANCE

The Heart of Splendid Lake
The View from Coral Cove
Something Old, Something New
Starstruck
Finding You
With This Ring
Second Chance at Sunshine Inn
Lighthouse at the Cove

THE AMISH LEGACY SERIES

Foundation of Love
Building a Future
Breaking New Ground
The Heart's Shelter

THE AMISH MARKETPLACE SERIES

The Bake Shop
The Farm Stand
The Coffee Corner
The Jam and Jelly Nook

THE AMISH HOMESTEAD SERIES

A Place at Our Table
Room on the Porch Swing
A Seat by the Hearth
A Welcome at Our Door

THE AMISH HEIRLOOM SERIES

The Forgotten Recipe
The Courtship Basket
The Cherished Quilt
The Beloved Hope Chest

THE HEARTS OF THE LANCASTER GRAND HOTEL SERIES

A Hopeful Heart
A Mother's Secret
A Dream of Home
A Simple Prayer

PRAISE FOR AMY CLIPSTON

"There is absolutely nothing I love more than discovering a new-to-me author who writes with emotional depth about compelling characters and charming small towns. Amy Clipston is one of those discoveries, and *The Lighthouse at the Cove* is one of those delightful stories that will draw me back to her books again and again."

—Sherryl Woods, #1 *New York Times* bestselling author of the Sweet Magnolias series

"Clipston (*With This Ring*) sets this charming romance against the idyllic backdrop of Coral Cove, N.C. . . . Clipston builds the chemistry between gruff Cade and chipper, can-do Everleigh through a satisfying mix of flirty exchanges and revealing conversations as the two work to untangle their problems and, with the aid of their faith, find their way to one another. Readers won't be able to resist this."

—*Publishers Weekly* on *Second Chance at Sunshine Inn*

"Amy Clipston's *Second Chance at Sunshine Inn* is like a warm hug on a rainy day. With relatable characters, tender emotions, and a charming seaside setting, this story of two strangers brought together by an unexpected inheritance will tug at your heartstrings. It's a beautiful reminder that love and second chances often appear when you least expect them."

—Rachel Hanna, *USA TODAY* bestseller of *The Inn at Seagrove*

"Amy Clipston masterfully weaves the grumpy-sunshine trope with a setting so charming you'll want to book a stay yourself. Readers will fall for Cade and Everleigh's undeniable chemistry, their emotional journey, and the delightful nod to *Sweet Home Alabama*. *Second Chance at Sunshine Inn* is a feel-good, swoon-worthy story that will leave you smiling long after the last page."

—Heidi McCahan, bestselling author of *Her Alaskan Family*

"Say 'I do' to *With This Ring*, a warm and fuzzy second-chance romance filled with family, forgiveness, and fairy-tale wedding feels. I loved the charming town of Flowering Grove, especially Dakota's bridal shop, and I was cheering for her and Hudson to make their own trip down the aisle from the very first chapter."

—Teri Wilson, *New York Times* and
USA TODAY bestselling author

"Once again, Amy Clipston delivers a heartwarming book about love and second chances. *With This Ring* is like a warm hug and a perfect feel-good read about the beauty of family, friends, and reconnecting with your first love."

—Rachel Magee, author of *It's All Relative*

"Clipston's latest is a sweet read of finding love and family."

—Rachel Hauck, *New York Times*
bestselling author, on *Finding You*

"Amy Clipston delivers swoon-worthy romance while addressing realistic issues of fame and long-distance relationships. Heather is a heroine to root for, and when she meets her opposite in Alex, humor and growth are the result. A thoroughly enjoyable love story."

—Lee Tobin McClain, *New York Times*
bestselling author, on *Starstruck*

"*Starstruck* is a lovely story filled with wonderfully drawn, fully relatable characters and a charming community. Amy Clipston writes with warmth and heart."

—RaeAnne Thayne, *New York Times* bestselling author

"Music, love, and dreams all combine in perfect harmony in this sweet romance."

—Sheila Roberts, *USA TODAY*
bestselling author, on *Starstruck*

"A rockstar and his 'Baker Girl' will warm your heart in this sweet, small-town, slow-burn romance!"

—Jennifer Snow, *USA TODAY*
bestselling author, on *Starstruck*

"Applause for *Starstruck*! Amy Clipston has masterfully crafted an endearing story of hope and taking chances. Readers will be instantly captivated by the charm of Bookish Brownies and Chocolate Chunk Novel cookies! A definite must-read for those looking for a feel-good romance."

—Lacey Baker, *USA TODAY* bestselling
author of *Snow Place Like Home*

"Hometown charm and swoon-worthy second chances make this a must-read."

—Kristen McKanagh, author of *Snowball's Christmas*,
on *Something Old, Something New*

"Amy Clipston writes a sweet and tender romance filled with a beautiful look at how love brings healing to broken hearts. This small-town romance, with an adorable little girl and cat to boot, is a great addition to your TBR list."

—Pepper Basham, author of *Authentically, Izzy*,
on *The View from Coral Cove*

"Grieving and brokenhearted, novelist Maya Reynolds moves to Coral Cove, the place where she felt happiest as a child. An old family secret upends Maya's plan for a fresh start, as does her longing to love and be loved. *The View from Coral Cove* is Amy Clipston at her best—a tender story of hope, healing, and a love that's meant to be."

—Suzanne Woods Fisher, bestselling
author of *On a Summer Tide*

"*The Heart of Splendid Lake* offers a welcome escape in the form of a sympathetic heroine and her struggling lakeside resort. Clipston proficiently explores love and loss, family and friendship in a touching, small-town romance that I devoured in a single day!"

—Denise Hunter, bestselling
author of the Bluebell Inn series

"A touching story of grief, love, and life carrying on, *The Heart of Splendid Lake* engaged my heart from the very first page. Sometimes the feelings we run from lead us to the hope we can't escape, and that's a beautiful thing to see through the eyes of these winning characters. Amy Clipston deftly guides readers on an emotionally satisfying journey that will appeal to fans of Denise Hunter and Becky Wade."

—Bethany Turner, award-winning
author of *Plot Twist*

"Amy Clipston's characters are always so endearing and well-developed."

—Shelley Shepard Gray, *New York Times*
and *USA TODAY* bestselling author

"Clipston's heartfelt writing and engaging characters make her a fan favorite."

—*Library Journal* on *The Cherished Quilt*

THE KAUFFMAN AMISH BAKERY SERIES

A Gift of Grace
A Promise of Hope
A Place of Peace
A Life of Joy
A Season of Love

YOUNG ADULT

Roadside Assistance
Reckless Heart
Destination Unknown
Miles from Nowhere

STORY COLLECTIONS

Amish Sweethearts
Seasons of an Amish Garden
An Amish Singing

STORIES

A Plain and Simple Christmas
Naomi's Gift included in *An Amish Christmas Gift*
A Spoonful of Love included in *An Amish Kitchen*
Love Birds included in *An Amish Market*
Love and Buggy Rides included in *An Amish Harvest*
Summer Storms included in *An Amish Summer*
The Christmas Cat included in *An Amish Christmas Love*
Home Sweet Home included in *An Amish Winter*
A Son for Always included in *An Amish Spring*
A Legacy of Love included in *An Amish Heirloom*
No Place Like Home included in *An Amish Homecoming*
Their True Home included in *An Amish Reunion*
Cookies and Cheer included in *An Amish Christmas Bakery*
Baskets of Sunshine included in *An Amish Picnic*
Evergreen Love included in *An Amish Christmas Wedding*
Bundles of Blessings included in *Amish Midwives*
Building a Dream included in *An Amish Barn Raising*
A Class for Laurel included in *An Amish Schoolroom*
Patchwork Promises included in *An Amish Quilting Bee*
A Perfectly Splendid Christmas included in *On the Way to Christmas*

NONFICTION

The Gift of Love

Candy Apple Kisses

AMY CLIPSTON

THOMAS NELSON
Since 1798

Candy Apple Kisses

Published by Thomas Nelson, 501 Nelson Place, Nashville, TN 37214, USA. Thomas Nelson is a registered trademark of HarperCollins Christian Publishing, Inc.

Thomas Nelson titles may be purchased in bulk for educational, business, fundraising, or sales promotional use. For information, please email SpecialMarkets@ThomasNelson.com.

HarperCollins Publishers, Macken House, 39/40 Mayor Street Upper, Dublin 1, D01 C9W8, Ireland (https://www.harpercollins.com)

ISBN 9781404122413

Library of Congress Cataloging-in-Publication Data

Names: Clipston, Amy author
Title: Candy apple kisses : a sweet romance novel / Amy Clipston.
Description: Nashville, TN : Thomas Nelson, 2026. | Summary: "In a pumpkin spice-drenched best-friends-to-lovers sweet romance, a struggling artist returns to her hometown to save her best friend's orchard. Their fight against a corporate giant ignites an unexpected romance full of heart and small-town charm"—Provided by publisher.
Identifiers: LCCN 2026004226 (print) | LCCN 2026004227 (ebook) | ISBN 9780840716491 paperback | ISBN 9780840716507 epub | ISBN 9780840716514
Subjects: LCGFT: Romance fiction | Novels
Classification: LCC PS3603.L58 C36 2026 (print) | LCC PS3603.L58 (ebook)
LC record available at https://lccn.loc.gov/2026004226
LC ebook record available at https://lccn.loc.gov/2026004227

Printed in the United States of America

26 27 28 29 30 LBC 5 4 3 2 1

For my mother, Lola Goebelbecker, with love, appreciation, and admiration.

You're my partner in crime, my movie buddy, my binge-watching pal, my cheerleader, my company while I write, my rock, and my best friend.

Thank you for all you do for our family.

Chapter 1

JAKE HUGHES COULDN'T stop the smile that overtook his lips as he jogged down the front steps of his parents' two-story farmhouse. A vaguely familiar 1960s pop song—was it The Beatles, or The Monkees?—blasted from the 2002 hunter-green Jeep Wrangler crunching up the gravel driveway.

His best friend since kindergarten, Emily Carmichael, was at the wheel. And he couldn't have been more relieved.

She's finally here! Everything's going to be all right.

The Jeep came to a stop just as Jake's work boots hit the gravel, and Emily jumped out.

"Carmichael!" he called as he pulled her in for a quick hug, lifting her off her feet for a few seconds. "It's about time you got here."

When he set her back on the ground, she gave him a friendly shove. "Whatever," she huffed. "I told you I'd be here by five."

Jake lifted his phone from the back pocket of his worn jeans and gave it a dramatic glance. "And yet it's almost six." He shoved the phone back into his pocket. "You're never on time. You were even late for our high school graduation."

"I was only *fifteen* minutes late to graduation, and you'd expect nothing less from me," she said with a flourish before reaching into the back of the Jeep for her huge black suitcase. At five-foot-four, her slight frame barely reached the back seat.

"I'll get it." He gently moved her to the side. "I don't know why you bought those big tires for this thing when you practically need a step stool to get in and out of it."

She lifted an eyebrow at him. "Uh, because it's cool."

He set the suitcase on the ground with a smirk as his gaze roved over her. Emily was nearly a foot shorter than he was, and she looked the same as he remembered. Her wavy, dark brown hair was styled in a thick ponytail that almost reached the middle of her back. Her well-loved blue jeans sported holes in each knee, and her signature pink Converse high-tops were splattered with a rainbow of dried paint. Her ivory skin was flawless and makeup free, and her eyes, a shade of brown so light they appeared golden, sparkled as she grinned up at him.

He could feel a snappy comment coming, and he relished it. He'd missed the barbs they'd always enjoyed throwing at each other since they were kids.

Standing on her tiptoes, Emily tapped the bill of his ball cap. "Why are you still wearing this ratty ol' Mets cap? I sent you a brand-new one for Christmas. But here you are, sporting the one you've had since high school."

"It's broken in." He adjusted the cap on his head.

"Broken in?" she exclaimed. "You've had it since we were sixteen. I think after almost fourteen years, it's time to retire it."

He shook his head. "Nah. Besides, I save yours for special occasions."

"Sure you do," she chirped with a laugh. "I knew I was wasting my money when I bought you a new one. But I just couldn't help myself." She inhaled a deep breath through her nose and spun around. "I love the smell of the orchard mixed with the lake. It never gets old."

"Which is why you need to come back to Western North Carolina more often, Carmichael. In fact, my mom and dad were heartbroken you didn't join us last year for Thanksgiving and Christmas."

Her ever-present smile wobbled. "Yeah. I know." She pushed her ponytail over her shoulder. "I should've come here instead of spending it with Steve and his family."

He lifted an eyebrow. This was news to him. He thought she and Steve were happy, that Steve might even pop the question. He was the first guy Jake could remember Emily gushing about in their texts and calls. "Trouble in paradise?"

"You could say that."

"You broke up?"

She examined her short, nibbled nails. "Yup."

He took a step closer to her. "When?"

"Um . . . it's been a couple months." She glanced up toward the clear blue sky, as if the answer was hidden there. "Maybe June? Yeah, it was definitely June."

So that was why she hadn't mentioned Steve when they'd texted and she'd dodged his questions about how things were going with him. "It's August, Em. Why didn't you tell me?"

"There she is!" Mom hollered from the porch. "You made it!"

Emily raced up the steps, and Jake followed with her suitcase.

Mom engulfed Emily in a tight hug. "It's been too long! We missed you at the holidays last year, sweetie. You must've been busy. I hope you'll come this year. It's not the same without you."

Emily gave Jake a guilty look, and he responded with an "I told you so" look.

"I'll definitely try." She fiddled with her mother's engagement and wedding ring, which hung from a silver chain around her neck. She hadn't taken them off since her parents had passed away four years ago. "How's Mr. Hughes doing?"

Mom jammed her hands on her hips. "Emily, you're almost thirty. When are you going to start calling us Diane and Leon?" Her expression brightened. "But thanks for asking. He's doing better."

"I'm so glad to hear it." Em shot Jake an accusatory look. "I would've come sooner if Jake had told me about the heart attack."

Jake held up his hands. "It was a crazy time."

"Too crazy to call *me*?" Her brown eyes challenged him.

Jake grimaced. She was right. He should've called her when it happened a month and a half ago, but Dad's heart attack had been such a shock that he'd barely remembered how to tie his shoes. "Sorry."

"Just don't do it again." Emily gave his bicep a playful punch before they followed Mom into the house, where the delicious scent of chili and cornbread drifted over them.

Emily gasped. "Mrs.— Uh, I mean, Diane, it smells fantastic in here."

"I made your favorite." Mom pointed toward the sweeping staircase. "Jake, help Emily get settled and then head down for supper. It's almost ready."

Jake nodded toward the staircase. "You know the way, Carmichael."

Emily gave him a mock salute and then jogged up the stairs to the spare room. Since Emily had sold her parents' house, the room basically belonged to her now. She flopped on the bed as he set the suitcase beside the closet door.

She crossed her legs under herself. "How's your dad—really?"

"Stubborn." He straddled the desk chair backward and rested his elbows on the back of it.

She waved him off. "Besides that."

"Huh?" He rubbed the stubble on his chin and considered the past month and a half. "Well, I guess I have lots to tell you."

"Sounds like we need to go out to the dock and talk after supper."

"Yeah." The muscles in his shoulders began to relax. "That's exactly what I need." He smiled. "I'm so glad you're here."

She laughed. "I could tell from your text that you needed me."

"How long can you stay?"

She shrugged. "As long as you need me."

"What about work?"

She hesitated and began fiddling with her mother's rings again. She was holding something back, and he was going to get it out of her.

"Supper's ready!" Mom called.

Emily popped up from the bed and hurried toward the doorway. "Yay!"

He shook his head. Emily was definitely keeping something from him, and he would get it out of her when the time was right.

The two friends sat across from each other while Jake's parents settled in their usual spots at either end of the oak table.

"So, Emily," Mom began as she passed the cornbread, "what have you been up to lately? Jake tells me you've been working at a coffee shop in Charlotte."

After taking a piece of bread, Emily pasted a bright smile on her face. "Yeah, I was, but being a barista just wasn't for me. I'm sort of between jobs now." She shrugged as if it wasn't a big deal.

Jake set his jaw. *So that's why Em is being so evasive,* he thought. *She's quit another job.*

"Oh." Mom's blonde eyebrows rose. "You quit?" she asked.

Emily nodded while spooning some chili into her mouth. She swallowed and pointed to her bowl. "This is outstanding, Diane. Your chili has always been the best."

"Thank you," Mom said, but Jake could see the concern in her pleasant expression. "Are you still teaching art classes at the community college?" she asked.

"Nope." Emily sipped her glass of sweet tea. "I quit after last semester."

"Mmm." Mom paused for a moment. "What about working at that other painting place? The one where you could have a little party and paint pictures. Oh, what was it called?"

"It was called The Art Spot, and I don't work there anymore either." Emily shook her head.

"So you're . . . not working at all?" Jake chimed in.

"I'm on the hunt for something different. They weren't the right fit." Emily turned to Dad at the end of the table. "How are you feeling, Leon?"

Jake sighed. Emily was deflecting. But he'd get the full story out of her. Somehow.

Dad made a face. "I'm just fine, but Diane is making a fuss as usual."

"You're not 'just fine,'" Mom chided. "You need to get your exercise and continue to eat right."

Dad rolled his eyes. "Blah blah blah," he muttered while sprinkling fat-free shredded cheddar cheese over his bowl of chili.

Emily shot Jake a look, and Jake took a sip of sweet tea to

suppress his laughter while Emily bit her lip to help swallow a giggle.

"How's Ally doing at UNC Chapel Hill?" Emily asked, referring to Jake's younger sister.

Mom beamed. "Great. She had an internship at a law office in Chapel Hill this summer. She's still working there part-time, and she's back in school now."

"Little Ally still wants to be a lawyer, huh?" Emily said. "I can't believe she's almost twenty. I remember rocking her on the porch and feeding her a bottle."

"And I remember her sneaking into my room and taking my stuff. Little stinker," Jake joked.

Mom chuckled. "I can almost still feel the hiccups I had every morning when I was pregnant with her."

Emily's diversion succeeded. She'd found a topic Jake's mother could talk about for ages: her children. They spent the rest of supper reminiscing about Jake and Ally's childhood.

After enjoying a piece of Mom's famous apple pie—which she now prepared sugar-free, much to Dad's chagrin—Jake and Emily cleaned up the kitchen before they headed outside.

"Let's go for a walk," he said, gently tugging her arm and steering her toward the path that led through the orchard.

Above them, the sun was beginning to set, bringing with it a kaleidoscope of vibrant colors while an ensemble of frogs and cicadas began singing the day into the night.

Emily skipped over to a tree and pointed to a small red apple. "Carolina crisp, right?"

"Yeah, but they're not quite ripe yet." He reached over her head and picked the apple before tossing it to her.

She took a bite and then danced around. "Whatever, tastes good to me! I love Carolina crisps!"

He laughed as memories of their childhood rolled through his mind. The summer before they started kindergarten, Emily showed up in the orchard one day and asked him if he wanted to play. And that was the start of their lifelong friendship. They'd grown up here in the orchard. He couldn't think of one single childhood memory without her in it. She'd always been at his side, through skinned knees, heartbreaks, and everything in between.

Emily finished the apple and tossed the core before her eyes lit up. "Race you to the dock!" Then she took off running.

"Hey!" he called, chasing her. "I'll catch you!"

"No, you won't . . ." she sang.

Jake followed her through the rows and rows of trees that had been passed down through his family for a century, defining the Hughes family's legacy from generation to generation.

He caught up to her just as she veered onto the path that led to Splendid Lake. He grabbed her arm. "Gotcha!"

She wriggled out of his grasp, giggling as they approached the lake. They made their way onto the dock, and she worked to catch her breath.

"You're still in much better shape than I am," she managed to say as she dropped down onto the wooden pier and hugged her knees to her chest.

He sat beside her and rested his arms on his bent knees. "Well, I actually *work* for a living while you make drinks."

"Ha ha." She rolled her eyes and turned toward the lake.

"Or you *used* to make drinks," he said. "Why'd you quit?"

She groaned. "Don't start."

The water sparkled in the early evening light while lightning bugs offered their nightly light show. The sound of the waves lapping up against the dock and rocking his small johnboat filled the air.

She pushed a few errant strands of her dark hair away from her face and lifted her gaze toward the sky. "Do you remember the time we went fishing and forgot the rods?"

Emily really was a master at deflecting. He'd give her a pass—for now.

"And the engine ran out of gas, so we had to yell for our dads to help us get back to shore?" He grinned. "Yeah, I remember."

She rested her chin on her knee. "Were we twelve?"

"Maybe." He shrugged.

"How about the time," she began while chuckling, "we snuck out late at night and went swimming and then got caught by Mrs. Monroe? Of course, she *had* to call our parents and spoil our fun."

"Yeah, we got that stern lecture about how dangerous it was to go swimming in the dark. How long were we grounded for that one?"

She scrunched up her nose. "A month?"

"That's right. A month." He snorted and bumped his shoulder against hers. "But it didn't keep us apart."

"Nothing could back then," she whispered as a strange expression flashed over her face, and he was sure she was wading through something in her mind. Her eyes cut to the path that led to the house where she'd lived from age five until her folks had passed away.

His chest clutched at the memory of the day her parents died. It was early summer, and the sky was cloudless and bright blue—such a contrast to the tragedy that changed everything. He'd never forget how she called him with the news. He could barely understand what she was trying to say, but he'd made out the words "my parents" and "plane crash," and the world had stopped. He'd rushed over to her house and held her against his chest while she wailed for what seemed like hours. He had no idea how to comfort her, except to let her know that he was there for her always.

The memorial service had passed in a blur, but she'd needed him at her side the entire time. He'd held her hand, wiped her tears, and kept her upright during the service. For the next couple of months, she couldn't stomach being alone in her family's large, beautiful house on the lake. He'd slept in the guest room, much to his girlfriend's disapproval, but he'd been steadfast. Still, Jake felt useless, never knowing what to say to offer her an ounce of comfort. She just seemed to need his presence.

Then six months after her parents died, Emily suddenly announced she was selling the house and moving a few hours away to Charlotte. He'd been shocked to his core. She couldn't stand living in her family home without them, and the house was full of too many bittersweet memories, she said. So she was finally going to pursue her dream of making art her career.

After she moved, Em had dove headfirst into her new life as an artist, and Jake had gotten so busy with helping his dad run the orchard that their friendship turned to weekly phone calls and random texts. He cherished their visits during the holidays and always looked forward to them, which was why he'd been surprised when she turned down his offer last year.

He gave her the space she seemed to crave, but not having Emily around had left a hole deep inside him. He wanted to give her time to heal after losing her folks, and he didn't want to burden her with his own problems. But being apart from her was . . . tough. She'd been a constant presence in his life for two decades. He longed for her to come home—and stay.

When Emily suddenly cleared her throat, he met her gaze

again. "So what's going on, Jake? Your texts were cryptic. You said you wanted to talk to me in person. Well, I'm here. Now spill it."

He appreciated her forthrightness. He could always count on Em to get right to the point and not be afraid to ask the tough questions. It was easy for her to do when the tough stuff wasn't about *her*.

"You know the McClains' orchard up the street?" He pointed in the direction of the other orchard at Splendid Lake, and she nodded. "They sold out to a corporation called Lancaster Properties. And Lancaster's made it clear that they're going to become our biggest competitor and possibly put us out of business."

She scoffed. "And how on earth would they do that?" She gestured around the lake. "Your family's orchard has been here for decades. No, a whole *century*. Hughes Family Orchard *is* Splendid Lake. No one can take that away."

"Actually, they can. They wanted to buy us out, but my dad told them no way. We're not selling, no matter how much they offer. This orchard is our family's legacy, and no one can take it from us. So instead, they're threatening to lower their prices, and I can't cut ours." He grimaced. "Since my dad's heart attack, I've been trying to talk my dad into allowing me to take the helm here. He's insisting that he can still do it, but I've been trying to convince him I'm ready." He snorted. "I've been ready since I was twenty-five, but you know how stubborn he is."

The corners of Emily's mouth curved up softly. "I sure do."

He shook his head. "Anyway, I've been dealing with my dad's hospital bills, plus Ally's tuition. I have too much riding on this place. I've worked here since I was a kid, and it's all I know. It's my family's livelihood. And now I need to prove to him that I can run this place as well as he has. That's why I need you."

She cocked an eyebrow as she absentmindedly moved her fingers over her mother's rings. "I don't understand how I can help."

"The orchard's hundredth anniversary is the last Saturday in September, and I want to do something big—*really* big." He held his hands up. "This is my chance to prove to my dad that I can run this place, and it's also a chance to show that corporation they haven't won. My family's orchard has always been here, and it always will be here." He pointed to her. "You're the most creative and talented person I know, and I need your help planning it. Will you help me?"

Her face broke into a bright grin. "Of course I will. You and your family are *my* family, the only family I have." She studied him and tilted her head.

He could almost hear her thoughts. "What is it?"

"You were there for me when my parents died." Her voice was soft, almost reverent, and he could barely hear her over the sound of the waves lapping against the pier. "Why didn't you call me when your dad had his heart attack? You know I would've been here as fast as my ol' Jeep could've driven."

His throat thickened, and he swallowed. The memory of the ambulance sirens overtook him, and he could still hear his mother frantically shouting, "Leon! *Leon!*" while his father lay on the floor, holding his chest. Jake sniffed and wiped his eyes.

"Hey . . ." Em shifted closer to him and rubbed his shoulder. "It's okay."

His breath hitched, and he tried to take a steadying inhale before he released it long and slow. "It was awful. My mom was a wreck, and I was trying to hold it together. I had to be strong for her and also for Ally. She rushed home. Thankfully her boyfriend drove her. I didn't want her coming all that way alone." He shook off the painful memories. "I thought about you, and I wanted to call, but it was just a lot. I didn't want you to have to worry about it too."

She nodded, but he was almost certain he saw hurt or possibly disappointment in her eyes.

"So what happened with Steve?"

Laughter burst from Emily's mouth. "Wow, way to change the subject."

He grinned. "Well?"

She moved her hands over her jeans. "It just . . . didn't work out. We wanted different things, and our relationship just ran its course. I've decided that I'm better off alone." She gave him a pointed look. "How's Claire?"

He stretched his neck and blew out a breath. He and Claire Chapman had dated since they were sixteen, and they'd had a lot of fun in high school—when things were easy. They'd managed to keep their relationship going even when she'd gone to college more than five hours away at the beach in Wilmington, North Carolina. But things got complicated after she graduated. Life happened, and they suddenly had different ideas about where their relationship would go, where they'd settle down, what their future would look like. Still, they couldn't seem to let go of each other—or the idea of what their relationship should be.

Emily's dark eyebrows lifted. "Are you off or on right now?"

"That's a good question. I'm actually not sure." He focused across the lake toward the lights glowing at the Splendid Lake Cabins and Marina Resort. "She's been out of town for a while. I think she's coming back soon."

Emily guffawed. "You think? Like, you don't even know when she's coming back? Then maybe you're 'off'"—she made air quotes with her fingers—"right now."

He frowned. They'd been "off" for a while, but neither of them seemed to want to face the truth that they'd outgrown each other. Or maybe she was holding on too hard. At this point, he wasn't sure about anything. "Her company consolidated, so she's been home working remote some, but also going out to Nashville—that's where the main headquarters are. So she's home for a few weeks and then in Nashville for a couple. Back and forth. She's in Nashville now."

"Gotcha." Emily cupped her hand to her mouth to shield a yawn.

"I think it's bedtime." He hopped up and held out his hand. She took it, and he lifted her to her feet.

The orchard was cloaked in darkness, and they used their phone flashlights to guide them past the tremendous trees stretching their thick branches up toward the dark sky. When they reached the path that led to his house, he tapped her arm. "I'll see you tomorrow."

"You sure will." She grinned and started toward his parents' house.

"Hey, Carmichael," he called to her.

She spun toward him, her silhouette backlit by her flashlight.

"Thank you for coming."

"It's my pleasure, Hughes." She bowed with a flourish, and he laughed.

He grinned as she continued toward the house. Emily was finally home again. Maybe, if he played his cards right, he could convince her to stay. Because he needed her. And Splendid Lake wasn't the same without her.

Chapter 2

EMILY STRETCHED AS her eyes flickered open. A beam of sunlight peeked through the slats in the white blinds, and for a moment, she forgot where she was. Then she scanned the room, finding the familiar white dressers and desk, along with the orchard photos that Jake's grandfather had taken in spring, summer, fall, and winter. A panoramic of the lake in spring, which Emily had painted for Jake's parents for Christmas when she was seventeen, hung on the far wall. She hugged her middle while taking in the bright colors in the painting—the greens, blues, and oranges—and recalled how she'd felt while working on the piece. She'd spent months getting the painting perfect for Jake's parents. Back then her muse had been her constant companion, prompting her to draw and paint almost nonstop.

But then her muse disappeared on the day that had changed everything.

Flopping back onto the pillow, she tried to dismiss the familiar grief that bubbled up inside her when she least expected it. This room had become her sanctuary after she'd lost her home and her parents. Her mom and dad had been on their second honeymoon, enjoying their twenty-fifth anniversary in the Caribbean. It was a decision that had destroyed the only life she'd ever known.

She closed her eyes and took a deep, cleansing breath as the events of last night scrolled through her mind. She was back in Splendid Lake with Jake.

Jake.

When she'd received his text three days ago, she was pleasantly surprised but also confused. They'd gotten into a routine of texting each other memes and jokes every couple of days, along with sporadic messages with actual words maybe once or twice a week. Although she craved more meaningful communication with Jake, she'd given up that hope years ago—four years ago, to be exact, when she'd lost her parents. After that, reality had smacked her in the face—her parents were gone, Jake had chosen Claire, and that was that. It was time to grow up and move on—*literally*—which was why she'd sold the house and fled to Charlotte with what few pieces she had left of her heart. Her plan was to start over and try to build a life centered on her art and her dream of falling in love with someone other than Jake, someone who loved her completely. So far neither plan had worked out. And although Jake was in love with someone else, she treasured their friendship.

When she'd gotten Jake's text on Wednesday, the tone was different from their usual "Hey, what's up?" She grabbed her phone from the nightstand and reread their text discussion from a few days ago.

Jake: Yo, Carmichael! Any chance you can come home for a bit? I need your help with something important.

Emily: What's up?

Jake: It's complicated.

Emily: Is your dad okay?

Jake: Yes.

Emily: Your mom and Ally?

Jake: They're fine.

Emily: Are YOU okay?

Jake: Yes! So can you come?

Emily: How soon?

Jake: Yesterday 😊

Emily: What's going on?

Jake: I'll explain when you get here.

Emily: Fine. See you Saturday.

Jake: Great. You're the best.

Emily: You know it.

Jake: 😊

While she was frustrated with Jake's secrecy, she was relieved to have a reason to go home—not that she needed one. But knowing that Jake needed her was comforting and gave her trip a purpose.

Although she treasured Jake and his family, the holiday visits were agonizing for her. She appreciated how Jake's parents treated her like their bonus daughter, but seeing Jake with Claire was painful. She'd accepted years ago that Jake would always pick Claire over her, but seeing them whisper, kiss, and cuddle felt like a stab to her heart, even after thirteen years. She'd done her best to appear nonchalant every time Jake touched Claire, but Emily was convinced Claire enjoyed basking in Jake's attention in front of her. And Emily couldn't blame her. She'd do the same if Jake were hers.

All right, enough of the pity party. Get your rear in gear!

Emily pushed herself out of bed and chose a pair of jean shorts and a T-shirt from the dresser. She'd unpacked before showering and climbing in bed last night.

It felt strange not to put on her khakis, black shirt, and yellow apron before heading to the dreaded coffee shop. She'd given notice the same day that Jake texted, and she tried not to smile as she told her manager that she had to go home due to a family emergency. She'd despised the job. The only fun part was doodling on the cups, and she relished when the customers complimented her artwork.

After styling her hair in a ponytail, she trotted down the stairs toward the savory smells of eggs and toast. Leon sipped coffee and read the paper as he sat in his usual spot at the table.

She reached the kitchen and stopped in the doorway while Jake flipped eggs in a pan and his mom buttered two pieces of toast.

Emily leaned against the doorframe and enjoyed the view for a moment. Jake had always been cute with his blond hair and striking blue eyes, but his easy sense of humor, tender heart, and unwavering loyalty to his family and friends were what won Emily over at a young age. She'd always sort of crushed on him. If she were honest, sometimes in their treehouse, she wondered what it would be like to reach over and kiss him on the lips. She just wanted to see what it felt like.

When he turned sixteen and sprouted up a foot taller than Emily, she began to notice that the way she looked at Jake felt . . . different.

Because all of a sudden he had become hot—*super* hot.

His baby face was gone, and his cheekbones looked as if they'd been chiseled from fine granite. When Emily watched him work in the orchard, she couldn't look away from his white T-shirt, soaked with sweat, clinging to the muscles rippling in his back, the way his biceps seemed to squeeze his sleeves. It didn't take long for his physique to capture the attention of all the girls at school. And it didn't take long for him to start returning their interest.

That's when Emily realized . . . she wanted to be more than just Jake's best friend.

Emily used to wonder: If she had asked Jake to the homecoming dance before Claire did, would she have snagged Jake's heart first? But the past was the past, and there was no escaping it, no matter how much Emily's stubborn heart pined for Jake—and he never noticed.

Still, as she watched him slip the scrambled eggs from the skillet onto a plate, she couldn't help but notice that his shoulders seemed somehow broader than the last time she'd seen him. And her eyes were glued to the thick, ropy muscles wrapped around his forearm as he set the plate on the counter.

Had the air-conditioning stopped working in the large farmhouse? Because boy, was it hot in here!

Jake spun to face her as if he'd heard her thoughts, and she tried to ignore the heat crawling up her neck to her cheeks. He flashed his heart-stopping, boyish grin at her. "Well, look who finally crawled out of bed," he joked. "We thought you'd sleep the day away."

"Ha ha," she retorted before sticking her tongue out at him.

Diane laughed. "You two have always acted like siblings."

It took all of Emily's strength to hold in the sigh building in her stomach.

Jake handed Emily a cup of coffee in a white mug sporting the Hughes Family Orchard logo. "Tons of sugar and more cream than coffee. Just the way you like it."

She took a sip. *Ahhh.* He knew how to make the best cup of coffee. "Perfect."

"I don't know how you drink that. It tastes like coffee-flavored creamer." Jake made a face and added the toast his mom had buttered onto the plate of eggs, along with a few pieces of bacon, before handing her the plate. "Have a seat."

At the far end of the table, Leon flipped through the *Splendid Lake News* while he continued to drink his coffee.

She sank down onto a chair, then took a bite of eggs. "My compliments to the chef."

"Tips are lousy," Jake teased before sitting beside her.

"What's on the agenda for today?"

"Well, I thought we'd—"

Jake's words were cut off by his ringing phone.

Emily tried to peek over at the name on the screen, but he answered it too fast. She assumed it was Claire and tried to shove away her jealousy.

After thirteen years, you should be used to it!

"Hi, Ms. Riley," Jake said with a bright smile. "What's up?" he asked and then he listened.

So it wasn't Claire! Ms. Riley was their retired elementary school teacher who lived down the street. Relieved, Emily took a bite of toast before drinking more coffee.

Diane sat across from Emily. "Jake has been helping Linda since her husband passed away last year."

"That sounds like Jake," Emily said. He had always offered to mow lawns for their elderly neighbors, and she would tag along and help with the trimming and weeding. They always had fun together, whether they were doing yard work for someone else or cutting loose with a swim in the lake.

"Okay, Ms. Riley. I'll see you soon." He disconnected the call and swiped a piece of Emily's bacon. "How about we run some errands and then help Ms. Riley?"

"Sounds like a plan."

* * *

Thirty minutes later, Emily climbed into the passenger side of Jake's black, mid-nineties Dodge pickup. The diesel engine chattered to life, and she smiled at the familiar sound. She'd taken hundreds of rides in the truck since Jake got his license at sixteen.

"It's so cool that you kept your grandpa's truck."

He rested his left arm on the door and drove out of his gravel driveway, steering with his right hand. "Claire thinks it's time to retire it and buy a new one."

"Don't listen to her." Emily waved off the suggestion. "This truck is so fun, and it sounds like a train too."

The truck bounced onto the paved road, and Emily looked out the window toward the orchard, taking in the ancient red barn that Jake's grandfather and possibly great-grandfather had once used to store equipment. It now featured peeling red paint and seemed lonely where it faced the orchard entrance. Emily and Jake had spent hours playing hide-and-seek in that barn back when they were kids. They'd also discovered litters of kittens tucked into a corner of the barn every spring.

She pivoted to face Jake again. "I haven't seen Dusty since I got here. Is she okay?" She always enjoyed seeing the black cat that had adopted the Hughes family a few years ago—and not the other way around!

"Oh yeah. She decided she likes sleeping on my sofa more than prowling around the orchard. You'll have to visit her later." He flipped on the radio. "I guess you want oldies, huh?"

She grinned. "Yes, please."

He found her favorite station, and The Turtles began to sing "Happy Together."

"I love this song!" she exclaimed before singing along at the top of her lungs.

Jake grinned and shook his head before switching on the air-conditioning. While she sang, she took in his profile—that blond scruff lining his jaw and his messy sandy-blond hair sticking out from under that old Mets baseball cap. She noticed the way his dark blue shirt hugged his biceps, and clearly his legs got an impressive workout lifting barrels of apples and heavy equipment in the orchard. Good grief, the man was nothing but muscle!

She shifted in the seat and turned her attention to the road ahead. She had to stop ogling him. He'd friend-zoned her years ago.

Now she just had to remind her heart and her head that they were better off as friends.

The song ended, and Emily turned down the volume as the DJ began talking about the hot and humid mid-August weather.

"Does Ms. Riley call you for help often?"

He slowed to a stop at a red light and rested his right arm on the steering wheel. "I do little jobs for her whenever she needs me."

"What's the job today?"

"Changing a lightbulb."

"Uh-oh," she sang. "Think you can handle it?"

He gave her arm a push and accelerated through the intersection.

"Hey!" She snatched his hat and set it on her head before pulling her long ponytail through the back. She flipped the visor down and checked her reflection. "Looks good on me, huh?"

"That's because it's broken in." While keeping his eyes glued to the road, Jake shoved his free hand through his thick mane. With his hair sticking up at odd angles, he looked somehow younger than twenty-nine and even more adorable.

Ugh! Stop obsessing!

Jake steered into the driveway leading to Ms. Riley's modest brick ranch. A happy scarecrow sat on her porch next to a large pumpkin and a hanging basket full of cheerful orange mums.

After killing the engine, Jake pinned Emily with a look that was supposed to be serious, but his twitching lips and the sparkle in his blue eyes gave him away. "Gimme my hat."

"Nope."

She shifted away from him. He reached for her, and she yelped as he reclaimed the hat and pushed it onto his head.

Emily rolled her eyes. "You have to admit it looks better on me."

"Get your own hat," he quipped, and with his lips curving

into the devastating smile she knew by heart, he climbed out of the truck.

They headed up the front path just as Ms. Riley appeared on the porch.

"Well, would you look at that? Emily Carmichael is back in Splendid Lake. Get over here and let me hug you, dear." The petite lady wrapped her arms around Emily's waist, and the top of her head came to Emily's shoulder. It was funny to think that Ms. Riley had seemed ten feet tall when they were in second grade.

"It's great to see you." Emily basked in the elderly lady's familiar scent of freshly baked cookies and lilac. It astounded her that Ms. Riley also had the same gray pixie cut that she'd had when Emily and Jake sat in her classroom at Splendid Lake Elementary. Had Ms. Riley been born with gray hair, or was she frozen in time?

Jake smirked. "I found Em wandering around the lake and thought I'd invite her to come with me," he teased before pinching the back of her arm.

"Ouch!" Emily swatted him away.

"You two come on in." The octogenarian beckoned them into the house. "I appreciate you always making time for me, Jake." She led them into the kitchen where a platter of chocolate chip cookies sat. The delicious aroma filled the room as if they had just come out of the oven.

And now Emily finally had the answer to one of her near lifelong questions—maybe Ms. Riley *actually* baked cookies every day. No wonder she was their favorite teacher!

"I hope you like chocolate chip." She held up the platter, and Emily and Jake each chose one.

Emily took a bite and closed her eyes while her taste buds danced with the sweet goodness.

"So, light bulbs," Jake began after swallowing a bite. "Which ones blew out?"

"Two in the master bath vanity and another in the hallway." She snapped her fingers. "Oh, and there's at least one out in my craft room. I've been struggling to see while I'm sewing for more than a week now. These old eyes aren't what they used to be." She tapped her tortoiseshell glasses and blinked her dark eyes.

"You should have called me sooner." He jammed his thumb toward the doorway. "Are the bulbs still on the shelf in the garage?"

"That's right. Next to the step stool," Ms. Riley said.

Jake finished his cookie. "I'll be back." Then he sauntered toward the hallway.

Ms. Riley smiled sweetly at Emily. "Let's have some tea with these cookies, shall we?"

A few minutes later, the two women were perched at Ms. Riley's little table, sipping their warm drinks and enjoying the cookies. A ceramic pumpkin surrounded by a few grinning ghosts sat in the middle of the table. It was still August, but Ms. Riley was clearly excited to celebrate fall.

Emily glanced toward the window overlooking the lush green yard and garden filled with colorful flowers and vegetables. Soon the humid days would fade into cool nights, and the leaves would transform into brilliant shades of gold, orange, and brown. Fall was the best part of living in the mountains of Western North Carolina.

"So," Ms. Riley began, "are you finally back for good?"

Emily shook her head. "No, ma'am. Jake asked me to come

home to help him plan a centennial celebration for his family's orchard. I'll probably go back to Charlotte when it's over."

"What have you been doing to keep busy?"

"This and that." She studied her cup of tea. "I was working in a coffee shop, and before that I taught art at the local community college."

"Why did you stop teaching?"

Emily met her elder's surprised expression. "It wasn't what I expected it to be."

"How so?" Ms. Riley studied her.

"I guess I thought it would be more inspiring, but it just seemed so . . . mundane. I felt like I was going through the motions."

"I'm sure your students were impressed with your talent." Ms. Riley smiled. "I clearly remember you glowing when I took your class to the art room. You were nearly bouncing off the walls when you came back to the classroom. You were always drawing something."

Emily chuckled. "I remember that too."

"And I was very impressed with your senior exhibit in high school. I thought for sure that you'd become a professional artist."

Me too. Emily hid her frown by biting into another cookie. She didn't want to discuss her failures.

Ms. Riley shook a finger at Emily. "Now don't you give up so easily. You have talent—*real* talent. Your art teachers always told me that. You shouldn't give up on your dreams, honey. You're still so young. Take it from someone who's made it to eighty and some change." The older woman peered at Emily, a sparkle in her eyes.

Emily moved her finger over the edge of the table. Ms. Riley made it sound so easy. Emily had tried to keep painting—really tried. But her muse seemed to have been destroyed in the crash that took her parents. She just didn't care about making anything beautiful anymore.

She swallowed a bite of cookie past the lump expanding in her throat. "How have you been doing?"

"Oh, me? I'm just fine. I'm happy here in my little house. I keep busy with my garden. I decided to start growing some vegetables this year." Ms. Riley sipped her tea. "I've been enjoying my tomatoes, cucumbers, and green peppers."

"Light bulbs are done," Jake announced, and with his tall height and broad shoulders, he filled the doorway. "When was the last time the batteries were changed in your smoke detectors?"

"Oh dear. I'm not sure."

He smiled. "Thought so." He tapped the doorframe. "I found nine-volt batteries in the garage, so I'll change them real quick."

"You don't need to—" Ms. Riley started.

"I don't mind." He disappeared into the hallway, and his footfalls sounded toward the garage.

"He's such a thoughtful young man," Ms. Riley said.

And hot too . . .

Emily sipped more tea. She needed to get her feelings for Jake under control. She'd thought she was over him, but who was she kidding?

"And so handsome."

Emily's eyes snapped to Ms. Riley's. Had she just heard her second-grade teacher right? Perhaps she had read Emily's mind? Or had she said those words aloud? She opened and then closed her mouth.

Ms. Riley pressed her hand to her chest. "I might be eighty-five, dear, but I'm not dead yet. I recognize a good-looking man when I see one, and I call it as I see it."

Emily burst out laughing, and Ms. Riley joined in.

"You two were always two peas in a pod," Ms. Riley continued. "Joined at the hip in the hallways, on the playground, and in the neighborhood. I thought you'd be married and on your way to starting a family by now."

Only in my dreams. "We're just friends."

"Hmm." Ms. Riley pressed her lips together. "Well, I think you two belong together, but I guess only time will tell."

A shiver raced through Emily at the notion of her dream coming true. *Yeah. Not gonna happen.*

"So, about that garden," Emily began, peeking out the window again. "Tell me what you do with all of those remarkable tomatoes."

Ms. Riley gave her a knowing look before launching into a detailed list of her many tomato recipes.

After several minutes, Jake returned to the kitchen. He disposed of the old batteries and then pointed to the window. "Would you like me to mow the lawn this week?"

"It's sweet of you to offer, but the lawn service comes tomorrow."

"I'd do it for free."

Emily's heart squeezed. Despite knowing Jake for nearly her entire life, she was still blown away by his kindness. She stacked plates and cups from the table and carried them to the counter before setting them in the dishwasher.

"Nonsense." Ms. Riley retrieved a couple of folded bills from her pocket and held them out toward Jake. "Take Emily out for coffee."

He gently pushed her hand back. "Already planned on it."

"Take the money. I insist."

Jake set his jaw, and Emily knew exactly what he was going to do. "Call me if you need me." He swept his arm toward the door. "Ladies first."

"Thank you for the delicious snack," Emily said while she and Ms. Riley walked out to the porch.

Ms. Riley grabbed her arm and peeked behind her shoulder, where Jake was making his way toward them. Then she leaned in conspiratorially. "You hold on to him. He's one of the good ones."

"I don't think—"

"Just trust me, dear. It's going to work out between you two." Behind them, the screen door opened with a squeak, and Ms. Riley patted her cheek. "You two have a good day now." She touched Jake's shoulder. "Thank you, sweetheart."

"Call me anytime."

They climbed into his truck, and Ms. Riley waved as Jake backed out of the driveway.

"You left the money on the counter, didn't you?" Emily asked.

"Of course I did." He steered down the road toward town.

Emily smiled. Jake was definitely one of the good ones.

"What was she whispering to you about when you got to the porch?"

"Oh, nothing." She shrugged. "Just girl stuff."

His blond eyebrows lifted. "What kind of girl stuff?"

"It's a secret. If I tell you, then I'll have to kill you, and I don't want to mess up your cool truck." She ran her hand over the dash.

He snorted and shook his head. "Whatever, Carmichael."

Emily settled back in the seat and tried to ignore how her stomach danced every time she imagined being Jake's girlfriend. She had to let that dream die.

If only she could convince her heart.

Chapter 3

THE DELICIOUS SCENT of coffee drifted over Jake as he pushed open the door to the Coffee Bean and held it open for Emily. The bell above them announced their presence, and the shop was buzzing with activity as customers sat at the tables or in booths enjoying their drinks and pastries. A few others stood in line at the counter, where Ava Burns, an acquaintance from high school, and her younger sister, Brooklyn, took and filled their orders.

Jake had heard that the sisters' dream of establishing this little shop had come true approximately five years ago when their father, a judge in their district, loaned them the money. It had quickly taken off and was known for being one of the most successful coffee shops for miles. A review from the local newspaper was framed and hung in a prominent place on a wall, raving that the Coffee Bean was far above the quality of the chain coffee shops in the area.

Emily waved to Ava behind the counter as she took her place next to Jake in line.

"Are you going to have your usual—lots of cream and sugar with a dash of coffee?" he asked.

"Yup." She adjusted her huge bag, which she called her purse, on her shoulder and glanced around the shop.

"Why don't you find a table, and I'll bring the coffee?" he asked.

"Sure thing." She gave him a mock salute and then hurried over to claim a booth in the far corner.

"Hey, Jake," Ava said when he got to the front of the line. "How are things at the orchard?"

"Fine. The season is about to start." He drew his wallet from his back pocket. "I see you're staying busy. How's Dylan's shop doing?" he asked. Ava's husband, Dylan, had also graduated with them and ran Burns Auto Repair with his father and brother.

"Good. Busy. What can I get ya?"

"I'll take an americano and a regular coffee," he said.

Ava rang him up, and he swiped his card before moving to the end of the counter, where Brooklyn was filling orders. Jake reclined against the wall and peered across the shop to where Emily sat in a booth, hunched over the table with a pen poised in her right hand while she doodled on a napkin. He grinned. Typical Em. Drawing was second nature to her, which was why he never understood why she quit teaching art to sling coffee cups all day long.

"Jake, how's your dad doing?"

He turned as Mrs. Smith, the owner of the Flower Shoppe across the street, moved to stand beside him. "Doing better. Thanks."

"I'm so glad to hear it." She pushed her pink glasses farther up on her long, thin nose. "I heard he had a massive heart attack, and I was thinking of him. That's so stressful."

"Yeah." She could say that again.

"I guess the orchard is getting ready to open, huh?" she asked, and he nodded. "What do you think about the McClain orchard selling out to a big company?"

He frowned. "I'm not sure what to think."

"I've heard that they're planning a big harvest festival–type opening. There's a rumor that they're going to have hayrides and things like that. And they're going to discount everything, from apples to jams."

Jake's stomach twisted. "I heard something like that too." This was why he'd asked Emily to come and help him with the anniversary. He knew he was up against a giant.

"Mrs. Smith?" Brooklyn called, holding up a cup.

The older woman patted Jake's shoulder. "Don't let it get you down. Your family's orchard is a part of what makes Splendid Lake special."

"Thanks." He hoped she was right.

After Brooklyn handed him the two coffees, he added copious amounts of cream and sugar to Emily's drink and then carried the warm cups to the booth, where Emily was still hunched over the napkin. He stood beside her and took in the elaborate doodle of a pickup truck. In typical Emily fashion, the doodle featured impressive details. The pickup truck's grill was nearly identical to his, down to the emblem, and the driver wore a baseball cap featuring the Mets' logo.

She'd drawn on a napkin every day at lunchtime when they were in school. Sometimes she'd draw a few flowers, and on others she'd create an elaborate landscape featuring the lake, the downtown area, or even his orchard. She'd spend nearly their entire lunch period drawing while still participating in conversations, and when she was satisfied that the doodles were complete, she'd pass them over to Jake and say, "For you." He cherished those things. When his pile of her napkin doodles on his dresser turned into a mountain, he'd found a box and kept them—each and every one.

One night a few years ago he caught Claire snooping in his old bedroom and rifling through the box. When she'd demanded to know why he'd kept Emily's "ridiculous drawings," he'd ripped the box out of her hands and told her to mind her own business. She hadn't liked that at all, but Jake stood firm that he'd never go through her personal things and, therefore, she shouldn't invade his privacy. Claire said she couldn't comprehend his "weird friendship" with Emily, but Jake didn't care.

And Claire obviously couldn't see that Emily had talent—*real* talent—and he would never understand why she wasn't putting it to good use.

"Not bad," he quipped, setting her cup on the table.

She gasped and sat back, clutching her chest. "You need to stop sneaking up on me. I'm going to have to put a bell on you."

He chuckled and slid onto the bench across from her. "Some of your best art has been drawn on a napkin."

"Right," she muttered before crumpling the downy paper.

"Hey!" He grabbed the napkin and smoothed it out. "This is too awesome to destroy."

She rolled her eyes, sipped her drink, and smiled. "The perfect coffee."

"If you say so." He tapped the napkin. "I kept every single napkin doodle you made in middle and high school."

Her brow furrowed. "You did not."

"Did too. They're in a box in my old room at my folks' house."

She eyed him with surprise. "You're lying."

"Am not. I'll find them for you." Jake took a draw from his

cup and savored the caffeinated goodness. *Ahhh.* The Coffee Bean served the best coffee in Splendid Lake—possibly even the state of North Carolina.

Emily gestured toward the counter. "What was Mrs. Smith saying to you?"

"She asked about my dad and then she mentioned that the newly revamped orchard has some big plans, like hayrides and all that. She said my family's orchard is a staple around here and to not let it get me down." His lips flattened. "I hope she's right."

"Of course she's right, silly. Hughes Family Orchard is the best." She dropped her pen into her ginormous purse. "I want to see the new one. Take me there."

"Now?"

"Yeah, now." She pushed herself out of the booth. "Let's go."

"Yes, ma'am," he teased. He folded the napkin and slipped it into his pocket as he followed her out into the humid late-summer air.

They hustled along the sidewalk toward his waiting pickup truck, and he took in some of the welcoming signs on that side of the street. The Christmas Shop was open year-round. The Warner, Splendid Lake's single-screen movie theater, stood next to Morningside Bakery, and the Flower Shoppe was next to Scoops, the local ice cream parlor. Each was owned and operated by local residents.

Glancing to the north, he spotted the town hall, library, fire station, and police station rimming the town square. He breathed in the lake and its familiar smell mixed with the delicious aromas coming from the town's longtime family restaurant, the Splendid Kitchen, and all the shops that served treats and beverages.

He loved his little town. It was home—and also why he couldn't imagine moving to Nashville with Claire. The familiar pit opened in his stomach when he considered his longtime girlfriend. They were at a strange fork in the road, but he couldn't think about that today. He was with Emily, and they were focused on the orchard—his family's livelihood and legacy.

"You okay?" Emily gave him a concerned look as they climbed into his truck.

He adjusted his cap and set his mirrored sunglasses on his nose. "Yup." He drove the short distance to the former site of McClains' Orchard and parked in the lot near the entrance. A brand-new sign declared the orchard was renamed "Apple Haven—Splendid Lake's Premier Orchard."

Emily bounced out of the truck and made a beeline toward the entrance. She peeked through the gate and took in the signs. Biting her lip, she moved her fingers over her mother's rings while she studied everything.

He came up behind her and read over her shoulder. The Coming Soon sign promised a "fabulous fall festival fun for all ages coming in September" with hayrides, a pumpkin patch, and "the most delicious apples in North Carolina," as well as "loads of activities for kids" at discount prices.

How could Jake's family's traditional orchard compete with that when they were dealing with his father's hospital bills and Ally's steep tuition?

Great. Just great.

His head started to throb.

"Quit frowning," she ordered, grabbing his hand and yanking him toward the truck. "Let's go. We have work to do."

Back in the truck, Emily grabbed a spiral notebook from her giant bag and began writing furiously.

"What are you doing?" he asked.

"Thinking," she quipped. "Just drive."

"Okay . . ." He exited the parking lot, and when they hit the road, his stomach growled. "You hungry?"

"Sure," she responded without peering up from her growing list.

"Let's pick up food and go to my place," he said before heading back toward downtown for takeout.

* * *

Emily looked up from her doodles and list just as Jake parked in front of his one-story ranch-style house. She recalled when he'd moved into the house nearly eight years ago when he'd decided it was time for him to grow up, move out of his folks' house, and get his own bachelor pad. The two-bedroom, one-bathroom, one-car-garage home had once been used as staff quarters when his father's former orchard manager lived on the grounds.

When the orchard manager retired, Leon asked Jake to take a more active role at the orchard, and Jake had recruited Emily, Claire, and a few other friends to help him repaint the entire home before he moved in. It seemed like only yesterday that they'd sat on the old beige carpet in the den and celebrated that the house had finally been painted. Emily could still smell the scent of paint mixed with their half dozen pies from the pizza parlor in downtown Splendid Lake.

"Home sweet home," Jake declared, gathering up their bag from the Splendid Kitchen and hopping out of the truck.

Emily followed him in through the front door and into a small foyer, where he hung his keys on a peg before moving to the kitchen and setting their bag of food on the counter. The delicious aroma of burgers and fries tickled her nose as she dropped her notepad on the table and hung her bag over the back of a chair.

She peeked into the den and spotted Dusty, Jake's old black

cat, curled up on the same brown sofa Emily had lounged on nearly a million times.

"Dusty!" Emily sang while rushing over to the kitty. "How are you?" Crouching down, she brushed her fingers over the cat's head. The feline rolled over to expose her chin, and Emily scratched while the kitty purred with delight.

Emily's eyes flitted to the flat-screen television, which was bolted to the wall above a brown credenza. Next to the TV sat a framed photo of Jake and Claire posing on the dock. Emily didn't recognize the picture, but she assumed they were dressed up for a wedding—possibly Claire's cousin's wedding, which Jake had mentioned they'd attended last spring.

Jake looked like he'd just walked out of a Brooks Brothers ad, wearing a dark blue suit coupled with a light blue shirt and a blue tie a shade darker. Emily couldn't remember the last time he'd worn a suit, but as she studied the photo, she wished he'd wear one more often. His hair was trimmed and perfectly styled, and he'd shaved, revealing that strong jawline and those dazzling cheekbones. The entire ensemble complemented his baby-blue eyes while accentuating his wide chest, muscular biceps, and tapered, trim waist. He was drop-dead gorgeous, and Emily suddenly felt a case of the vapers coming on.

Beside him in the photo, Claire looked perfect, as usual, in a simple green dress that matched her eyes. Her long blonde hair was perfectly straight, which was something Emily could rarely accomplish with her wild dark waves—no matter how strong the product or flat iron. Claire's angelic face had the perfect amount of makeup. She wore cute wedge heels, and since she was a few inches taller than Emily, Claire looked like she belonged beside Jake, who had his arm wrapped around Claire's perfect little waist.

They had always been the perfect couple. So perfect that it was nauseating.

Emily swallowed a sigh. She'd once longed to be Claire and garner all of Jake's golden attention, but she'd realized that was a ridiculous dream. Still, the heart wanted what it wanted, and hers still longed for Jake to allow her a chance to break out of the friend zone.

"Do you like where I hung your painting?"

Jake's question hauled Emily back from her ridiculously pathetic spiral. He had wandered over to the sofa.

She stood, and when he held out a french fry, she took it. Then he stared at her, as if he were awaiting an answer to a question.

What had he asked?

Oh right, the painting!

She snapped to attention while her eyes focused on the painting she'd sent him for Christmas hanging in a place of honor above the television. She'd painted it partly by memory and also with the help of a photo she'd found on the Hughes Family Orchard Instagram account. The piece featured the old barn that sat facing the road near the entrance to the orchard. She'd spent hours perfecting the piece, pouring all her love for Jake, his family, and their home into it. And she could see that love in the brushstrokes and the care she'd taken.

"Isn't that the perfect spot for it?" He handed her another fry. "I look at it every night while I watch TV."

She nodded, and suddenly all the pieces clicked together in her mind. "I got it," she whispered. "See ya later, Dusty," she told the cat before heading out the front door and down the porch steps.

"Where are you going?" Jake trailed after her to the driveway.

Emily pointed toward the entrance to the orchard. "How long has that barn been out of commission?"

"I don't know." He rubbed the blond scruff lining his jaw. "Twenty years? Why?"

She started down the dirt road toward it.

"What are you doing?" he demanded.

"Going to the barn." She beckoned him. "Come on, slowpoke!"

"What are you up to?"

"Just trust me," she said.

He took a few long strides and fell into step beside her. "I always do," he said, and his words sent a warm glow curling through her.

Up close the barn's age and neglect were even more apparent. The two humongous wooden doors hung loosely from rusted hinges, while rotting boards held nests for who knew how many birds. The peeling red paint had flaked off, leaving the barn looking naked in the overgrown field.

But the old building still held beauty along with its legacy. And its potential was endless!

Emily started inside.

"Whoa!" Jake grabbed her arm and tugged her toward him.

He held on to her, and she enjoyed the feel of his warm and rough skin as she breathed in his familiar scent—sandalwood mixed with soap. She'd missed that comforting smell more than she'd realized. She'd missed *him*. Staying away from Splendid Lake for so long had been more difficult than she'd understood.

He released her arm. "It's not safe in there."

"What would it take to make it safe?"

"I don't know. Why?" He studied her with a mixture of confusion and intrigue.

"What if we made it into a market?"

He chuckled. "What are you talking about?"

"The new orchard is offering a fun-filled fall festival—their words, not mine. That means we need to offer something equally as amazing, right?"

He nodded, and his eyes were crystal blue in the afternoon sunlight.

"What if we had a market?" She pointed to the barn. "Let's restore the barn and invite local vendors to sell cool stuff here. That could be a whole new revenue stream when the orchard opens for the fall season."

When his brow wrinkled, she kept talking. "You can invite the community to be part of it—like, Mrs. O'Connor can sell her pies, and Mrs. Randolph can sell her jams. Then there's Mr. Williams, who always made donuts. You know, things like that."

His eyebrows rose, but his expression conveyed he wasn't buying any of it.

She huffed out a frustrated breath. "Jake, why did you invite me to come here?"

His face warmed. "Because I missed you."

She blinked. She'd missed him too. *A lot.* Had he missed her the same way? Her stomach flip-flopped at the idea of finally getting Jake to care about her as more than a friend. But that was a crazy thought. If he did, then why hadn't he told her how he felt? She frowned.

He clocked her expression and scoffed. "You don't believe I missed you?"

"I thought you wanted my help."

"I do."

"Then why are you so skeptical about this?"

He paused, seeming to consider the barn, and then clasped his hand around hers and tugged her toward his house. "Our lunch is getting cold. We can talk while we eat."

* * *

Sitting at his kitchen table, they unwrapped their burgers and fries. She turned to a fresh page in her notepad and started sketching the barn in between bites of her bacon cheeseburger. After completing the outside, she added booths inside. When she finished, she set her jaw. It was a lousy diagram, but it would have to work.

She angled the picture toward Jake. "Okay, this isn't the best barn, but you get the idea. We could clean it up and then section off the inside for a variety of vendors. All the orchard has ever offered is apples, right?"

"Yeah." He took a sip of his Coke. "It's an orchard."

"But what if you offered more? Then we'll get customers that the other place doesn't. There wasn't anything on their fancy signs about an autumn *market*."

He tapped his lips, and she wondered what they tasted like.

Stop it, Emily! Stay on task!

"I like it," he said, but his expression was grim.

"You sure? 'Cause you're not acting like it."

He blew out a long breath and slouched in the chair. "I don't know if my dad is going to go for this. He's all about tradition."

"But times change. If the orchard doesn't, then it won't exist anymore."

"You're right." His smile returned. "Let's make a list of things to sell and then we can work on a plan to convince my dad to agree."

They finished their lunch before creating a list of possible vendors for their market and then discussing the barn renovations.

Later, when his phone dinged, Jake fished it from the pocket of his athletic shorts, consulted it, and frowned. He sent a brief text before turning his attention back to Emily. He seemed to shake off his frustration as he tapped her notepad. "So, about the barn. I definitely need to fix the doors and replace the hardware so they don't fall on someone."

She touched his forearm. "Everything okay?"

"Yeah." He cleared his throat. "We should start a list for Lowe's." He fetched a notepad and pen from a nearby drawer and wrote *Lowe's* at the top before listing supplies. His movements were stiff and jerky, and frustration came off him in waves.

"Jake."

He ignored her and continued writing.

"Jake!" she exclaimed, and he finally met her gaze with a frown. She rested her hand on his bulky bicep. "You can't lie to me. We've been friends for nearly twenty-five years, and I can tell when you're upset. You know that, right?"

He sagged in the chair.

"Do you want to talk about it?"

"It's Claire." He scrubbed his hand over his mouth. "We had an argument before she left, and she's been bugging me to talk to her about it. Things have been . . . strained."

This was news. Jake and Claire had had their share of arguments—some of them pretty intense—but they always worked it out. "I thought things were going great between you two. What happened?"

"You know she works for a big medical supply company," he began, and she nodded. "Well, the company was bought out, and the main offices are in Nashville. She's able to work from home, but she has to check in with her manager and team in Nashville periodically, which is where she is now. Her dream is to be CFO. Even though she had a good offer with a company over in Asheville, which is a short commute, she's still trekking out to Nashville and waiting for that promotion."

Emily nodded. "Okay . . ."

"Well, she wants to move out there permanently." He paused, and his lips turned down. "And she wants me to go with her."

"Oh." Emily worked to keep her expression blank, but the thought of Jake moving to Nashville felt like a stab to her chest. Not only would he be more than seven hours away from Charlotte, but a move to Nashville with Claire would lead to a commitment—a *real* commitment—marriage, a family, a future. And then for sure Emily would lose him forever.

She couldn't stomach the idea of not having Jake in her life. What would she do without him?

But she needed to focus on Jake's needs, not her own.

"What do *you* want?" she asked, working to keep her voice calm.

"What do you *think* I want?" He threw his hands up. "The orchard is my life. It's been in my family for a hundred years. How can I leave, especially with my dad's health being so fragile? My family is depending on me to bring the orchard out of its slump. It's our livelihood, our history, our legacy."

Whew! "Doesn't she understand that?"

"She thinks I should hire someone to run the orchard." He set his jaw. "She keeps telling me that I don't support her, but it's not that. Of course I want her to do well and fulfill her dream of becoming a CFO. But I'd like her to do that here." He pointed to the floor. "Like I said, she had one good offer when a competitor tried to poach her. It had great benefits and a salary bump, along with the room to grow her career. Maybe not the direct line she might have in the Nashville company, but still. I'd never ask her to give up her dreams for me. But what about what I want?" He pointed to his chest. "Doesn't it matter that I want to stay here?"

He leaned back in his chair and stared up at the ceiling. "I feel so torn." He sighed. "That's why I told her we needed a break for a while."

Emily's stomach dropped. Had she heard him right? They broke up? And he didn't tell her?

Whoa.

"You b-broke up?"

"Yeah." He nodded, and he looked stricken. "It was my idea. And it totally crushed her." He rubbed his forehead. "I feel like the biggest jerk on the planet."

"You told her it was over?" Emily's leg began to bounce under the table.

"Yup. I said we needed space and that maybe we should see other people. Maybe she'll find someone who will give her what she wants, because apparently I can't."

Emily worked to wrap her brain around this bombshell.

Jake and Claire broke up. They were over.

And he asked Emily to come home to Splendid Lake.

Her heart gave a bump.

But Jake had kept that news—*big news*—from her.

"When did this happen?" she asked.

He studied his hands as if the answer were written on his palms. "Two weeks ago."

Hold on!

Two weeks ago. And he'd kept this from her!

"So why didn't you tell me?" Her question vibrated.

He grimaced. "I guess I've been trying to come to terms with the fact that it's finally over between Claire and me after more than a decade."

Emily nodded. "If it's over, then why is she texting you?"

"She still wants to talk about it."

"If you want me to leave so you can call her . . ."

"No, no, no." He pointed to her notebook. "Let's put a plan together and then talk to my dad about it. Even though he's stepped back, he wants me to keep him informed of all my ideas."

"Okay." Emily tried to focus on their harvest market idea, but her mind was spinning while she tried to comprehend that Jake was single.

Single!

And maybe that meant she finally, after all these years, had a chance with him.

Chapter 4

"Em and I are working on some ideas for the orchard's hundredth anniversary celebration, Dad. I think you're going to like them."

Jake glanced around the kitchen table. It was suppertime, and Mom had made her famous (to the Hughes family, anyway) pork chops, along with baked potatoes and green beans. He hoped Mom's delicious meal would soften his father's stubborn streak. He peered across the table at Emily, who nodded, encouraging him to continue, while Mom watched him with interest from the other end of the table. Dad pressed his lips together before eating a forkful of pork chop.

Jake cleared his throat. "We stopped by the McClains' old orchard. Lancaster's opening it in a couple of weeks and doing a fall festival theme."

"Figures," Dad grunted.

"Em and I were throwing around ideas, and she came up with something I'd never thought of. What if we restored the old barn and turned it into a market?" When Dad's expression turned to stone, Jake continued talking at a fast clip. "Think about it, Dad. It's a whole new revenue stream. We could have a variety of vendors, like food and collectibles, and we'll invite members of the community to join us for—"

"No." Dad's response was swift and firm. "This is one of your impulsive ideas like you had in high school. Remember when you tried to convince me to have a demolition derby out in the west field? I said no to that lousy idea too."

The room fell silent. While Dad continued eating, Mom and Emily shared an awkward expression.

Jake set his fork down and took a deep breath, trying to curb his frustration. His father refused to let go of the mistakes he had made in high school—the parties, the stupid pranks, the mediocre grades. Dad acted as if Jake were still that same immature kid, but he wasn't. He'd grown up and matured. Although Jake respected his father too much to contradict him, he couldn't allow Dad's bullheadedness to destroy their livelihood. He studied his baked potato and tried to think of something that would make his father entertain their idea.

"Leon, could I please show you what we had in mind?"

Jake's eyes flickered to Emily, who had spread out her diagram in front of his father. Dad eyed it with cautious curiosity.

"Since the new McClains' is going with a fall festival theme, I was trying to think of something different to make this orchard stand out. I've always loved the abandoned barn." She chuckled. "I have so many memories of playing in it when we were kids, and when I saw the painting I sent Jake for Christmas, the ideas clicked together." She tapped the barn drawing. "I think it could be really neat if we restored the barn and turned it into a market featuring local fare. We'd draw so many locals, especially if we highlight all the vendors who make Splendid Lake so special."

She began listing names of local folks who might want to have a booth there, and the most incredible thing happened—Dad's scowl warmed ever so slightly. "You could charge a fee for the booth, so it would be a win-win for the vendors and for you. What do you think?"

Dad studied her diagram with his lips pursed.

"I think it's a wonderful idea, dear," Mom said.

Silence drifted over the dining room for a moment, and Jake held his breath. He felt Emily watching him, and when he turned toward her, she gave him a sweet smile.

Dad pushed the drawing away from him. "This isn't what my parents and grandparents wanted for their orchard. They always said that the apples would sell themselves. We don't need this nonsense to get customers here."

Jake opened his mouth to protest, but Emily cut him off.

"I know this is different from what people expect from Hughes, but I think asking the community to participate will drive new customers here." Emily's voice was calm. "Everyone loves a fun market with different booths to visit. And utilizing the barn is a way to keep the Hughes legacy alive. Didn't your grandfather build that barn?"

Dad's blue eyes lit up. "He did. I was about five years old, and I helped paint it."

He's actually smiling!

Jake settled back in his chair and grinned. Em was brilliant!

"I think he'd be happy to know that his great-grandson was bringing the barn back to life," Emily declared.

Dad nodded, but then his smile flattened as his stare settled on Jake. "How are we going to pay for this? You know funds are low since our trees didn't produce as many apples after last year's storm, and with Ally's tuition . . ."

"Dad, we have to spend money to make money."

The older man frowned. "But you have to *have* the money to spend it, Jake."

Emily held her hand up. "I'll pay for it."

All eyes in the room settled on Emily.

"Why on earth would you pay to renovate my family's barn?" Jake asked.

Emily flipped over her barn drawing and began to doodle. "I have the money from the sale of my parents' house," she whispered, her voice barely audible. "I haven't touched it."

Jake stilled. She'd sold the house three and a half years ago. He'd assumed she'd been living on it all this time.

Mom touched Emily's shoulder. "Honey, we don't expect you to invest in our orchard."

Emily kept her eyes focused on the paper, and soon a dock and lake took shape. "I'd love to spend some of the money on something that's important to me, and this place is like my home."

Jake's heart turned over in his chest. He'd always known that Emily felt comfortable here, but having her call the orchard home was overwhelming in a way he couldn't quite comprehend.

Mom met Jake's gaze with a warm smile. "Thank you, Emily. But we can't let you do that."

Jake took a long drink of sweet tea, hoping to quench his suddenly dry throat.

"It's a nice gesture, but the orchard is fine as is," Dad said.

Emily's head popped up. "What was the barn used for, Leon?"

"Storage, years ago."

"We can keep that spirit." Emily opened a fresh page in her book and started a new drawing. "Tell me what it looked like."

"I still don't think . . ." Dad's voice trailed off.

Emily grinned. "Just humor me, okay?"

Jake's phone began to ring, and he found Claire's face grinning at him on the screen. His stomach twisted. It was time to stop avoiding the painful conversation and tell Claire she had to move on.

He stood. "Excuse me, I need to take this." Then he slipped into the den, took a deep breath, and answered the call. "Hello?"

"Jakey," Claire crooned into the phone. "It's so good to hear your voice."

He dropped onto the sofa and reclined his head against the back. Claire was the master at avoiding big conversations, so it was just like her to call and act like everything was normal between them. It had been two weeks since he told her that they should see other people, but she was acting like nothing had changed.

"How are your folks?" she asked.

"Fine." He rubbed his forehead with his free hand. "We were just eating supper."

"Your dad's okay?"

"Yup."

"That's good."

An awkward silence expanded over the phone line, and he knew he had to end this conversation and get back to his folks and Emily.

"Look, I really can't talk long," he said.

"Just give me a minute, okay?" Claire's voice sounded thick, and his stomach clenched. "I know you said we need to move on, but I don't want to. I still think we can work this out. Just consider coming out to Nashville—maybe over a weekend. Then you could see how great it is here. I know you'd love it. There's so much opportunity, and we could finally settle down and build a life here. Get married. Start a family."

Whoa, whoa, whoa!

Hadn't she heard a thing he'd said? Maybe he hadn't made it clear that he wasn't ready for any of that.

She sniffed. "I want a future with you—and *only* you. I don't want to see other people."

He squeezed the bridge of his nose as the all-too-familiar guilt crept back into his chest. He felt like a jerk for breaking her heart, especially after all they'd been through.

Claire had been in town when his dad had the heart attack, and she'd heard the news through the Splendid Lake grapevine. She'd shown up at the hospital with food for him and his mom. He'd told her he needed some time alone, and Claire had held his mom's hand while he went outside to get some air. When he returned, he found Claire hugging his mom while she cried.

Whether he wanted to face it or not, Claire had been there for him, and vice versa. He'd held her hand at her grandmother's funeral and helped clean out her apartment.

Both of their families believed that Jake and Claire would eventually get married and grow old together.

But if that were true, then why did Jake want to end this conversation with her right now?

"Why don't you come see me next weekend?" Claire asked.

"Can't."

Laughter drifted into the den from the kitchen. He moved to the doorway. His father's bright smile took him by surprise, and Jake found the corners of his mouth begin to lift.

"This isn't a good time," he told Claire.

Mom said something, and when Emily guffawed, the adorable sound seemed to echo throughout his parents' old farmhouse—and apparently into the receiver.

"Who's that?" Claire asked.

Jake crossed to the back of the den and stared out the wall of windows facing the orchard. "Em."

She paused for a moment. "Is she visiting?" Claire's question was hesitant.

"Yeah."

"For how long?"

"Not sure." He studied the grove of trees, trying to imagine it full of visitors filling baskets with ripe apples.

"Why is *she* there?" Claire's words were flinty. Sharp.

"She's helping me figure some things out with the orchard." He was done with this conversation. Time to wrap it up. "I gotta go, okay? We'll talk later."

"When?"

He sighed. "I don't know."

"Wait." Her voice was urgent. "Is there a chance we can make this work?" Her voice trembled.

He pushed his hand through his thick hair. He longed to tell her no, but something was holding him back. A sense of loyalty forbade him from cutting her off completely. He couldn't stand the idea of ruining their friendship after nearly fourteen years.

"I still love you," she continued, "and I believe in us."

He was certain he cared about Claire, and he wanted her to live a happy life. But did he still love her? No, not in the same way he once had. Yet he couldn't bring himself to say the words back to her, and that sent more guilt burrowing in his stomach.

"Don't give up on me," she said, her voice wobbling.

"I need some time to figure things out. Right now I'm focused on my family and the orchard."

"Yeah, okay." She sniffed again, her voice trembling as she said, "Call me when you're ready."

"I will."

* * *

Emily smiled while Leon shared another story about his childhood growing up at the orchard. She enjoyed hearing about his adventures, but what she really loved was how Jake's father beamed as he reminisced. She could feel how much he treasured his family's legacy, and she could envision him working in the barn next to his grandfather while he detailed his memories.

Jake's soft voice sounded in the den, and Emily had the sneaking suspicion he was talking to Claire. Emily tried to swallow back her jealousy. Jake had been with Claire since sophomore year, when Claire had moved to Splendid Lake. It made sense that they would work things out and get back together again. Her heart would just have to accept it. Somehow.

"That barn has been here nearly as long as I have," Leon said.

"Which is why we should honor your family and turn it into a market," Diane said. "Let's give Emily's idea a try."

"Fine," Leon said.

Emily shared a victorious smile with Diane. "And I'll pay for the renovations." She took another bite of pork chop. "This is delicious," she declared.

"Thanks," Diane said, her eyes sparkling. "Now, Emily, are you settled in Charlotte for good? Or can we convince you to come back to Splendid Lake?"

"I'm not sure." Emily shrugged and cut up her loaded baked potato. Splendid Lake was her home, but the memories were painful—bittersweet, but definitely painful. She missed her parents so much that her heart ached for them, and being so close to her childhood home, seeing places where they used to be a family . . . it was all too much for her.

Jake slid onto the seat across from her and kept his eyes focused on his half-eaten meal. "Sorry about that," he muttered.

Emily's heart squeezed as he scooped a forkful of green beans into his mouth and avoided her stare. His conversation clearly hadn't been pleasant. She'd have to convince him to open up about it later when they were alone.

"I've decided that when the orchard opens for the season, I'll allow you to give the market a try," Leon said.

Jake's eyes snapped to his father's. "You will?"

"Yes." Leon wagged a finger at his son. "But if it flops, then never again. Understood?"

"Yep, understood." Jake gave Emily a half-hearted smile. "I guess that means we need to get to work, Carmichael."

Emily grinned. "I'm ready when you are, Hughes."

"I'm looking forward to seeing what you dream up here," Diane said. "Oh, and who was that on the phone?"

Jake's expression flattened instantly. "Claire." He lifted his glass of sweet tea and took a long draw.

"How's she doing?"

Emily hated how Diane's expression brightened when she asked about Claire, and she hated herself for being jealous of Claire. *Again.*

Jake shifted in his seat. "Okay, I guess."

"Is she in town?"

He shook his head. "Nashville."

"That's right. Her mom told me that when I ran into her last week." Diane pointed at Leon. "Sherry said that we need to have dinner with her and Ron. It's been too long. I miss our weekly dinners." Then she faced Jake again. "When is Claire coming home?"

"Not sure." Jake continued to stare at his plate, moving the food around absentmindedly.

Diane frowned. "Listen, I'm not going to pry about whatever's going on with you two. But I promise, whatever it is, it'll get better." She gave Leon a sad smile. "Your dad and I had plenty of rough patches when we were dating, and plenty after we got married. But we soldiered on and got through it. You and Claire will do the same. Those tough times will make you stronger as a couple."

Emily tried to ignore the queasiness that overtook her stomach as she imagined Jake and Claire beaming at each other at the altar, their current tiff a distant memory and a happy future together stretched out in front of them.

Then she gave herself a mental head slap. She was Jake's friend. And if he was suffering, she was going to help him through this hard time, whether Claire was in the picture or not.

Uncertainty flickered in Jake's eyes. More than ever, Emily longed to get him alone for a few minutes and force him to open up to her.

Diane turned to her. "You mentioned that you and Steve broke up. Are you seeing someone new?"

Emily was so stunned by the shift in the conversation she couldn't answer for a moment. "Uh . . . n-no."

"Well, don't give up, sweetheart. You'll find the right guy. Just don't be afraid to put yourself out there and meet new people."

Emily was suddenly dragged back in time to senior year, when she'd had her heart broken by her prom date. Since Jake was glued to Claire, Emily had agreed to go to prom with a sweet guy in her Spanish class named Lawson. He'd asked her out nearly a half dozen times before she agreed to go. And they'd had a great time at the dance. Lawson was funny, attentive, and cute, and Emily had started to like him. She thought maybe they'd become a couple. But a week after prom, she spotted him kissing a gorgeous blonde in the hallway.

Once again, she'd lost out to a prettier and more exciting girl.

And when her mother found her crying in her room, Mom had given her almost the exact same advice as Diane was sharing now.

Emily's heart ached. She missed her mother so much.

"I think I'm better off alone," Emily said. "I've given up on love for now."

"Now don't do that," Diane instructed. "My meemaw used to say that there's a lid for every pot, and I agree." She turned to her son. "I'm anxious for Jake to settle down. You're going to be thirty in January. You and Claire just need to learn how to compromise, and then we can plan a wedding. After you're married, I'll finally have some grandkids running around the orchard."

Yup, that definitely was bile rising in Emily's throat.

She needed to find a way to shed her jealousy. But there it was, tying her insides into a knot. Again.

Sighing, Emily took another sip of sweet tea.

Chapter 5

EMILY GRASPED JAKE'S hand and tugged him toward the back door. They'd cleaned up the kitchen, and Mom and Dad had retreated to the den to watch television.

"Where are we going?" he asked.

She dragged him outside, where the evening air was warm, and he breathed in the comforting scent of the apples mixed with the smell of the lake.

"You need to get out. I can't stand it when you're sad or upset."

"Who said I'm sad and upset?"

She snorted. "Your good mood dissolved after your phone call. You've only managed to string two or three words together since you hung up with Claire. Now, follow me into the orchard."

He complied, and they started down the path toward the lake side by side.

"Does our fort still exist?" she asked.

"Yeah, but it's a little worse for wear. It hasn't been touched since we were twelve."

She picked up speed with a spring in her step. "Let's find it!"

He grabbed her arm before she could sprint away. "Wait a second. I need to know how you managed to win my dad over on the market idea."

She shrugged. "I just asked him about the barn. Soon he was sharing stories. I told him it would be a great way to honor his parents and grandparents if we restored it, and I said that would play into the orchard's hundredth anniversary."

For the second time that evening, Jake felt a warm rush of admiration for Emily wash over him. "You're pretty awesome, you know that?"

She chuckled. "Not really. I just know that your dad wants to keep within tradition, and we can do that *and* open the market by bringing together the past and the present." She turned off the worn path. "This way, right?"

"I think so."

They walked in silence, their shoes crunching along the grass. He began a mental list of tasks for renovating the barn, and when he considered the budget, he recalled Emily's confession that she hadn't spent any of the money from the sale of her family's home. He knew how much money she'd gotten for the large lakefront home—seven figures—and he couldn't understand why she hadn't used any of it to restart her life.

"Why haven't you spent the money from the house sale?"

Her steps faltered, but she kept moving forward. "Wasn't the fort over here?" she asked before she took off running.

"Wait up!" He raced after her, catching up when she stopped under a tall tree.

She pointed toward the branches. "Red delicious, right?"

"Yeah." He picked one off the branch and held it out to her. "They probably need a couple more weeks."

She shook her head and rubbed the apple on her gray T-shirt. “Nah.” She took a bite and closed her eyes. “So good.”

Jake smiled. He’d always been proud of his family’s apples, and seeing someone enjoy one never got old.

She held it out to him. “Try it.”

“I know what they taste like.”

“Please?” She stuck her lip out in what he’d always called her puppy dog look. “Pretty please with sugar on top?”

He laughed. He couldn’t resist her when she did that, and she knew it. “Fine.” He bit into it and enjoyed the sweet goodness. Then he gave it back to her. “Finish it.”

“I will.” She took another bite.

While he watched her eat, the evening sunlight was at the perfect angle to not only illuminate her golden-brown eyes but also highlight her dark hair with streaks of red. He’d never noticed the highlights in her thick, wavy mane until that moment, and an unexpected urge to touch her hair overcame him.

Yikes.

Jake shook his head. *Uh, that was weird.*

She finished the apple and then tossed it aside. “Now. Let’s find that fort!”

They continued past the line of trees until they came to the part of the orchard that was off-limits to customers. He unlocked the combination on the fence, and they continued walking to their wooden fort. It still sat on a high branch overlooking the lake.

She ran her fingers over the bark and found the initials they’d carved there when they were ten. “Our tree,” she said softly. She pointed to the scratches that read, *JH + EC*.

He touched his initials too. “Seems like it was yesterday.”

"Yeah, and you got in so much trouble for swiping your dad's pocketknife off his dresser."

He laughed. "Yeah. Well. I still don't regret it."

She grabbed the rope ladder and started to climb.

"What are you doing?" He grabbed her leg. "This thing isn't stable, and we both weigh more than we did when we were kids. If you fall from that height, you'll get seriously hurt."

She made a face, shook off his hold, and continued to climb the ladder. "Don't be such a Debbie Downer." She stopped midway. "Come on! Are you chicken?"

"I don't know if it can hold me."

She rolled her eyes and shimmied upward. "Your dad made this solid. It's survived windstorms and hail. We're fine. Stop stalling and get your butt up here!"

He groaned. "You make me crazy."

"That's why you love me . . ." she sang.

He laughed. She'd always kept him on his toes, and although he could usually predict her reactions, sometimes she shocked him, like when she insisted on selling her parents' house, moving to Charlotte, and leaving Splendid Lake and him in her rearview mirror. It had broken his heart. But he'd kept that little tidbit to himself.

But now that he'd convinced her to come back to visit, he wanted more than anything to persuade her to stay.

He took hold of the ladder and tried to judge whether the old wooden platform could actually hold his weight now that he was six-foot-three and close to two hundred pounds.

But if he sat in the fort with Emily, maybe she'd finally open up to him.

He slowly climbed up the rope ladder until he reached the top and managed to squeeze up through the entrance to the platform.

The canvas tarp that served as their roof was riddled with holes, allowing him to see the sun begin to set above them. But the floor was solid, just as Emily had predicted. He crawled over to her and sank down beside her with his long legs dangling over the side.

Emily glanced around. "I remember it being bigger."

He chuckled. "We were a lot smaller back then."

She rested her arms on the wooden railing that lined the perimeter of the small fort.

"Whoa!" He grabbed her arm. "That might not be secure. Are you determined to fall off and break something?"

She held on to the railing and shook it. "See? It holds together just fine."

He groaned. "My nerves are shot right now."

"You worry too much." She tapped the tip of his nose and then rested her elbows on the railing and her chin on her palms while she stared out toward the lake. The water glistened with a prism of bright colors as the sun began to set. Frogs croaked with delight and cicadas chittered while fireflies sparkled in the air.

For a moment, Jake basked in the beautiful late-summer evening. He was sitting in his fort with Emily nearly seventeen years after the last time they'd perched themselves in this tree. He longed to freeze time.

"Sometimes I wish I could go back to when all we did was play in the orchard and sit in our fort. Things were much simpler then," she said softly.

"I was just thinking the same thing." He leaned back on his hands.

A few moments stretched out between them as they watched a sailboat pass on the distant lake.

Emily turned toward him. "Tell me about your conversation with Claire."

He sat forward and crossed his arms. "It's not worth repeating."

"Jake . . ."

"I really don't want to talk about it."

"Too bad." She poked him in the middle of his chest. "You're going to tell me what happened whether you want to or not, because I said so."

He growled out his annoyance. "Fine, but it was the same conversation Claire and I have been having for more than a month." He stared out toward the lights glowing on the other side of the lake. "She asked me to come out to Nashville. She says we can have a life there. She told me she still loves me, and she begged me not to give up on our relationship."

Emily nodded slowly and licked her lips. "Do you . . . love her?" Her question was soft, almost hesitant.

He scrubbed his hand over his jaw. "I mean . . . I care about her. I always will." He looked down at the ground. "But my life is here, and she knows that."

"Did you tell her it was time to let go?"

He sighed. "No."

Emily was quiet for a long moment, but he could almost feel her working through something in her mind. "Why are you so afraid of letting her go?" Her voice was uncertain, which wasn't something he heard from her often.

He considered her question, and he couldn't come up with an answer. "It's complicated."

"Okay." She angled her body toward his. "I'm ready to listen."

He chuckled.

"I'm serious. You told me that you broke up with her, but you're allowing her to hound you and beg you to try again. Why don't you stop answering her calls?"

"Because I've known her since we were sixteen. We grew up together. I can't just shut her out."

Emily pivoted back toward the water and focused on the dock.

They sat in silence for several moments before he turned toward Emily's childhood home and focused on her. "Let's talk about something else."

"Okay." She brightened.

"Why haven't you spent any of the money you made on the sale of the house? I thought you were going to use it to start a new life."

Her mouth opened and then closed. "I don't want to talk about it." She shook her head, wiggled out from under the railing, and pushed herself toward the hole in the floor that led to the rope ladder. "Let's go for a night swim before it gets too cold."

"Oh no you don't." He gently rested his hands on her forearms, and she stilled. "You're not going to escape."

Her eyes searched his. "Please let me go." Her expression pleaded with him, and the pain he found there sucked the air out of his lungs.

"I didn't mean to hurt you, Em. You know I never would."

She looked down at the fort floor. "I just don't want to talk about it."

"Why not?"

She rubbed her eyes and swallowed.

"Hey, it's me." He tapped his chest. "You can say anything to me. You know that."

She stared at her lap and moved her hands over her denim shorts.

"Look at me," he whispered. "Please."

When she met his gaze, her striking golden-brown eyes were

glistening with tears. "If I spend the money from the sale of the house or my inheritance," she began, her words quivering, "that means they're *really* gone—*forever*." Her voice broke as a sob tore from her throat, and she covered her face with her hands.

Jake's heart fractured at the sound of her agony. He held her against him. "It's okay. I'm here," he murmured in her ear. "I'm so sorry. I didn't mean to make you cry."

Emily wrapped her arms around him and buried her face in the crook of his neck.

He rubbed her back and rested his cheek on her head. "You're not alone," he whispered. "I'm here for you always. I mean that."

Jake closed his eyes and held her close while he breathed in the sweet scent of her shampoo mixed with the orchard and listened to the cicadas and frogs sing. When Emily relaxed against him, he felt his nerves finally settle down. Everything seemed to be right in his world, and he felt like she belonged in his arms.

She sniffed and moved her fingers through his hair at the base of his skull, and the sensation sent electric pulses dancing through his veins, causing him to draw her closer.

He stilled when that action registered in his mind. He'd consoled her dozens of times after she'd lost her parents. The first few nights, he'd held her for what felt like hours while they sat on her sofa. But that was platonic. When he'd had her in his arms four years ago, they were only friends.

But this moment felt different. It felt . . .

Romantic.

And suddenly the urge to kiss Emily overcame him.

They'd never kissed. He'd hugged her thousands of times over the years, and he'd never even thought about kissing her, even when his buddies at school asked him if he and Emily were secretly more than friends.

But at that moment, he found himself wondering . . . if he lifted her chin and tasted her pink lips, would she kiss him back? If he raked his hands through her long, thick, wavy hair, would she push him away?

His hands began to tremble as he wondered what he should do with them.

As if she could read his thoughts, Emily wriggled out of his arms, sat up, wiped her eyes, and forced a smile. "That's enough of that." She slid toward the ladder. "Let's go for a night swim," she said while disappearing through the floor and down the ladder.

He scrubbed his hands over his face and tried to get his wits about him.

Emily would never want him as more than a friend. He needed to suppress those foreign thoughts before they destroyed their friendship.

After a few deep breaths, he shoved himself through the hole in the floor and descended the ladder.

Emily squinted up at him. "You look a little pale. You okay?"

"Yeah." His voice sounded rough, and he cleared his throat. "I'll take a rain check on that swim. I think it's time to head to bed."

She frowned. "When did you become such a fuddy-duddy?"

"We have a lot of work ahead of us, so it's probably best that we get some rest."

They walked in silence back through the orchard toward his parents' house, though his mind was anything but quiet. His thoughts raced at a million miles an hour.

When they reached the path that led to his house, she gave him a little wave. "Good night," she said softly before continuing toward his parents' house.

Jake jammed his hands in his pockets while he watched her petite shadow disappear into the night. He needed to get his confusing feelings for her under control before he did something stupid—like kiss her—and destroyed their friendship. He couldn't imagine losing her. If that happened, he'd be completely lost.

* * *

You're not alone. I'm here for you always. I mean that.

Jake's words were still echoing in Emily's mind hours after she'd climbed into bed. She'd tried staring at the ceiling through the darkness, counting sheep, and counting backward from one hundred, but nothing worked to stop her mind from reliving her conversation with Jake in the treehouse.

When he'd asked about the money from her parents' house, she'd tried to keep it together. But all the grief she'd kept buried deep in her heart had poured out of her like a tsunami, and the next thing she knew, she was wrapped up in Jake's muscular arms, where she felt safe and protected.

She'd yearned to curl up in his lap and stay there forever. He'd held her so tight, just as he had in the days following her parents' death. After several moments, she relaxed, and she lost herself in imagining what it would be like to be his girlfriend. Her fingers wound their way through his soft hair as she basked in his familiar scent and listened to his heartbeat echoing in his brawny chest.

Then reality crashed down around her, and her silly fantasy evaporated as his words about Claire repeated in her mind like a broken record.

He still cared about Claire. He couldn't let her go because things were "complicated." Emily would never have a chance with Jake, and torturing herself with her immature dreams was just plain stupid and bad for her health.

And that was why she'd disentangled herself and suggested they go swimming, to put some distance between herself and Jake. A swim in the cold lake was just what she needed to cool down her raging emotions.

Emily groaned and yanked the sheet over her head. She needed to get over Jake once and for all. But the more time she spent with him, the deeper in love with him she became.

"I'm doomed," she told the empty room before she snickered. Yeah, she was doomed. But she'd been doomed since she was a kid. Jake had hijacked her heart years ago.

With a harrumph, she kicked off the sheet and sat up. It was clear she wasn't going to get any sleep. The glowing green numbers on the clock declared it was 1:45 a.m. She needed something to occupy her crazy mind.

For a moment, she considered going down to the basement to finally sort through the dozens of boxes and plastic containers that Jake's parents had stored for her after she'd sold her family's home. But she didn't want to risk waking up his parents. Plus, she wasn't ready to face those memories—not yet.

Instead, she dragged her laptop and sketch pad out of her bag, sat down at the desk, and started researching ideas for their fall marketplace. Hopefully by plunging her mind into the orchard, she'd eventually get sleepy and find a way to rest before the sun rose.

Chapter 6

WHEN DID YOU draw these?"

The next morning Emily stood with Jake outside the barn as he flipped through her detailed sketches of the renovation for the market, one of the outside and three of the inside. She had included details of the booths and also customers milling about. She'd added shading and even utilized her colored pencils to complete the drawings.

Emily jammed her hands into the pockets of her jean shorts. "Last night."

"They're pretty enough to frame." He flipped to the last one and then met her gaze, eyeing her with something that looked like shock or possibly wonder. "Did you sleep?"

"I mean, yeah," she said quickly with a shrug. "Why wouldn't I?" She tried to laugh, but it came out as a squeak.

Way to be obvious!

She'd finally fallen asleep after five and then woke up at eight when she heard Diane rattling pans around the kitchen. The truth was that she'd tried drowning thoughts of her parents and her feelings for Jake in the sketches, but she still couldn't turn off her brain. The thoughts haunted her while she drew, and after she fell asleep, she dreamed about marrying Jake in the renovated barn with her parents, his parents, and the entire town of Splendid Lake in the congregation. But if she admitted that out loud, then Jake would know that not only was she crazy about him, but she was just plain crazy.

Jake lifted a sandy-blond eyebrow, and a blush creeped up her neck to her cheeks.

Oh boy. Time to take the focus off me!

"If you flip to the next page, you'll see I started a shopping list for Lowe's. It complements the one you wrote yesterday." She pointed to the sketch pad. "We can go now if you want."

He consulted her list and nodded. "Vince, the new manager at the orchard, gave me a list of roofing supplies too. The guys are going to help me with the roof and then we'll worry about the walls and the interior." He grabbed a piece of paper from the pocket of his athletic shorts. "We can take my truck."

"Great."

She followed him to his truck and tried to focus on their to-do list and not her insane wedding dream or the way he'd wrapped his strong arms around her last night.

* * *

Jake steered his pickup through the Lowe's parking lot a couple of hours later. The bed of his Dodge was loaded down with roofing supplies, and with the windows open, a warm breeze swept through the cab.

Emily flipped on his radio, and when a hard rock song came through the speakers, she switched it to the oldies station and sang along with "Louie Louie" by The Kingsmen. Turning, she grabbed Jake's ball cap and yanked her long ponytail through the back before adjusting it on her head.

"You change my radio station, and you steal my hat," he grumbled while slowing to a stop at a red light. "You're awfully bold."

She batted her eyelashes. "Yup, and I'm also cute."

"That's true, but now my hair's a mess."

"I can help with that." She threaded her fingers through his soft hair, doing her best to arrange it. "There you go."

His baby-blue eyes assessed her, and her stomach fluttered.

Oh boy.

She settled back in her seat and folded her arms. "You're not getting this hat back."

"Typical," he muttered, but the corners of his mouth lifted in a ghost of a smile. He turned onto Main Street, which ran through downtown Splendid Lake, driving past the town hall and the library. When he came to the line of stores, he chose a spot in front of Scoops.

"What are we doing here?"

He shifted into Park and plucked his keys from the ignition. "Getting ice cream," he said, his brow furrowing. "What else is there to do at Scoops?"

"Oh, okay." She pushed open the door and met him at the front of the truck.

Jake held the parlor door open and made a sweeping gesture for her to walk in. The little shop was decorated in a 1950s theme with a black-and-white checkerboard tiled floor, red vinyl booths, chrome high-top tables, and red vinyl stools. Photos of ice cream sundaes, banana splits, and cones dotted the walls.

The shop buzzed with conversations as people enjoyed their sweet treats, and Emily nodded and waved to acquaintances as she stood in line beside Jake.

"Are you going to get your usual?" he asked her.

She tipped her head to the side. "What's my usual?" she asked, quizzing him.

He rolled his eyes. "Chocolate chip cookie dough in a waffle cone with chocolate sprinkles."

"Very good." She poked his impressive bicep. "And I know you're getting chocolate peanut butter in a waffle cone. You never deviate."

They made their way to the counter and placed their orders before Emily retrieved her wallet.

When Jake started to protest, she held up a hand. "My treat. I insist." She swiped her card and took the receipt.

"Emily?"

She spun just as Andi Wingate rushed over and hugged her. "It's been forever."

"Andi!" Emily squealed. "How are you?"

"I'm great." Andi looked up at Jake. "Hey, Jake." Then she focused on Emily. "I was across the street at Morningside Bakery, and I thought I saw you two walk in here. Are you back for good?"

Emily shook her head. "No, but I'm here for a while." She could feel Jake watching her while she spoke. "How's your hubby?"

"Seth's great." Andi pushed her hand through her short brown bob. Her brown eyes sparkled while she talked about her husband, who was their high school classmate and one of Jake's good friends. "His landscaping company has really taken off. He has three crews working for him now and pretty much makes his own hours floating from jobsite to jobsite. He's doing more managing and less landscaping."

"Good for him. Want some ice cream?" Jake asked.

"Sure," Andi said. She gave him her order before she and Emily found a booth and sat.

"Are you and Jake . . . ?" Andi asked once they were seated in a booth.

"Together?" Emily asked.

Andi nodded.

Emily gave her a nervous laugh. "No, no, no. He asked me to come home to help him plan a celebration for the orchard. What have you been up to?"

"I'm the bookkeeper for our landscaping business. How about you?"

"I've been doing this and that."

"With your art?" Andi actually seemed hopeful.

Emily shrugged. "Sort of." She was grateful Jake arrived with their ice cream just then. She didn't want to discuss failures—not even with an old friend. "Here's our ice cream." She slid over to make room for Jake on her side of the booth.

Jake sank down beside her and handed Andi her cone. "Pistachio for you." Then he held out Emily's. "Chocolate chip cookie dough for Em."

"Thanks," Emily said before taking a bite.

They spent the next hour enjoying their treats and catching up with Andi. After their ice cream was gone, they walked out to the sidewalk.

Andi hugged Emily. "Don't be a stranger. If you need any help at the orchard, give me a call. My number's the same."

"I will," Emily promised.

"Tell Seth hi for me," Jake told her before climbing into the truck.

* * *

Emily rested her elbow on the console as she looked out the back window toward the truck bed. "I guess the plan is to start with the barn roof."

Jake nodded. "That's right, but I need to hit one more place on our way back to the farm." He stopped the truck at a stop sign and snuck a glance at Emily. She hummed along with a song on the radio while she wound her finger through her thick dark hair and peered out the windshield. She looked adorable wearing his hat. No, *adorable* wasn't the right word. She was striking. His eyes lingered on her high cheekbones, her radiant golden-brown eyes, her cute button nose and pink lips. Her ivory skin was makeup free, but honestly, she didn't need any makeup. She was naturally pretty. He'd always considered her attractive, but lately she seemed . . . different. Or maybe he was the one who had changed.

Emily met his eyes, and her dark brows lifted. "Why are you staring at me?"

He narrowed his eyes and pretended to assess her. "I'm plotting how to get my hat back."

She touched the bill, and those sumptuous lips presented a coy smile. "It's mine now."

"Is that right?" He wagged a finger at her. "We'll see about that."

He drove through town and steered into the parking lot for the Splendid Lake Food Bank.

"You still donate apples here?" she asked, looking impressed.

He parked near the building and retrieved two large bags of apples from behind the driver's seat. "Of course I do."

They jogged up the front steps and into the building, where he headed toward the office.

"Jake!" Ms. Alexander hurried out from behind her desk. She divided her smile between him and Emily. "Hi, Emily. What have you two brought us?"

He set the bags on a nearby chair. "These ripened early."

"Oh my." Ms. Alexander examined the bag. "They're perfect." The middle-aged woman studied him. "How are you feeling about the new orchard? What's it called now?" She snapped her fingers. "Apple Haven. I heard from Joyce Robbins that they're going to have a petting zoo and face painting for kids. It'll be like a festival every day for the entire season."

Jake's posture stiffened. "I heard something about that."

"Could be some stiff competition for your orchard. You have always been so traditional—just apples and atmosphere, which is great, but customers expect more of an experience now. What are you going to do about it?" Ms. Alexander asked.

A warm hand rested on Jake's forearm as Emily stepped closer to his side. "We've got it under control. We're planning some exciting upgrades to the experience at Hughes Family Orchard."

"Oh! What kind of upgrades?" Ms. Alexander's hazel eyes sparkled.

"It's a surprise." Emily's pretty face lit up like a kid watching fireworks on the Fourth of July. "You'll have to come see." She gave Jake a warm smile, and the tense muscles in his shoulders and neck began to ease.

"Well, I'll pass along the news that exciting things are coming to Hughes Family Orchard. Be sure to let the community know so that folks come check it out," Ms. Alexander said.

"Oh, we will," Jake responded, resting his hand on Emily's shoulder. "We'll also bring some more apples soon."

Jake and Emily headed back out to the truck, waving to familiar faces on the way.

"Thanks for the save," he told Emily as they crossed the parking lot on the way to his truck.

She bumped her shoulder against his side. "It's going to be okay. We got this."

When they reached his truck, he unlocked the passenger door and then snatched his hat off her head and stuck it on his. She watched him with a look of awe. "Are you staring at me because the hat looks better on me?" he joked.

She shook her head. "I'm just really impressed by how you take care of everyone around here. You're like Splendid Lake's very own caped crusader."

He snorted.

"Seriously, you are. You're helping the downtrodden and taking care of neighbors. You're kind of amazing."

He rolled his eyes. "Get in the truck."

"Yes, Superman." She saluted, and he laughed.

* * *

Later that afternoon Jake crouched on the roof of the barn and swiped the back of his arm over his forehead and his face. He glanced back toward where Vince, Rico, and Eddie hammered plywood to replace the rotted boards. The afternoon sun was brutal, and he was convinced it was at least a hundred and fifty degrees.

Jake took a long draw from his bottle of water and moved to the edge. Below him, Emily sat on a stool and wrote in her notebook. He grinned as he recalled how she'd begged and pleaded, trying to convince him that she was perfectly capable of hammering pieces of plywood. While he'd been impressed with her enthusiasm, he told her there was no way he was going to allow her to stand on the roof and risk her life.

An amusing argument ensued, during which she lectured him on equal rights, girl power, and how she'd take all the necessary safety precautions, and Jake had somehow managed not to smile at how adorable she was. Finally, Emily conceded, and then she settled on a stool and spent the next couple of hours pouting and drawing while he and the orchard employees worked.

"Hey," he called down to her. "How are things down there?"

She tented her hand over her eyes and squinted up at him. "Boring. Why don't you take a break?"

"That sounds like a great idea." Jake pivoted toward where the three other men worked. "You guys up for a break?"

They all nodded and wiped their foreheads.

"Let's call it a day and get back to it tomorrow," Jake said, and they all agreed. "Thanks for your help today."

After gathering their tools, the men climbed down the ladder. Once on the ground, Jake thanked the workers again and then stowed the tools and supplies.

Emily linked her arm with his. "Let's go for a walk."

Jake allowed her to steer him through the orchard, and soon they were out by the dock. He breathed in the fresh scent of the lake and scanned the path leading to her childhood home. "You want to take a walk over there?"

"Over where?" She scrunched her nose and turned her back to him.

"To your folks' house," he told her gently. "Maybe it would be good for you to go visit it. I'll stay with you the entire time."

She kicked off her Birkenstocks and then began to yank off her shirt, revealing a black tank top, before she placed her phone on the dock.

"Whoa!" He tried not to stare at how the tank top hugged her curves. "What are you doing?"

She held her hand out to him. "Give me your phone."

"Why?" He lifted it from his pocket.

She took it and set it on the dock next to hers. "We're going for a swim. Take off your shoes."

He did as he was told and kicked off his sneakers and socks. Then he reached up behind his neck and pulled off his T-shirt.

Her eyes meandered over his chest for a few moments before she snatched his hat off his head and dropped it beside their shoes and shirts.

Then she grinned. "You first," she said, pushing him toward the end of the dock.

Stumbling forward, he grabbed her arm, and she shrieked as they crashed into the water together. Jake released Emily's arm when the cool lake water swallowed them up. He bobbed up to the surface and pushed his hands through his wet hair and sighed. The cool water soothed his aching muscles. How had Emily known that this was just what he needed after spending a few hours hammering on the barn roof?

She appeared beside him and flipped her long hair out of her face before she splashed him. "That's what you get for pulling me in with you," she joked.

"Oh yeah?" He splashed her back, and she giggled and swam away from him. He loved how impulsive she was, keeping him guessing and pushing him out of his comfort zone.

"How many times have we swam in this lake?" She treaded water beside him.

"A million?" He splashed her.

She splashed him back. "That sounds about right."

Soon they were in a splashing war, with water and their laughter raining through the air.

Emily reached over and grabbed his shoulder while gasping for air. "Truce. Okay?"

Her warm hand on his shoulder sent a shock wave of heat rushing over his skin.

He pretended to consider the request. "I don't know. You

started it, but now you can't take it, huh?" He rested his hands on her shoulders. "What if I dunked you? Maybe then we'll be even, after you pushed me in the lake and then splashed me."

"Please don't." Her words came out in a squeak.

He chuckled and then swam to the dock and pushed himself up out of the water. He stood and reached over. "Come on."

She held up her arms, and he lifted her out of the water as if she were as light as a feather. She hugged her arms to her middle, and he tried not to stare at her. Water dripped from her long hair, and her clothes stuck against her skin. He couldn't help but think she was gorgeous.

He cleared his throat and tossed her the T-shirt she'd left on the dock. She pulled it over her head and shoved her feet into her shoes.

"I guess we need towels," he said as he put on his T-shirt. "Let's go to my place."

Chapter 7

EMILY HUGGED HER arms around her waist while droplets of water dripped onto Jake's concrete driveway, forming puddles around her Birkenstocks.

Jake tapped in the code for his garage door, and the motor hummed while the door lifted. His plain tan T-shirt was damp and sticking to his shoulders and back, and as much as she tried to look away, her eyes defied her and studied how the taut muscles in his torso flexed as he moved. The magnificent sight was almost as intoxicating as the view of him with his shirt off. She'd been so mesmerized by him that she'd pushed him into the water to shake herself from her momentary stupor.

He sauntered into the garage. "I'll get us some towels."

Emily glanced around the garage, which contained shelves of tools and supplies, lawn equipment, and a bicycle.

When she spotted a shelf holding jugs containing an orange liquid, she rushed over to it. "Jake Hughes! How long have you been making cider?"

He brushed his hand over his sternum. "A while. Hasn't worked out yet."

"Can I try some?" she asked.

"Don't bother. It's not any good." He started for the door. "I'll be right back with a towel for you." He disappeared inside the house.

Once the door clicked shut, she began to examine the jugs. According to the dates scrawled on the surface, he'd been working on cider for more than a year, and he'd never mentioned it to her once. Curious. She'd always assumed they told each other everything. She was both impressed by his effort and disappointed that he'd never shared it with her. Perhaps she didn't know everything about him after all.

Emily tugged open the refrigerator door and found two more jugs of cider on the top shelf beside a few bottles of water. One of the jugs was three-quarters full. After locating a cup on a nearby workbench, she poured herself some and took a long drink. The tart goodness slipped down her throat, and she smiled before taking another long drink. Jake had brewed some delicious nonalcoholic cider! Why had he kept this to himself? Soon the cup was empty, and she refilled it before drinking more.

The back door opened, and Jake walked down the garage steps dressed in fresh athletic shorts and a blue T-shirt that complemented his gorgeous eyes and brawny torso.

"What are you doing?" he asked while holding out a large beach towel featuring multicolored surfboards in one hand and a shirt and shorts in the other.

She placed the cup on the workbench and wrapped the towel around herself. "I'm enjoying the homemade cider you hid in your fridge, and I'm also trying to figure out why you've kept it a secret."

"Aren't you supposed to ask permission before going through someone's fridge?"

"Not when I'm at your house." She lifted a corner of the towel and rubbed it over her long hair. "The cider's delicious. You need to sell it. Seriously."

"No, it's not good enough." He held up the shorts and shirt. "Here are some dry clothes. The shorts have a drawstring. They're good enough to get you back to my folks' house."

"Thanks." She climbed the stairs leading into his laundry room.

"Hey," he called, and she spun to face him. "Next time we swim, how about we change into our swimsuits first?"

"Where's the fun in that?" she asked, and the grin she received in return made her insides turn to mush.

Emily hurried through the laundry room to the bathroom, where she stripped out of her wet shirt, tank top, and shorts. She lifted the gray shirt he'd given her over her head and breathed in the cozy smell of his laundry detergent while hugging the soft fabric against her body. Then she stepped into his black athletic shorts and tied the drawstring as tight as she could.

She gathered up her wet clothes and exited the bathroom, meeting Dusty in the hallway. "Hey, girl." Crouching down, she rubbed the cat's head. Dusty lifted her chin and purred with delight. "I'll see you soon, okay?"

"Meow!"

Emily left the wet towel on his washing machine and found a grocery bag for her soggy clothes before returning to the garage, where Jake rested against a metal shelf while talking on the phone. Her stomach sank as she imagined Claire on the other end, spewing her undying love for him and begging him to run away to Nashville with her.

Way to be dramatic, Emily!

"All right," he said. "We'll be there soon." He disconnected the call and dropped his phone into his pocket before rubbing his hands together. "We've been summoned for supper. It's taco night."

Emily almost sagged with relief. "Great!"

He started out the open door.

"Wait." She sidled up to him and pointed to the jugs of cider sitting on the shelf. "We're going to sell your cider in the barn. I'll design a label."

He shoved his hand through his wet hair, and his messy locks reminded her of when they were in high school. "It's not ready."

"Then we'll work on it until you think it is."

He pursed his lips for a moment before taking her hand in his. His warm skin sent a thrill zipping down her spine. "You know my mom doesn't like it when we're late for supper. Let's go." He took a step and tugged her hand, but she stood firm, unmoving.

She held on to him. "Have your folks tried your cider?"

"No, they don't need to know about it."

"You should tell them."

"Not until it's perfected." His expression sobered. "It's a secret. Please keep it to yourself, okay?" he asked, and she nodded. "Promise me."

She pretended to lock her lips with an invisible key.

He laughed. "Let's go eat."

* * *

"Why is Emily wearing your clothes?" Mom asked while Jake loaded the dishwasher with their empty plates after supper.

The sound of the shower running in the upstairs hall bathroom hummed above them. While they'd eaten Mom's delicious tacos, along with rice and refried beans, Emily entertained his parents with hilarious stories about customers she'd encountered at the coffee shop in Charlotte. He appreciated how Emily happily chatted with his folks and how she felt like part of the family—like she always had.

And he couldn't help thinking about how cute she looked in his clothes.

After supper, he'd told Emily to go shower while he helped Mom with the dishes. Emily had tried to protest, insisting she needed to help, but after a little pouting, she finally agreed to go upstairs.

"We went for a swim after I worked on the barn roof with Vince and the guys. We were both soaked, so we stopped by my place and got some dry clothes."

"I'm sure the lake was refreshing after that hard work," Mom said as she packaged the leftovers in containers. "I love having Emily here. Feels like old times. If only Ally were here too."

Jake nodded and added the utensils to the dishwasher.

"Emily gives you a run for your money, that's for sure. I can see her pushing you into the lake." She chuckled.

"How'd you know swimming was her idea?" he joked.

Mom chuckled. "I know how she is."

Jake grinned while he recalled splashing her in the lake. And how good she looked with her clothes clinging to her and her long hair cascading down her back and dripping on the dock. His heart skipped a beat.

Dude, she's your friend! Knock it off!

"She's never been afraid to challenge you. I've always loved that about her."

Me too. Along with many other things.

Jake stacked the glasses on the top shelf of the dishwasher and tried to cool the temperature inside his head.

"When are you going to see Claire again?" Mom asked.

"Don't know." He kept his eyes focused on the dishwasher.

"Jake," Mom said, and he busied himself with adding the serving platters. "Look at me."

He blew out a long sigh and faced her.

The concern in her blue eyes pricked his heart. "I can tell you and Claire are having problems." Her face was solemn. "Do you want to talk about it?"

"Not really."

Mom patted his cheek. "Honey, you're almost thirty. You might want to start thinking about settling down. Especially if you want to start a family."

Jake let out a slow breath. "I hear you, Mom. Right now I'm focused on the orchard."

"Don't let life pass you by. That's all I'm trying to say." Her eyes reddened as they began to pool with tears.

Oh no.

"Your dad's heart attack made me realize how—how precious life is."

He touched her arm. "I know." His voice was gravelly.

She cleared her throat. "That's why you need to get married, son." She clasped her hands together. "Your dad's health is fragile. I know a wedding and some grandbabies would lift his soul so much."

Jake pressed his lips together. "Listen, a wedding isn't on my agenda right now. But maybe Ally will get married first and give you and Dad some grandkids."

Mom wiped her eyes. "We almost lost your dad." Her voice sounded thick. "I'm so afraid of losing him. We've been together thirty-five years."

Ugh.

Seeing his mom cry was too much. He tried to swallow back the guilt clogging his throat.

"You and Claire have been through so much. You can't give up on her now. She was your rock after your dad's heart attack."

He agreed that he and Claire had history. But a future together? He wasn't so sure about that.

Mom turned her attention to stacking the containers of leftovers in the refrigerator. When the shower stopped running above them, an idea hit him.

He added a detergent packet to the dishwasher before starting it.

"I need to go look for something," he told his mom.

As he jogged up the stairs to his old room, he tried to shake off his mom's emotional discussion. He needed to focus on the present—which was the orchard. He'd ponder his future later.

* * *

Emily sat on the edge of the bed, clad in a pair of cotton shorts and a green tank top as she brushed her waist-length dark hair. Not only had supper been delicious, but the conversation was lively and fun. She enjoyed laughing and bantering with Jake and his folks.

When she was younger, Emily used to imagine she was married to Jake, and his family was her family. Such a ridiculous fantasy, but tonight the feeling overcame her once again. She tried to tamp it down, but the more she laughed and talked with them, the more her dream of Jake being more than a friend pulsated and morphed.

Get ahold of yourself! He's not ever going to let go of Claire!

A knock sounded on the door, and she set the brush down beside her. "Who is it?"

"Take a wild guess," Jake deadpanned, and she laughed. "Come in."

He pushed the door open and held up a shoebox. "You need to see this." His eyes roved over her as if he were checking her out. A wave of warmth washed through her.

Surely she was imagining it. He'd never noticed her in that way before.

She patted the spot beside her. "Sit."

He sank down beside her, and the bed shifted under his weight. Then he held out the box. "Open it."

Emily lifted the lid and gasped. It was full of the napkins she'd doodled on—hundreds of them! Shock rolled through her as she combed through them, her brain traveling back in time on a wave of memories. She recognized some of the doodles, but others weren't familiar.

"Jake," she whispered, her heart squeezing. "This—this is crazy."

"I told you I kept them."

She met his gaze. "Why on earth would you want to?"

His smile was adorable. "Why wouldn't I? *You* drew them." He gave her shoulder a gentle shove, and once again, Jake Hughes had managed to overwhelm her with his thoughtfulness. No wonder this man had stolen her heart back when they were kids.

She flipped through the napkins and laughed as she picked up one featuring an illustrated food fight in their middle school cafeteria. "I remember this day like it was yesterday! The jocks across the cafeteria started a food fight and were all sent to the principal's office."

"Right!" He chuckled. "The cafeteria monitor was so angry that her face turned as red as one of our apples."

They both laughed.

Emily folded her legs under herself and chose another napkin with a doodle of the lake and a little boat with two people sitting in it. She turned it over, hoping to find a date, but she didn't see one. "I wonder why I drew this?" She gave the napkin to Jake.

"I don't remember, but it's good. All of your doodles are good." He tossed the napkin into the box.

"Right," she replied with sarcasm. She examined a few more. "I remember this one." She handed him a napkin covered in a drawing of Jake's grandfather's truck with people sitting in the bed. A banner with "Hughes Family Orchard" adorned the side of the truck. "That's when we were in the Splendid Lake Apple Festival parade."

He grinned. "That was a fun day."

"It was." Emily had sat in the truck bed, along with Ally and a few friends. Claire had insisted on being in the cab with Jake. She could still recall how her stomach roiled every time Claire stole a kiss from Jake.

"What about this one?" Jake held up a napkin with a doodle of the football field. "This was when Splendid Lake High School was in the run for the state championship."

"Which we lost."

"But the games were still fun," he countered.

"They were." She'd always loved sitting in the stands with Jake and their friends during the football games. She assumed Jake was there to watch his girlfriend cheer with the rest of the squad, but Emily cherished sitting beside him.

When she found one featuring a bouquet of flowers, her stomach constricted. She remembered that day vividly.

Senior year. Valentine's Day. Claire had spent their entire lunchtime bragging about the bouquet of roses that Jake had given her. Emily had poured her jealousy into drawing a bouquet as a way to cope with her feelings—and also avoid looking at Claire. All these years later, Emily could still feel that envy boiling low in her stomach. It hadn't faded one bit.

Yanking herself from that memory, Emily glanced up at Jake, and his intense expression sent a chill through her.

"What?" she managed to say, the air stuck in her lungs.

"Why did you give up on your dream of being an artist—a professional, full-time artist?"

She shook her head and began stacking the napkins neatly into the box. She didn't want to have this conversation—not now, not ever. Her failures were something she needed to overcome without his help. He wasn't going to be here forever. He would surely find his way to Nashville. With Claire. And without her.

"Hey." Jake took her hands in his. "Look at me, Emily."

Hearing his voice say her full name sent a jolt directly to her heart. She could count on one hand how many times Jake had called her by her full name since they'd met nearly twenty-five years ago, and each time he'd said it, they were either having a serious conversation or in some kind of peril.

She slowly lifted her eyes to meet his, and his blue orbs were full of concern and something she couldn't quite identify that made her feel all fluttery inside.

"*Please* tell me the truth." His voice pleaded with her. "Why did you give up your dream?"

She sighed. "It just didn't work out." She did her best to sound casual, but she heard the thread of pain in her voice.

He looked unconvinced. "Did you *really* try?"

"Jake, I don't want to talk about this." She tried to stand up, but he hauled her back down onto the bed.

"We've always told each other the truth, right?"

She nodded.

"Then tell me. I remember you helping the other kids in art class when we were in school. You were so good at it. And you were a wonderful art teacher here at the community center, and I know you loved that job. You beamed every time you talked about it."

She nodded. That was true. She had loved her job at the community center, teaching art to both kids and adults. But once her parents died, everything changed—including her love for her job. Nothing seemed to make sense anymore. Everything felt sort of . . . pointless. Her parents' death was a bomb that had exploded her life—every single aspect.

"You've floated from job to job since you moved to Charlotte. Why would you stop teaching art, something you love and excel at, to work at a coffee shop?" His eyes searched hers. "It doesn't make any sense to me. So please, help me understand."

Her throat dried while she tried to form a response. How could she explain she'd lost her muse? Plus, if she told him that, then he'd want her to completely open up to him.

The truth was, her muse wasn't just this nebulous thing. After a while she'd realized . . . *Jake* was her muse. And he'd been her muse for so long. But she'd finally forced herself to give up on him, finally accepted that she could never have him. She couldn't allow herself to bare her soul to him. They'd always been honest with each other—to a point. She'd kept her love for him locked up deep within her heart. She couldn't allow herself to be that vulnerable. If she did, then he'd tell her that he didn't care about her that way, and it would not only destroy her heart but also demolish their friendship.

Instead of responding, Emily scooted away from him slightly, trying to put some space between them. "Jake, being an artist, a full-time artist, is not as easy as you think."

"Nothing that's worth it is easy."

He was right, but she wasn't going to admit it.

Silence drifted over the room, and Jake's brow furrowed while he studied her as if she were an intricate puzzle. Tension filled the space between them, and she longed to read his thoughts.

Finally, Jake stood and held out his hand to her. "Come with me."

She threaded her fingers with his before he lifted her to her feet and towed her across the hall to his old bedroom, which his folks had converted into an office after he moved out. A desk, a few filing cabinets, and a sofa replaced his double bed and dressers. But the walls were still the same pale blue as they'd been when it was Jake's room.

"Check it out." He pointed to the far wall where a large painting of downtown Splendid Lake decorated for the holidays hung.

Emily sucked in air while she perused the painting. She'd created it for her senior project, and she'd spent weeks on it—adding the details of the glowing Christmas tree, the lights illuminating each store window, decorations adorning every light post, and the townspeople enjoying the evening.

The painting had won first prize in a local art show, and it had hung in her parents' den from the day she brought it home until she sold the house. After that, it had been packed up in the Hugheses' basement for the past four years.

"When did your mom hang it here?" she asked Jake.

"I hung it here shortly after you left for Charlotte. I went down to the basement looking for something and came across your paintings. When I saw this one, I decided it needed to be enjoyed, not hidden away and forgotten. This is your masterpiece." He rested his hand on her shoulder. "You're talented—really, *really* talented. You need to share that talent with the world, not hide it away like you hid this painting in my parents' basement."

She cupped her hand to her mouth as his words unlocked something deep inside her. She tried in vain to swallow back the emotion and spun away from him, but it was too late. Tears filled her eyes, and her shoulders began to shake.

"Hey." He came up behind her and rested his hands on her shoulders. "I didn't mean to upset you." His voice was low in her ears, sending a quiver dancing up and down her spine. "I just wanted to say that I believe in you."

"You were always the only one who ever did." Her voice was raspy.

"That's not true."

She spun to face him. "It is." She pointed to the painting. "When I won that art award, I got a small scholarship. I told my parents I wanted to be a professional artist, and they said I was wasting my talent. They wanted me to become a college professor like my dad or a pediatrician like my mom, but all I ever wanted to do was draw and paint. They were so disappointed in me when I went to school to become an art teacher."

"You never told me that." His words were soft, and he looked stricken. "Why did you keep it from me?"

"Because it was too painful to share." She rested her hand flat against his chest. "You're the only one who thought I could be an artist, and I let you down." Now her tears were flowing like a waterfall, and she felt like an idiot for losing it in front of him—*again*!

Why couldn't she keep it together when she was around Jake?

"Get over here." He pulled her into his arms.

She basked in the comfort his strong arms provided, and she worked to get her tears under control. For a few moments, she imagined Jake was hers and they were in a real relationship, but then she shook herself back to reality and stepped out of his arms.

Emily plucked a tissue from a box on the desk and wiped her eyes and nose.

He touched her arm. "I still believe in you. You need to learn how to believe in yourself."

"Right." She cleared her throat and pointed to the painting. "Thanks for getting my painting out of the basement." She tossed the tissue into a small trash can under the desk and picked up a notepad and a pen. "Let's make a plan for the barn." She sat in one of the office chairs, then studied the notepad and tried to ignore how her heart suddenly craved more hugs from Jake than ever. "When do you think the roof will be done?"

"I'd imagine by the end of the week, since four of us are working on it." He sank down beside her, and while he discussed the barn, she tried to dismiss her longing to crawl back into his protective arms and stay there forever.

Chapter 8

JAKE SAT BACK on his heels and scanned the roof. It was Friday evening, and the roof renovation was finally done. He hadn't expected it to take all week, but thanks to quite a bit of rotten wood, the project was bigger than he'd planned, and it had taken more money than expected. He was dipping into his savings, but it was for a good cause—his family's legacy. He refused to let Emily pay. Instead, he'd rely on his savings and then his credit card.

The evening was actually cool, and he was grateful that the late-summer air was finally letting go of some humidity and hinting that autumn would be here soon.

Jake stood up to his full height and turned toward the orchard employees. "Thanks so much for staying late so we could finish this up. Next week we'll start on the barn walls."

"Sounds good, Boss," Vince said, and Eddie and Rico nodded.

They all climbed down the ladder.

"Have a good weekend." Jake waved as they climbed into their pickups and took off.

After stashing his gloves and supplies in the barn, he glanced around the area in search of Emily. They'd texted earlier, and she'd mentioned she was helping his mother with a few chores and would join him soon.

He pivoted toward an old picnic table, where Emily worked on her sketch pad. His lips turned up in a grin. He should've known she'd be drawing.

She was completely focused on her project. Her right hand flew over the paper, and her head bopped along with a beat only she could hear in her AirPods. Her dark hair fell in waves past her shoulders, catching the evening light in a way that cast an almost imperceptible red glow.

He liked the way the corners of her mouth curved up slightly as she sang along softly with an oldies song. Her vibrant golden eyes sparkled as she concentrated. And with her perfect nose, high cheekbones, and symmetrical face, he suddenly realized Emily was . . . captivating. His pulse quickened as he felt an unfamiliar spike of adrenaline in her presence.

He stilled for a moment as a strange feeling washed over him. He felt something unlock deep inside him—something he hadn't felt for years. Was he imagining it? But if that were true, then why were his hands trembling?

He took a deep breath and tried in vain to dismiss this crazy notion that he had romantic feelings for her.

"Hey," he called, and his voice sounded hoarse. He cleared his throat. "Carmichael!"

But Emily kept singing and drawing.

He crept up behind her and peered down at her sketch pad and found what looked like a label with the words "Hughes Family Orchard Cider" in the center of a logo featuring a grove of trees. She continued to sing the lyrics to "Do You Believe in Magic" by The Lovin' Spoonful while she shaded the label with a red pencil. As usual, the drawing was impressive. He'd always been blown away by her level of detail—even the leaves on the trees were lifelike. But as great as her logo was, he still wasn't going to try to sell his cider and risk ruining his family's reputation.

Emily shifted, and when her golden eyes focused on him, she gasped and removed an AirPod from her left ear. "I hate it when you sneak up on me," she exclaimed.

"Sneak? I've been calling you, but you're too busy drawing and singing to hear me."

She worked to catch her breath. "That's it! I'm buying you a collar with a bell on it."

He chuckled before jamming his thumb toward the water. "We finished the roof. Let's go."

"When did you become the boss of me?" She shot him a look, but the twinkle in her eyes made him grin.

"I've been the boss since you showed up uninvited in my orchard when we were five and never left. Now come on."

She closed up her sketch pad and stored her AirPods in their case before stuffing them, along with her colored pencils, into her giant bag. "Where are we going?" she asked, hefting the bag onto her shoulder.

"For a boat ride."

"Now?"

"Yes, right now. The guys and I have been busting our rears on the barn all week. I need a break and so do you."

They traipsed down the path to the dock, and he climbed into the old aluminum johnboat that Jake was convinced was as old as he was—if not older. But the small boat still did its job. Jake held his hand out to Emily, and she took it. When her warm fingers entwined with his, he tried to ignore the zip of heat that traveled up his arm.

What was wrong with him? He'd held Emily's hand a million times over the years. Maybe he was coming down with something. Scarlet fever? Yup, that had to be it. It was just a hot flash caused by a terrible illness. That was the only explanation that made any sense.

Emily settled on a seat in the center of the boat, and he started the engine before they glided out toward the middle of the lake. Above them, the sun began to set. He turned off the engine and the boat bobbed gently while the waves lapped up against it.

Soon his aching muscles began to relax. He relished being out on the lake—breathing in a whiff of the water and taking in the sound of the happy frogs croaking nearby while he peered at the familiar lights on the shore. This was his lake. Well, technically, it wasn't *his*, but it was home, and being out here with Emily made it feel even more special.

She opened her giant shoulder bag, plucked out her sketch pad, and flipped to the picture of the logo before shoving it into his hands. "I know you saw it earlier. What do you think?"

"It's great, but you're wasting your talent. I'm not selling the cider. Not now, not ever."

She eyed him. "Did you get your stubbornness from your mom, your dad, or both of them?"

He chuckled.

"Yup. Definitely from your dad. Your mom is more apt to compromise." She took the sketch pad back. "The cider will be a great addition to our fall market. I'll find a way to convince you to sell it. You'll see." She paused for a moment, her eyes flashing with determination. "You really haven't told your folks about it?"

He shook his head. "Nope. You're the only one who knows."

He held up a finger. "But I need to add that you were snooping when you found it, so I technically didn't tell you about it."

"You haven't told *anyone* at all?"

"No, no one." He tilted his head. "What are you getting at?"

"What about Claire?"

He snorted. "She'd never want to hear about my lame attempt at making cider. She just wants me to move to Nashville with her." He turned on the engine and motored out farther into the lake.

The boat glided through the water, and Emily looked lost in thought while she squinted up at the sky above them. The radiant prism of colors from the sunset created a halo around her, making her dainty features even more striking.

Why hadn't he ever noticed how pretty she was?

He shoved down that question just as Emily focused on him. "You're staring at me again. What's up?"

Oh no.

Had she heard his thoughts? His stomach constricted.

"Nothing." He shrugged and tried to sound casual despite his rocketing heartbeat. "I was trying to read your thoughts, but my Carmichael ESP is a bit rusty. So tell me—whatcha thinkin' about?"

She pointed to the sky. "The sunsets are always glorious here in Splendid Lake." She paused. "And they're the best to paint," she added, her words soft and full of reverence.

"So paint it."

"I can't, silly. I don't have my easel or my paints."

He pointed to her humongous bag. "Use your sketch pad and your colored pencils. Take your time. We can sit here as long as you want."

Her hand fluttered to her necklace, and she began twiddling

with her mother's rings. "No." She shook her head while keeping her eyes focused on the heavens above them. "Not tonight." She turned her attention back to him and smiled, but her smile didn't quite reach her eyes. "Let's head back." She rubbed her hands over her arms. "It's getting a little chilly."

He started the engine before piloting the boat back to the dock. After tying it up, he climbed out and then held his hand out to her. Emily threaded her fingers with his and allowed him to guide her up onto the dock.

"Thanks for the ride, Captain Hughes."

He chuckled, and she released his hand before bumping his side.

They headed down the path, using the flashlights on their phones to guide their way. When they reached the path leading to her former childhood home, she hesitated.

"Do you want to walk over to your old house?" Jake rested his hand on her shoulder. "I'll go with you."

She craned her neck over her shoulder and gave him a sad smile. "Thanks, but no."

They continued until they reached the turnoff for his house. When they stopped, she threw her arms around his neck and hugged him.

"Good night," she whispered before hurrying toward his parents' house.

* * *

Emily flipped Jake's radio to the oldies station and began singing with The Beach Boys' "Good Vibrations." The sky above them was cloudy, and a pleasant breeze drifted in from their open windows. It was Tuesday morning, and they'd just left the home improvement store after filling the bed of his truck with sheets of plywood and other supplies to continue fixing the barn walls.

When she snuck a glance at Jake, she spotted him resting his left arm on the truck door while he steered with his right hand. He wore his usual Mets ball cap, and he tapped his fingers along with the beat of the song.

She leaned toward him. "So you actually like the oldies, but you don't want to admit it."

"What?" He scoffed. "No way."

She pointed to his left arm. "I have proof. You're enjoying it."

He shook his head.

"You're going to let me help build the walls on the barn today, right?" she asked. "Having me 'supervise,'" she continued, making air quotes with her fingers, "is insulting to everyone of my gender. I'm capable of hitting a nail. Don't you remember when I built that diorama of the town square for art class in middle school? That required a hammer and nails, and I escaped without injury and got an A." She lifted her chin.

He stopped at a stop sign and faced her, his grin making her want to melt into the bench seat. "You're cute when you're annoyed."

Oh yeah. Just call her a puddle, because she was definitely liquefying after that compliment.

But wait—he avoided her question!

"Jake, are you going to let me help or what?"

He accelerated through the intersection. "We'll see."

She harrumphed. "Such a nonanswer," she muttered.

He snickered and drove up a hill. When he came down the other side, a small dark sedan was parked by the side of the road with the trunk opened. An older man squatted beside the rear driver-side tire and seemed to be struggling to loosen the lug nuts.

"Is that Mr. Tompkins?" Emily asked.

"I think so." Jake slowed the truck and parked behind the sedan before flipping on his hazard lights and climbing out. "Sir, do you need help?" he called.

Emily hopped out of the passenger seat and met him at the back of the sedan.

The older man stood and swiped his hand over his balding head. "Why, Jake Hughes. Good to see you, son." He nodded at Emily and then held up the tire iron. "I can't get these old lug nuts to budge. I'd sure appreciate it if you gave it a try."

"Happy to." Jake took the tire iron, and squatting down, he slipped it onto the first lug nut and spun it as if it had never been tightened. As he loosened the remaining lug nuts, Emily folded her arms over her middle while enjoying the view of the taut muscles in his shoulders and arms flexing.

Jake was so fit, so kind, and so . . . *amazing.*

She swallowed a sigh.

Get it together, Emily!

"I tell ya," Mr. Tompkins began, "I'm not as young as I used to be. Forty years ago, I could've removed those just as fast as you did."

Jake stood up and adjusted his ball cap. "It's no problem." He pointed to the back of the car. "I'm assuming the jack is in the trunk?"

"Sure is."

Jake scooted around the car and returned with the scissor jack and spare tire.

"It's good to see you, Emily," Mr. Tompkins said. "Last I heard you'd sold your folks' place and moved out to Charlotte. Are you back for good?"

She shook her head. "I'm here helping Jake with some plans for the orchard."

"I'm hoping to convince her to stay." Jake gave her a wink while he removed the flat tire. Then he slipped on the spare and began replacing the lug nuts.

Mr. Tompkins shoved his hands in the pockets of his khaki shorts and began jingling a pocketful of change. "It's a good idea to get some help with your orchard. It looks like your competitor is going to give you a run for your money."

"What makes you say that?" Jake's posture and expression went rigid while he tightened everything into place.

"I've heard some things." The portly older man shifted his weight on his feet, and the change in his pocket jingled.

"What kinds of things?" Jake lowered the car and shielded his eyes from the sun.

"Well, I'm not the type of person to tell tales, but . . ." *Jingle jingle jingle.* "My wife has her schoolmates over for tea every Friday, and last week those ol' biddies were just gossiping away."

Emily took a step toward him. "Go ahead and tell us, Mr. Tompkins. We won't share it with anyone." She shrugged. "And if we do, we won't say where we heard it. Right, Jake?"

Jake's lips flattened as he nodded.

Mr. Tompkins cleared his throat. "Folks are saying that the new place is going to put the Hughes Family Orchard out of business since it's been . . . *ahem*, going downhill." He held his hands up. "Those aren't my words. I'd never say that about your family's place. I remember picking apples there when I was a child. Your orchard is a fixture here."

Jake's face pinched as he loaded the flat tire into the trunk and shut the lid.

Uh-oh.

"We have some plans that will knock your socks off, and we'll show everyone that Hughes Family Orchard is still the best around." Emily rested her hand on Jake's forearm and smiled at him. "Right, Jake?"

"Yeah."

He nodded, but she could feel his worry in his tense muscles.

Mr. Tompkins shook Jake's hand. "Well, thank you for stopping to help me. I really appreciate it."

"No problem," Jake said. "You're all set. If you take the tire to Burns Auto Repair, they can fix it for you."

Emily waved to Mr. Tompkins and then climbed into Jake's Dodge pickup.

Jake took his spot in the driver's seat. A frown clouded his handsome face while he turned the key, and the truck chattered to life.

Emily rested her hand on his thick bicep. "Hey. Look at me."

He met her gaze.

"Everything is going to be fine."

His forehead puckered. "How can you be so sure?"

"Because I believe in you, and I believe in the orchard. And you should too."

His expression warmed slightly.

"And mark my words . . ." She gave him her best mischievous smile. "We're going to have a blast kicking Apple Haven's butt."

He snorted, and when a smile turned up his lips, her heart tripped over itself.

"There's that smile I love." The words slipped out of her mouth before she could stop them, and when heat infused her cheeks, she tried to look casual.

"Thanks," he said before steering the truck onto the road. "We'd better get back to the barn."

Chapter 9

EMILY STEPPED OUT of her bedroom and headed toward the stairs Wednesday afternoon. A sweet, decadent smell filled her senses, sending a whirlwind of happy childhood memories scrolling through her mind as she made a beeline for the kitchen.

"Are you making—?" Emily gasped when she found a row of candy apples lining the counter. "You *are* making candy apples!"

Diane chuckled while setting another one on the paper to cool.

"Those are part of some of my favorite childhood memories," Emily continued. "Jake and I ate them until we got sick every fall. Do you need help?"

"Nope. This is the last one." She dipped it in the syrup, turned it a few times, and then set it down to cool. "Take one."

"Are you sure?"

Diane waved her off. "Don't be silly."

Emily chose one of the cool ones and took a bite. She closed her eyes as the flavors of syrup and apple overtook her mouth.

"You make the best candy apples in the state of North Carolina, if not the world." She bent toward Diane and lowered her voice. "Are you ready to tell me your secret recipe?"

Diane wagged her finger at her. "Now, you know better than that. I can't share the Hughes secret family recipe with anyone."

"Rats." Emily snapped her fingers and then took another bite. *Delicious!*

Diane rested against the counter beside her. "How are things going with the barn project?"

"It's coming along. We're still working on the walls. I just came in for a minute, but I'm heading back out there. Hopefully we'll be painting soon." She paused, lowering her voice. "Jake wouldn't let me help with the roof, but I'm grateful I'm allowed to help with the walls." She rolled her eyes, and Diane laughed.

"He always was overprotective of you. I remember when you dated that guy your senior year." She tapped her chin. "What was his name?"

Emily sighed. "Evan. Jake couldn't stand him."

"That's right," Diane exclaimed. "I think he told me nearly every day that you could do better. He said that Evan was a liar and a cheat."

"And Jake was right. I found out the hard way."

Diane smiled. "You two have been through a lot together."

That's true. Emily nodded and ate more of the apple.

"I was so relieved when he told me he was going to beg you to come home to help out here. He's been so stressed out since his dad's heart attack." Diane's expression filled with concern. "How's my son doing? Really?"

Emily wiped her mouth with a paper napkin. "He's worried about the orchard. But I keep telling him that we've got this and it's going to be okay." She decided to keep the rumors about the competitor's orchard to herself. No need to upset Jake's mom.

"Having a market in the barn is a brilliant idea, and I think it just might work."

Emily glanced down at the row of candy apples as an idea filled her mind. "Could I take a couple of these outside to share?"

"Of course you can."

"Thanks."

* * *

Jake frowned and glanced around the side of the barn, where Vince continued to hammer new sheets of plywood over where the rotten boards had been removed.

Vince had arrived right at eight that morning, ready to work, but Jake hadn't heard from Eddie or Rico, despite his efforts to text and call them. They'd both seemed off yesterday—very quiet instead of their usual jovial selves. Jake had a feeling that something was up, but he'd let it go since everyone had bad days.

But having only Vince's and Emily's help with the barn walls was going to put them behind. He'd wanted the walls done by Friday so they could focus on getting the interior ready for the vendors. At this rate the barn would never be ready in time for the anniversary celebration.

His phone dinged with two texts almost simultaneously—one from Rico and one from Eddie.

> Rico: Hey, Jake. I took a job with Apple Haven. Sorry to do this, but I need the higher pay. I have to think of my family. Anyway, I'll stop by Friday for my last paycheck. Hope you understand. Thanks.

Eddie: Yo, Boss. Sorry to bail, but I accepted a position with Apple Haven. Got a raise and benefits too. I appreciate the opportunity, but you know how it is. Anyway, I'll be there Friday for my last paycheck. Thanks, man.

Jake's stomach bottomed out, and his jaw clenched.

Not only was Apple Haven threatening to take his customers, but now they were stealing his *employees*. What was next? Would they come for his parents' home? Their land?

With a growl, Jake dropped his phone in his pocket and picked up his hammer and a piece of Sheetrock. He lined up the sheet of plywood with the barn frame, lifted the hammer, and set the nail in place. He banged the nail into the wood with all his might, doing his best to release all the stress and anger swarming his chest. He repeated the process until the piece of plywood was secured in the wall.

Mr. Tompkins's warnings about Apple Haven came to the forefront of his mind as he set another piece of the plywood against the barn's wall frame. He held it steady with his left forearm while holding a nail between his finger and thumb.

Folks are saying that the new place is going to put Hughes Family Orchard out of business since it's been . . . ahem, going downhill.

The words echoed through Jake's mind, and he lost his concentration and missed the nail, sending a shock wave of pain from his thumb through his hand and up his arm. Sucking in a deep breath, he dropped the hammer and began to dance around. Shaking his hand and stamping his foot, he groaned and tucked his hand under his opposite arm.

"Jake!" Emily's frantic voice sounded behind him. "Are you okay?"

She appeared beside him and grabbed his arm. "Let me see."

Her golden-brown eyes were full of concern, and her empathy made his mouth dry.

He held out his hand, and she examined his thumb, now bright red. She brushed her fingers over his hand, and her warm skin made his heart flop around like a fish out of water.

"Can you move it?" she asked.

He did, and when the pain flared, he hissed.

"I'll go get you some ice," she said, and she started toward the path.

"No," he said, and she stopped moving. "I'm fine." She raised her eyebrows, and he added, "Really, I am. But thanks." He brushed his hand over his stubble and frowned.

She studied him. "What's wrong?"

"I bashed my thumb. Remember?"

"You need to turn the frown upside, and I have just the remedy. I have a surprise for you and Vince." She looked past Jake. "Hey, Vince! You still here?"

"Yeah." Vince came around from the back of the barn and pushed his hand over his dark hair.

Emily jogged over to the picnic table and returned with two candied apples. "Jake's mom is making her out-of-this-world candy apples. I snagged two for you." She handed them over. "She still won't tell me what's in her secret recipe."

"Oh man, I love these things! They're the best," Vince said before taking a bite.

Jake nodded and did the same, and the crisp treat brought back a rush of childhood memories.

"I have an idea," Emily suddenly announced.

Jake swallowed another bite. "I'm listening."

She bounced on the balls of her Birkenstocks. "Let's put a kitchen in the barn!"

He blinked and then blinked again. Had he heard her right? "A kitchen?"

"Yes!" She danced a little jig. "That way we can sell these beauties." She pointed at the candied apples. "Along with your cider."

Vince did a double take. "When did you start making cider, Boss?"

So much for Em keeping a secret.

Jake ignored the question and took another bite of the apple.

"Just listen. Okay?" Emily took his arm and half pulled, half dragged him into the barn while Vince followed close behind, chewing his apple. She took off and stopped in the middle of the barn before pointing to the back corner. "We can put the kitchen over there. It'll be like a little booth, and then your mom can make her candy apples, and we can keep your cider on shelves. And then we can—"

"Whoa," Jake began, interrupting her. He rubbed his free hand over his forehead. "Do you realize what you're asking us to do? We have to get a permit, hire contractors, and then—"

She held her hand up, and her happy expression faded. "I'll pay for it. You haven't let me pay for anything yet, but I want to do this. For you." Something flashed over her face, and she quickly added, "For your family. For Splendid Lake."

Jake blew out a deep breath and glanced around the barn. It was still a mess, and they had so much work to do: replacing the rotten wood in the floor, painting the entire inside of the barn—after painting the outside, of course—and then building booths for the vendors. He met Emily's hopeful expression and then shook his head. "We have a little more than a month before the anniversary, which is barely enough time to clean this place up. There's no way we can build a kitchen."

"I'll pitch in," Emily said. "You think I'm not capable, but I can do it."

"I believe in you, but right now it's just the three of us doing all of the work."

"What do you mean?" Vince asked.

Jake pressed his lips together. "Eddie and Rico quit."

"What?" Vince's dark eyes rounded. "When?"

"They both texted me earlier. They went to work for Apple Haven." Jake grimaced at Vince. "Tell me you're not going there too."

Vince shook his head. "No, I'm not. I had no idea they were even considering leaving." He paused for a moment. "I'm shocked."

"Yeah. Me too." Jake sank down onto an old bale of hay. "I have no idea how we're going to make this happen. Even if I advertised to replace their jobs, I'm running through our budget with all of these supplies."

Emily came to stand in front of him. "We got this. And I've already told you I'll pay for it." She pointed around the barn. "Let's forget my kitchen idea. It was silly. Instead, your mom can make the candied apples in her kitchen, and we'll bring them out here to sell them. We just need to go forward with our plan of cleaning up the inside and retrofitting the booths. We can install counters and shelves."

"And we need someone to sell the candy apples if we're running the place." Jake pointed to the three of them.

"We'll figure that out, Debbie Downer," Emily quipped.

Vince chuckled.

Jake ate another bite and shook his head while his lips twitched. "You know you drive me crazy."

"That's why you love me," she sang with an adorable smirk.

Yeah, that's absolutely true.

The thought caught Jake by surprise, but he forced his brain to focus on everything they had to do before the orchard opened. He pushed himself up. "That's enough chitchat. We need to get back to work."

"All right, Boss." Vince started for the barn door.

Emily looped her arm in Jake's. "We got this. I promise you." She rested against him, and he cherished the feel of her body heat mixing with his.

"I'm putting my faith in you. Don't make me regret it," he teased, and her smile made his heart buoyant.

* * *

Jake pushed his loaded shopping cart over to the front of the home improvement store the following afternoon. All his muscles ached after working until dark last night, but he was grateful that he and Vince had finished one side of the barn. Emily had insisted that he and Vince continue concentrating on the barn walls while she started painting. He couldn't help himself from checking on her frequently while she was balanced on the scaffolding, and each time he peeked around the side of the barn, she waved him off, promising to yell loudly if she fell. As if that would calm his nerves at all.

He moved forward in the line and chuckled to himself. He was enjoying having Emily at the orchard. Not only did she keep him entertained with her jokes, sarcasm, and quirky personality, but he felt more settled around her. She'd always known how to calm him down when he was stressed.

But it wasn't just that. There was something different about her. He couldn't put his finger on it, but he was almost certain something had shifted in the way he felt about her. But surely that was just his stress talking.

Jake loaded the painting supplies on the conveyor belt and retrieved his credit card. He was easing ever closer to his limit, but he was determined not to accept Emily's money. The orchard belonged to his family and wasn't her problem—no matter how much she insisted she wanted to help him.

After paying, Jake began loading the supplies into the bed of his truck. When he thought he heard someone call his name, he spun just as Seth Wingate rushed toward him. "Seth! What's up?"

"I thought that was you." Seth picked up a gallon of red paint and set it in the bed of Jake's truck. "Andi told me she ran into you and Emily the other day. She said you're working on some projects at the orchard."

"That's true."

"Well?" Seth raised his palms. "What are you working on?"

Jake summarized the rumors that were going around about Apple Haven and then gave him a rundown of what they were planning with the barn. "I'm hoping we can get it all together in time, but I found out that two of my three employees quit to go work at Apple Haven. So now they're not only threatening to take my customers, but they're also poaching my employees." He pushed the cart into the nearby cart corral. "Maybe it's a blessing since I'll save on their salaries and can put those funds into the supplies. But how can we get it all done in time?" He rested against the open tailgate. "Em says it's going to work out, but I'm not so sure."

"Man, that's a lot. Want some help?"

"Thanks, but I'm sure I can't afford you."

"Don't worry about it." Seth leaned beside him. "I'll do it for some of your mom's apple pie and a candy apple."

Jake lifted a suspicious eyebrow.

"Seriously," Seth insisted with a chuckle. "I have three crews working for my landscaping business, and I pretty much spend my days handling clients while Andi takes care of the books. I can handle client calls while I'm working at the orchard." He held up his cell phone. "You know, technology and all. So do you want my help or what?"

"I definitely want it, but I don't want you to feel obligated."

Seth gave him a look. "And how many times did you drive me to and from school when my jalopy was in the shop?"

"Um." Jake adjusted his hat on his head. "Pretty much all of junior and senior year."

Seth chuckled. "That's true." Then he tapped the side of the pickup truck. "I'm glad you kept your grandpa's truck. It suits you." He held out his hand. "Do we have a deal?"

"Deal." Jake shook his hand, and the tension in his back released. Emily was right—things *were* going to work out. He made a mental note to ask his mom to start on some apple pies after she finished the candy apples.

"I haven't seen you in a while. How's Claire?"

Jake closed the tailgate. "Things are . . . rocky right now."

"Really?" Seth seemed surprised. "I thought y'all would be married and have a couple of kids by now."

Jake shook his head. "Nope." Time to change the subject. He gestured toward the truck. "I need to get back to the orchard, but it was great seeing you."

"I'll come by tomorrow."

"Thanks, buddy." Jake climbed into the truck and headed home.

* * *

The sound of a diesel engine drew Emily's attention toward the dirt road spanning the short distance from the orchard entrance to the barn. She climbed down the scaffolding and met Jake at the back of the truck as he hopped out.

"How'd it go at the store?" she asked while lowering the tailgate.

"Great." He climbed in and began handing her supplies. "I got us some more help."

"What do you mean?"

"I ran into Seth Wingate. He's going to come over tomorrow and start helping in exchange for some of my mom's apple pie and candy apples."

She clapped. "Yay! I told you it was going to work out."

He grinned, and her pulse tripled. "You sure did, and you were right."

"Maybe Andi will come too." She picked up a bag of paintbrushes and an extender. "These are perfect."

Jake jumped down to the ground. "Yeah, I thought—" He stopped speaking when his phone began to ring. He studied the screen, and when Emily spotted Claire's name, her belly twisted. He glowered and locked the phone.

She hesitated, waiting for him to say something about Claire. She yearned to know why he didn't accept the call. Was he over Claire, or was there another reason? She longed to read his thoughts. But instead of commenting on the rejected call, he pocketed the phone.

"Need help carrying the paint up the scaffolding?" He hefted a gallon of paint and strolled toward the barn.

Emily followed him. "Yeah. Thanks." She focused on her task at hand and tried to shove away her nagging curiosity about Claire.

Chapter 10

WE'RE SO GRATEFUL that you and Seth came to help," Emily told Andi the following morning. It was the perfect early September morning—not too hot—and the sky was bright blue. A few birds sang in the nearby trees while Emily and Andi used paintbrush extenders to work on the side of the barn.

She had managed to finish the highest part of the wall last night, and despite her sore arms and back, she was determined to finish painting the side of the barn by the end of the day. She was so grateful when Andi and Seth had arrived shortly after eight, and while Jake, Seth, and Vince worked on the walls of the barn, she and Andi set to work painting.

"When Seth told me he ran into Jake and offered to help, I said I'd love to come too since it'll be like old times. Some of my best memories are from when the four of us hung out together. We were never bored." Andi snickered. "Do you remember that time we had a bonfire down on the beach?"

Emily pivoted toward her. "And you set your shoe on fire by accident?"

"Yes!" Andi cackled. "I was like, 'Why is it so hot all of a sudden?'"

"And I was like, 'Uh, Andi . . . look down!'" Emily guffawed and wiped her eyes. "I'll never forget the way you danced around while stamping your foot. I thought Seth and Jake were going to fall down from laughing."

Andi hugged her middle while gasping for air. "Oh my goodness," she said as she got ahold of herself. She leaned her paintbrush extender against the wall and sat on a folding chair before choosing two bottles of water from a nearby cooler. Then she patted the chair beside her. "It's time for a break. Sit." She held out a bottle of water.

Emily sank down onto the chair, opened the bottle, and took a long drink while scrutinizing their work. "We're good painters."

"Now *that's* funny," Andi declared. "An artist is calling me a good painter." She sipped from her bottle. "But the barn is coming together. I can't wait to see what it looks like when it's done."

"Me too." Emily twiddled the bottle cap in her fingers.

The rumble of low conversations drifted over from the other side of the barn.

Andi angled her body toward Emily. "How about the time we got together to dye Easter eggs, and Seth and Jake started horsing around and spilled the egg dye all over the kitchen?"

"I thought your mom was going to lose it." Emily groaned. "I felt so bad about that."

"Yeah. We scrubbed the kitchen until it was glistening." Andi snorted.

Emily began peeling the label off her bottle while the events of that long-ago day flashed through her mind. She had just broken up with Evan a few days earlier, and she had been the fifth wheel with the two couples. She was positive that Claire had been shooting her dirty looks the entire day, which didn't make any sense. Claire had Jake, and Emily was single. But Emily always had the feeling that her existence irritated Claire. Lifting the bottle, she took a long drink of water.

"I always thought you and Jake belonged together."

The comment caught Emily off guard, and she began choking on the water. She tried to suck in air, but she continued to cough.

"You okay?" Andi asked.

Emily sputtered and coughed while trying to respond.

Jake appeared around the side of the barn and rushed over to her. "Hey." He knelt beside her and rubbed her back. "Just breathe."

The worry reflected on his face just made the entire situation even more embarrassing. Behind him, Andi gave her a knowing look.

Finally, the coughing subsided and Emily was able to breathe again. "I'm fine," she told Jake. "Get back to work."

He stood, but his face was full of concern. "You sure?"

"Get out of here," she insisted.

He nodded and then sauntered toward the other side of the barn.

"Like I said . . ." Andi lifted her dark eyebrows.

Emily twisted the cap onto the bottle. "We're—"

"Just good friends, right?" Andi finished her sentence and then pointed her bottle toward her. "You care about him."

Emily threw her arms up. "Of course I do. He's my best friend."

"But you *really* care about him, don't you?"

After peering down toward the corner of the barn, Emily lowered her voice and said, "It doesn't matter, because he doesn't feel the same way about me."

"What makes you say that?"

Emily sighed. "He can't let go of Claire even though it's been rocky for years." She summarized how Claire was splitting her time between Splendid Lake and Nashville and had been begging Jake to move to Nashville with her. "He told me that he still cares about her, and he can't just tell her that it's over because things are 'complicated'"—she made air quotes with her fingers—"between them." She slumped back in the chair. "It's obvious he still cares about her. He says they've broken up, but she calls him all the time and begs him to give it another try. That sounds to me like they're still holding on to each other."

Andi touched her arm. "He cares about you too, Em. Don't give up hope."

"I'm not giving up, Andi. I'm just facing reality."

"I disagree." Andi pointed toward the far end of the barn. "If you paid attention to the way he just ran over here to check on you and make sure you were okay, then you'd agree with me."

Emily stood and picked up her paintbrush extender. "We need to get back to work." But while she continued to paint the barn, she couldn't ignore the hope that took root deep in her heart.

When she heard a car pull up near the barn, she turned just as Ms. Riley climbed out of her gray Honda Accord. "Hi," Emily called as she hurried over. "Is everything okay?"

"Of course it is, dear." Ms. Riley waved a greeting to Andi. "I drove by earlier and saw you all working on this old barn, and I thought I'd bring some of my husband's tools to use. I filled up the trunk for you."

Emily and Andi shared a look as the older woman popped her trunk.

"Ms. Riley," Jake called as he and Seth hurried over to join them. "What's up?"

"She brought us some tools to use while we work on the barn," Emily said. "Isn't that sweet?"

His smile sent warmth swirling in her chest. "It sure is."

They all gathered around the trunk of the car, where they found paintbrushes, rollers, extenders, and trays, along with hammers, saws, and other tools.

"This is very generous of you," Jake said while he and Seth began pulling tools from the trunk. "We'll bring them back when we're done."

"Nonsense," Ms. Riley said. "I'd just be grateful to see you using them, especially for this wonderful place." She glanced around the orchard. "Your orchard is part of what makes Splendid Lake home. If there's anything else I can do to help you, you just let me know."

After carrying the tools and supplies to the barn, they waved to Ms. Riley as she drove away.

"We have some of the nicest neighbors here," Andi said.

Emily smiled. "Yeah. I definitely agree."

* * *

"When was the last time we all had pizza together?" Andi asked while glancing around Jake's small table later that evening.

Jake swallowed a bite of the delicious pepperoni pie. "The last time we were all together was high school, so it had to be senior year."

He was so relieved at the progress they'd made today. While the women had worked on painting one side of the barn, Jake, Seth, and Vince had finished replacing all the rotten boards. Tomorrow they would start on the doors before Emily and Andi helped with the painting.

Vince had left at his usual time, but Seth suggested that the four of them keep working until sundown. When they began running out of light, Jake invited everyone back to his place for pizza. Once the pies arrived, they gathered around his small kitchen table and began to reminisce. Dusty, that lazy cat, continued to snore on her favorite chair in the den as if it were an ordinary evening.

"That's actually not true," Emily said. "We got together a year after graduation. Seth and Andi were home from college, and we had a pool party over at Seth's folks' place. I remember it clearly." When she took a drink of sweet tea, there was something in Emily's eyes that he couldn't quite decipher.

Andi took another piece of pizza. "I remember that." She tapped Seth's arm. "You invited everyone you could track down, and we swam until midnight, when the neighbors complained we were too loud."

"Well, the music was too loud, but we weren't noisy," Seth joked, and everyone laughed. "We were never rowdy."

"Riiight." Andi drew out the word and then giggled.

Jake recalled the party. He'd been so excited to see some of his school friends, but Claire hadn't wanted to go. She finally conceded, but she'd been in a foul mood the entire evening, forcing him to leave early. He'd been disappointed—angry, really—that they'd had to leave because she wasn't having a good time. Looking back on that night, he realized that things were beginning to change between them. He'd once been attracted to the way she loved to be the life of the party, the center of attention, the most interesting person in the room, but that attraction faded as he grew up, and they started growing apart.

He could think of dozens of times when Claire's mood had ruined their time with friends. He'd always made excuses for her, but after a few years, he began to realize how controlling Claire tended to be.

"I know we're turning the barn into a market," Andi began, "but what do you plan to sell there?"

Emily took a breadstick from the box in the center of the table. "I was thinking we'd contact local vendors and really showcase what Splendid Lake has to offer." She rattled off the list of vendors she planned to contact.

"We can help with that," Seth said. "Many of our customers are folks who either own stores or sell merchandise."

Emily beamed. "Great!" When she shared a smile with Jake, his heart thudded against his rib cage.

"When is the orchard going to open?" Seth asked.

"Well, the hundredth anniversary is the last Saturday in September, so we need to open at least a few days or so before," Jake offered.

Emily tapped the table with her finger. "Which is why we need to start contacting vendors now."

"I can put together a list of vendors I recommend." Andi met Jake's gaze. "Maybe you can sell some fall favorites, like pumpkins or cider. Have you ever considered selling a cider using apples from your orchard?"

Emily gave Jake a look. "Gee, Jake. What a *great* idea. Wouldn't it be *fantastic* if you could sell your own cider?" Her words were measured.

He set his glass down and leveled his eyes with Emily's.

Andi locked eyes with her husband. "Uh, babe," she began, "I feel like we're missing something here."

Seth nodded. "Me too."

Silence permeated the kitchen, and Jake was certain he could've heard a pin drop.

Emily rested on her elbows, her eyes challenging him. "Should we tell them?"

"Don't . . ." he warned her. Out of the corner of his eye, he spotted Seth and Andi exchange confused expressions.

Suddenly, Emily jumped up and grabbed his hand. "Let's go. It's time for you to share your cider with someone other than me."

"You make cider?" Andi asked.

"No way," Seth exclaimed. "You need to sell it, man!"

Emily jammed her hands on her small hips. "That's what I've been trying to tell him." She grabbed Jake's arm and tugged again, but he remained cemented in place. When she bent down to him, the flowery smell of her shampoo wafted over him, and his senses began to spin. "You told me I need to believe in myself," she said softly. "Well, now it's time for you to do the same. *You* need to believe in *yourself*."

Jake pressed his lips together while her words warmed him from the inside out. She'd always supported him, encouraged him, believed in him. And at that moment, he realized she had always been his most loyal cheerleader, no matter what.

He worked to keep his smile from coming up to the surface. "I hate it when you use my words against me."

She grinned, and his lips defied him and lifted.

"Fine," he said with a groan. "Let's go."

Emily did a cute little dance before the four of them headed out into the garage, where she gathered four plastic cups and filled them with cider from the container in the refrigerator.

Seth took a drink and then examined the cup. "This isn't bad."

"Yeah. It's tart," Andi agreed.

Jake took a long swig and shook his head. "It needs work."

"Then work on it," Emily insisted. "You can do it. I know you can."

His chest swelled as he absorbed her expression. She truly believed in him, and for a moment, he was completely overcome with appreciation for her.

"Okay," he said. "I'll give it a try."

Emily beamed, and Jake had to squelch the sudden yearning to hold her in his arms and kiss her.

Dismissing the thought, he headed for the door. "Let's finish our pizza before it gets cold."

* * *

"Thanks for a fun night," Andi said as they walked out to Seth's black, late-model Chevrolet pickup truck.

After finishing the pizza, they played a few rousing rounds of Uno, which included quite a bit of laughter, before the exhaustion from their hard work finally caught up with them.

Their shoes crunched along the rock path leading to the driveway, and the sky above them was dark and peppered with bright and shining stars. The only light came from the metal fixture above the garage door.

Jake chuckled. "I think I should be thanking you and Seth instead of you thanking me."

"We'll do it again tomorrow, man." Seth shook his hand before hitting his key fob to unlock the truck and climbing in.

Emily hugged Andi. "Thank you for helping me paint."

"It was fun." Andi waved at Jake and then hopped up into the passenger seat beside her husband.

Jake looped his arm around Emily's shoulders and held her against him as Seth started the truck and motored down the rock driveway toward the orchard exit. "So I guess I have to admit that you were right about everything."

"Everything?" She squinted up at him and pushed her thick ponytail over his arm. "Can you be a little more specific?"

He released her, but she didn't move. She continued to rest against his side, and he reveled in their intimate contact. "You said it would work out. You said we'd find help. And you were right about it all. It's all coming together."

"Well," she began with a dramatic tone, "it's about time you trusted me."

"I've always trusted you."

She studied him, and her smile faded. "Same."

They were both silent for a moment, and he felt something move between them—something intangible.

"I'm beat, so I'll see you tomorrow." She powered on the flashlight on her cell phone and started down the path toward his parents' house.

"Hey," he called, and she spun to face him, her outline silhouetted in the lights coming from the back of his parents' house. "Thank you."

"For what?"

"Just thank you."

"Um . . ." She chuckled. "You're welcome?"

Jake crossed his arms over his chest and smiled as she waved before hurrying down the path.

* * *

Jake jogged up his parents' stairs to the second floor the following Tuesday evening. They'd spent the weekend working on the outside of the barn. Seth and Jake had replaced the two barn doors on Saturday while Emily and Andi finished painting one side of the barn. Then the four of them continued painting on Sunday. Vince joined them again Monday morning, and the five of them finished the painting earlier in the day. Jake had to admit that the barn looked not only presentable but good—really good. In fact, it looked brand-new, and he was anxious to get started on sprucing up more of the inside tomorrow.

After Seth, Andi, and Vince left, he and Emily had eaten supper with his folks. He enjoyed watching her glow while she talked about the barn and all of their work. She'd even encouraged his parents to see it, and although his mother promised to come out tomorrow, his father had only grunted. But Jake had faith that Emily would convince his father too.

He and Emily had cleaned up the kitchen before she excused herself and disappeared to take a shower. He had expected her to join him and his folks in the den, but she'd been gone for more than an hour, which was why he headed to her room to check on her and tell her good night.

He knocked on the door and waited.

"Come in," she called.

Jake pushed open the door and found her sitting at the desk working on her laptop, clad in a pair of shorts and a tank top. Her dark, wavy hair was styled in a thick knot on top of her head with wavy tendrils falling past her neck. His gaze meandered over her shapely legs, her bare neck, and a spot behind her ear. That strange hankering to touch and kiss her swelled inside him, along with a craving to get out a phone and snap a photo of her.

Get ahold of yourself, Jake!

She swiveled on the chair to face him. "What's up?"

"I was wondering what you were up to since you didn't come back downstairs." He dropped onto the corner of the bed behind her chair.

"I'll show you." She typed on the keyboard, and a flyer advertising the grand opening of the market and the anniversary celebration filled the screen. "I was inspired during supper. What do you think?"

The document included a fall theme with the orchard's logo and detailed their schedule. "It's perfect."

"Glad you like it. We can have a billion copies made and then distribute them all over."

He nodded. "Sounds great."

"Also, I was thinking about the website." Emily typed on the keyboard, and the orchard's homepage filled the small screen. "I need to update it, and I can add the flyer too." She snapped her fingers. "And then social media too. We need to start promoting the grand opening and the anniversary celebration."

"Go for it." While Jake studied her, sadness washed over him. In less than a month, they would have their grand opening, and then Emily would go back to Charlotte.

How would he adjust to life without her again?

Okay. Something was up with him. Why was he suddenly so ridiculously sentimental? Maybe he was coming down with something.

Yup, that had to be it. It was definitely scarlet fever. He should call his doctor first thing tomorrow.

"I will." She folded her legs under herself and studied him. "All right. You have a super-weird expression on your face." She drew an imaginary circle in the air in front of his face. "What's goin' on in that head of yours?"

He brushed his knuckles over his sternum. "Have you considered moving back to Splendid Lake? Like, permanently?" he asked.

She sat up straight, and an unreadable expression flickered over her face. "I don't know if I could since I don't have a place here anymore."

"But you said you haven't touched the money your folks left you, or the money from the sale of the house." He pointed in the direction of the lake. "You could buy any house you wanted."

"But I don't have anyone keeping me here anymore."

He scoffed. "Really? Is that right?" He pointed to his chest. "So I'm chopped liver now?"

"No, no, no. I mean, I don't have *family* here." She counted off on her fingers. "My grandparents are gone, and my folks are gone. I have cousins out west somewhere, but I don't know them. I don't have anyone here."

He frowned as an ache radiated from his gut. "Seriously? What about me and my folks? You said we were your family and being here felt like you were home, but now we suddenly don't count?"

"Of course you count. But you have your own life here."

"I do?" He couldn't stop his sardonic smile. "I have a life, and that's why I texted you and begged you to come home and help me because I have my own life?" He shook his head. "I obviously need you." He hesitated. "And I miss you—*a lot*."

Her golden eyes glistened. "I miss you too," she whispered.

Silence stretched between them for several moments while they stared at each other, and the air seemed electrified. Jake held his breath as all of his feelings for Emily rose to the surface. He longed to reach for her, pull her against him, and beg her to stay in Splendid Lake.

But then suddenly she spun back toward her computer, and the moment was gone. "So I'll finish up the flyer, and I'll also work on the website and the Instagram page. I'll add the flyer to both and also detail the schedule."

Emily discussed the details of her plans for the website, but Jake was lost in his thoughts. What would life be like if Emily returned to Splendid Lake permanently? They could spend every weekend together. They would share everything with each other. They could possibly expand their friendship.

Take it to the next level?

His pulse pounded at the idea.

"Jake?" she asked, slamming him back to the present. "Are you okay?"

He sat up straight and cleared his throat. "Yeah. Sorry." He pointed to the screen. "Everything sounds great. Thanks for doing it." He stood. "I'm going to head home. I need to shower and feed Dusty. I haven't been home since lunch, and she's probably starving."

"Okay." She nodded, but her features pinched with concern. "See you tomorrow."

He moved to the door and then tapped the knob. "You should think about staying. Seriously." He headed down the stairs and tried to shove away the yearning that was building inside him.

But more than ever, he wanted to know if Emily cared for him the way he cared for her.

He planned to find out soon.

Chapter 11

THE FIRE CRACKLED and popped on Wednesday evening, sending its glowing red tentacles reaching toward the dark sky. Behind the flames, tiny waves lapped against the sandy beach while fiery reflections danced on the water in the cool mid-September night.

Emily and Jake, along with Seth, Andi, and Vince, had spent the past week tirelessly renovating the inside of the barn. They started by fixing the floor before moving to the walls. After painting the entire inside of the barn, they began to assemble the booths for the market, using movable shelves and walls to accommodate multiple vendors. The barn was actually starting to look like a market, and Emily couldn't wait to see the final product on opening day. The entire project had gone so smoothly that she was convinced they'd be done by the end of the week.

Aside from working on the barn, Emily had also spent the last week contemplating her conversation with Jake in her bedroom. She couldn't stop thinking about how he'd nearly begged her to stay in Splendid Lake. A lump expanded in her throat as she recalled the mist in his blue eyes. He'd seemed wounded when she explained there was no family to keep her here anymore. There was something in his eyes that felt almost like . . .

Love.

No, no, no.

She had to be misinterpreting it all. If Jake truly loved her as more than a friend, then he could let go of Claire. Emily couldn't bear the thought of staying in Splendid Lake and watching Jake and Claire get back together, let alone get married and start a family. It would rip her heart out. And that was why she was better off going back to Charlotte and working on getting her life together after the orchard was up and running.

But leaving this time would be more difficult than the last.

She shivered and hugged her arms to her waist.

"Cold?"

Jake shifted toward her, and she breathed in his aroma—laundry soap and sandalwood mixed with the fire. He shucked his sherpa-lined jean jacket and draped it over her shoulders. "Here."

"Thanks," she said, pushing her arms into the sleeves and hugging the jacket against her body. She couldn't help but press her nose against a sleeve to bask in his warm, comforting smell.

She snuck a glance at Jake and savored the view of him in the flickering firelight. He wore a gray-and-blue-plaid shirt, his signature worn blue jeans that fit him oh so well, and work boots, along with his Mets cap. She wanted to run her fingers against the blond scruff lining his jaw. And boy, did his blue eyes sparkle in the light of the bonfire.

The sound of his laughter at something Seth said broke her out of the spell for a moment. Emily shook her head. She needed to make sure no one knew she was mesmerized by this man.

At that moment, her fingers itched to grab her sketchbook

and draw Jake looking so heart-stoppingly hot on this beautiful autumn night. It would be the perfect drawing. No, if she had her easel, it would be the perfect *painting*—one she would cherish forever.

Emily felt someone watching her. When she turned toward Andi, her friend was smirking.

Great. Andi caught her mooning over Jake.

Oh well. Who could blame her? The man was drop-dead gorgeous!

"This is the best fire," Andi announced. "And I didn't manage to light up my shoe this time!"

Everyone laughed.

"That's because Jake and I set up the fire, and you and Em didn't, babe." Seth drew his wife against him and kissed her before releasing her.

"I think it's time to make s'mores." Andi lifted the bag of ingredients they'd picked up at the grocery store earlier.

"Yes! S'mores!" Emily distributed the skewers. Soon they had their sticks filled with marshmallows and were roasting them over the fire and then building their delicious treats. When Emily's marshmallow began to burn, she yelped, yanked her skewer back, and examined the charred mess.

"I think you held it too close to the flame," Andi quipped.

Emily gave her a mock glare. "Gee, thanks for the advice."

"Well, she's right," Seth chimed in, chuckling.

With a sigh, Emily replaced the burned marshmallow with a fresh one.

"Em."

Turning, she found Jake had moved his folding camping chair closer to her. He held up his s'more toward her. "Take a bite," he said.

"No, thanks." She held up her skewer. "I'll just try again."

"Go on." He angled his body toward her.

She hesitated, but then something in his expression beckoned her. She took a bite of the sweet little sandwich, and as she licked her lips, the intensity in his blue eyes stole her breath for a moment.

He'd never looked at her that way before. What were his eyes trying to tell her? Was he attracted to her? But how could that be after so many years? Why would he suddenly see her in a different light?

"Finish it." He held out his hand. "I'll make another one."

It took her a second to find her words. "Th-thanks."

"Sure." He smiled before adding another marshmallow to his skewer.

"I think the market is going to be a hit," Seth announced, and Emily was grateful for the change in focus. "You won't have any trouble finding vendors."

Andi built her s'more. "We need to get working on that."

Emily glanced toward the barn in the distance while she imagined a bustling orchard with customers hustling in and out of the old building. But as she looked at the barn, her eyes roved around the land surrounding it.

There was other available space. What could they do to make the orchard even more inviting for customers?

Suddenly an idea hit her. "What if we had some outdoor activities too?"

"Yes!" Andi agreed. "You need to host an open-air painting workshop."

Jake licked his fingers, which were covered with gooey marshmallow. "And you can teach people how to paint."

"They can paint the orchard or the lake," Seth added before handing Andi a s'more.

Emily considered that. Was she ready to try to teach again? Did she even want to? "Maybe."

Jake gave her a look that conveyed they were going to talk about this later before he turned his focus to Seth. "So tomorrow I think we should finish up painting the shelves in the booth areas."

The friends spent the rest of the evening discussing the barn. Once they were full from their s'mores, they extinguished the fire and cleaned up the beach before carrying the chairs and supplies to Jake's house.

While the guys stood on Jake's small front porch and discussed the plan for the next day, Andi grabbed Emily's arm and steered her out to the driveway. "Listen, Em. I have never been more convinced that Jake's totally into you," she gushed.

"Shh!" Emily hissed before peeking back toward the porch. Thankfully, Jake had his back to her while he listened to Seth go on about refinishing the inside of the barn doors one last time. She locked eyes with Andi. "No, he's not. And keep it down or they'll hear you."

Andi's brow wrinkled. "Didn't you see the look on his face when he fed you his s'more?"

Yeah, Emily had seen it all right. But she had tried to convince herself she'd imagined it.

"I thought he was going to kiss you!"

The words rang in Emily's ears. Suddenly she found herself drifting into a daydream, trying to imagine what it would feel like, taste like, for Jake to kiss her. A shiver zipped through her belly. "Nope. No way. Jake has never, and will never, want to kiss me."

Andi's furrowed brow smoothed out, a sparkle dancing in her eyes. "I predict that you two get together."

Emily's heart raced, but she tried to keep her expression calm. "I'm telling you, Andi, it's not gonna happen." She saw the guys begin to descend the porch steps and saunter toward them.

"When it does, I will take a *great* amount of joy in saying, 'I told you so.'" Andi hugged her and whispered, "Chin up, my friend."

And before Emily could say another word, the guys walked up to them.

After saying good night, Andi and Seth climbed into Seth's pickup and motored toward the orchard exit.

"What was that about?" Jake asked as their taillights disappeared into the dark.

Emily jammed her hands into his jacket pockets. "What?"

"You know." He gestured around her. "You and Andi looked like you were having a pretty intense conversation when Seth and I came over. What were you talking about?"

"Nothing."

"Huh." He moved his fingers over his scruffy throat. "It looked like something to me."

She shrugged and hoped her cheeks wouldn't flush. "It was . . . top-secret girl stuff."

"Top secret, huh?" His gorgeous smile came out to play. "Like the girl talk you had with Ms. Riley?"

"Yup. Exactly." She wagged a finger at him. "If I tell you, then I'll break Girl Code, and I'll get in trouble with all my friends." She frowned dramatically. "Trust me. We don't want that to happen."

He chuckled, and she enjoyed the sound. "If you say so." Then the corners of his lips began to fall, and his blue eyes seemed to search her eyes. "Why don't you want to teach painting in an open-air workshop?"

She swallowed a sigh and looked out toward the orchard. She couldn't possibly tell him how being back in Splendid Lake made her feel so . . . emotional. All the time.

"You should do it," he pressed. "You're such a phenomenal teacher. Just think about it, okay?"

"Okay." She turned toward him, and that intense expression that had surprised her earlier in the evening flickered over his face once again. She stilled as Andi's words echoed in her mind:

I thought he was going to kiss you!

Her pulse pounded. She'd been dreaming of his kiss since she was sixteen. Maybe their time had finally come!

Kiss me, Jake. Please!

He took a step closer to her, and she thought her heart might beat out of her chest. Reaching over, he pushed her hair behind her ear with his fingertip, and his featherlight touch sent goose bumps chasing each other down her arms. "Well, I . . . Good night, Em."

Before she knew it, she released a breath she didn't know she was holding.

"Good night," she said softly before starting down the path. When she realized she was still wearing his jacket, she spun to face him. "Hey, your jacket." She started to shuck it.

"Keep it," he called. "I have more jackets. It looks better on you anyway."

Her stomach quivered as she hugged the jacket to her middle. "See you tomorrow."

A small grin lit up his face. "I'll be here."

* * *

"We did it! We got it painted!" Emily sang while dancing around the barn. "It looks amazing. Just plain amazing!" She rushed over to Jake and gave him a high five.

It was Friday, and Andi and Seth had left for Hickory earlier that day to spend the weekend with family and celebrate Seth's grandmother's eightieth birthday. Jake and Emily had eaten breakfast with his folks before heading to the barn to finish up the last small details. They'd teased each other and laughed all day long, only stopping to eat a quick lunch and supper. He couldn't help but think that he and Emily made a good team—a *really* good team.

"It looks great in here, Em."

She rested her hand on his bicep, and his heart skipped a beat. He loved how casually she touched him. It felt so right.

"We're ready to get the vendors in here," she said.

"Yeah. That's next on the agenda." He linked his fingers with hers and gave her a gentle tug. "I have a surprise for you."

Her pretty face lit up with a smile. "Oooh. I love surprises."

"I know." He towed her toward the barn entrance. "Let's go."

"What is it?"

He smirked. "A surprise." His phone vibrated in his pocket, but he ignored it. Most likely it was Claire, and he had no interest in talking to her.

She groaned. "I hate it when you keep things from me."

He laughed. "You'll like it."

Jake and Emily strolled through the cool, cloudy day to his garage. He punched in the code, and the door hummed as it made its journey upward.

"Close your eyes," he said.

She did as she was told, lids pressed together tightly. He didn't think she could get any cuter.

His phone vibrated again, but he continued with his plan. After taking her hands in his, he guided her over to the refrigerator. Bending down, he whispered in her ear, "Stay here, okay?"

He was almost certain she shivered as she nodded. But he must've imagined it. Why would he make her shiver?

He filled a cup with cider and then returned to where she stood with her eyes closed. "I'm going to give you something to drink, but I need you to keep your eyes closed."

"I will," she promised.

"Here, put your hands out." He placed the cold cup in her hands. "Drink this."

While Emily complied, his phone vibrated again in his pocket, but his eyes were focused on her lips. He tried to dismiss the rush of heat that moved through his veins, whispering to him over and over that he should cover her lips with his.

As if reading his thoughts, Emily's golden-brown eyes flew open. "Jake! What did you do to this cider? It's out of this world!" She brought the cup to her mouth and took another sip.

"I've been working on perfecting it at night, and I realized I needed to ferment it more," he explained. "I wanted you to be the first one to drink it. I think it's ready to be sold now."

She beamed at him. "For real, are you serious?"

He nodded.

She whooped, pumping her fist in the air. "Fantastic! We can use the label I already created. I'll get them printed ASAP."

"Yeah, let's do it."

In the distance, Jake could hear a siren begin to wail faintly. His phone started vibrating again. The world may have been trying to distract him from this woman, but he couldn't pull himself away from her. He kept his eyes focused on Emily as something passed over her face. She set down the empty cup on the chest freezer beside her and touched his shoulder.

Then she wrapped her arms around his neck and held him against her. "I'm so proud of you, Jake. Truly." She said the words softly next to his ear, sending an avalanche of emotions racing low in his stomach.

He rested his hands on her hips as he inhaled the scent of her perfume, smelling faintly of flowers. Holding her now, like this, definitely felt different. The familiar yearning that had burrowed into his chest weeks ago awakened once again. He couldn't ignore it any longer.

He was attracted to Emily.

And he needed to know if she wanted him as much as he wanted her.

The sirens in the distance grew closer and closer, but he couldn't really hear them. His attention was set on the beautiful woman nestled in his arms.

"Emily," he whispered.

Her golden-brown eyes lifted to his.

He trailed his finger over her cheek, and she trembled while holding on to his shoulders. Yup, there was no mistaking it: He definitely made her shiver.

"Emily." He repeated her name, and he watched her eyes grow round.

At that moment, he was certain that they were meant to be more than friends.

Placing two fingers under her chin, he tilted her mouth toward his, and his eyes locked on her luscious pink lips. He wanted more than anything to kiss her. No, he *needed* to kiss her as much as he needed air to breathe.

He leaned down toward her, and he could hear her breath catch.

Suddenly, red lights flashed in his peripheral vision and reflected off the garage walls around them. He froze.

The sirens sounded like they were right outside his garage.

Wait. What?

His gaze moved to the entrance, and the hunger that had consumed him faded as the roaring sirens slammed him back to the present. The flashing lights were moving toward his parents' house.

My parents' house.

Oh no!

He released Emily and grabbed his phone from his pocket before examining the screen. There were four missed calls from his mother.

His insides turned and dropped.

Emily touched his shoulder as her eyes widened. "Jake, what's wrong?"

"It's my dad!" he yelled before taking off toward his parents' house.

Chapter 12

JAKE'S HEART WAS in his throat when he found his parents' front door wide open and an ambulance with lights flashing parked in the driveway. He raced into the house, and his world tilted as he took in the scene.

Two EMTs were loading his father onto a stretcher at the bottom of the stairs. Dad moaned while cradling his right arm to his chest. A gash stretched across his forehead, and a bright purple bruise lined his cheek. His left leg also sported a splotch turning black and blue.

Oh no. Oh no, no, no. Not again!

Jake sagged against the wall and tried to shove down the tide of panic rising in his gut.

"Son!"

Mom rushed over to him. Her eyes were red and puffy, and tears streaked her cheeks.

"What happened?" Jake asked in a strained voice.

"Your dad said he wanted to get something, and before I could stop him, he was halfway up the stairs, and then he fell. I tried to call you, but when I couldn't reach you, I called 911."

Jake tried to swallow past the guilt lodged in his throat.

A warm hand covered his forearm, and Emily came to stand beside him. "It's going to be okay." Her voice was comforting.

He nodded dumbly, wanting to believe her. No, *needing* to believe her.

"Ms. Hughes," one of the EMTs called, "we're going to take him to the hospital."

Mom took a shuddering breath. "Is he going to be okay?"

"Ma'am, we can't say for sure, but I think he's sprained or broken his arm. We'll let the doctors check him out. Do you want to ride with us?"

"Yes, of course." Mom nodded and wiped her eyes with the back of her hand.

Emily gave Jake's arm a reassuring squeeze. "We'll see you there."

The EMTs loaded Dad into the ambulance and then helped Mom in before the doors slammed, and soon the ambulance took off, sirens blaring.

Adrenaline shot through Jake, and he took off toward his house. He fished his keys from his pocket, and they jingled as he fisted them.

Emily's footfalls sounded behind him on the rock path. "Jake!" Her footsteps sped up before she grabbed his arm and tugged him, causing him to stumble. "Stop!"

"We need to go *now*." He tried to rip his arm out of her grasp, but her fingers clamped down on him. "What are you doing? We have to go!"

"You're not driving." Her expression was somber.

He made another attempt to shake his arm free, but she doubled down, grabbing his other arm.

"Jake, *stop*."

He froze.

"Take a breath."

He pulled in a ragged breath through his nose, and his eyes began to sting. He lifted his gaze toward the gray clouds clogging the sky and tried to blink back the tears that threatened to spill onto his cheeks.

Hold it together. It's your job to be the strong one.

But guilt weighed heavily on his shoulders, and he drew in another deep breath to try to calm himself down.

"Hey."

He closed his eyes and worked to rein in his raging emotions.

"Jake, look at me."

He shook his head. "We need to go," he whispered, his words sounding hoarse.

A warm hand cupped his cheek. "Please look at me," Emily pleaded.

When he opened his eyes and saw the compassion in her face, he felt as if his soul were covered in a blanket of warmth.

"You don't have to shoulder this alone. I'm going to be by your side, no matter what happens."

He couldn't help it then. A few tears escaped his eyes, and she brushed them away with the tips of her fingers.

He cleared his throat and attempted to find his voice. "When my dad fell, my mom tried to call me at least four times, but I didn't answer," he croaked out. "I should've been there."

"It's not your fault." She threaded her fingers with his.

He nodded and wiped away more tears.

Ugh! Stop blubbering like an idiot. You're almost a thirty-year-old man!

Emily wrapped her arms around his waist, and Jake closed his eyes, resting his chin on her head until his tears subsided. Then he released her and dried his eyes with his sleeve. "We need to go," he said.

"Fine, but I'm driving. You're in no shape to get behind the wheel."

He nodded.

They jumped into her Jeep, and his leg bounced while she steered out of the orchard.

Emily stopped at a red light and rested her hand on his thigh. "Deep breaths." She reached for his hand, then entwined her fingers with his. "I'm here."

"Thank you," he managed to say as he felt a tiny ribbon of relief swirl in his chest.

* * *

Emily shifted on the pine-colored vinyl chair. She tried crossing her legs and folding one underneath her, but she couldn't find a comfortable position. Not that she would on hospital furniture.

She glanced at the clock on the wall and then scanned the crowded waiting area of the emergency room. A television mounted in the corner showed a weatherman discussing the forecast for the weekend, but there was no way she could concentrate on what the man was saying. All she could think about was Jake and his parents.

She couldn't believe that two hours ago she was standing in Jake's garage, where he had almost kissed her.

He almost kissed me!

But . . . none of that mattered now. There were more important things to worry about.

She could still hear the pain in Jake's voice when he told her that he should've been there to help his parents. And seeing the trails of tears down his cheeks had fractured her heart. She couldn't stop herself from holding him—she'd do anything to comfort him—and she was grateful he'd allowed her to.

But sitting out in the waiting area and not knowing what was going on was making her crazy. She'd almost texted Jake a hundred times, but she knew he'd share an update with her if he had one.

She longed for someone to talk to, any sort of distraction, so she unlocked her phone and shot off a text to Andi.

Emily: Hi! I hope you and Seth are having fun in Hickory. I wanted to let you know that Jake's dad fell, and we're at the ER. I'm waiting on an update.

Andi: Oh no!!! Please let us know how he is and if you need anything. We can head home earlier if you need us.

Emily smiled. Andi and Seth were the best kind of friends.

Emily: Thanks. I'll keep you posted.

She dropped the phone into the front pocket of her hoodie and then picked up a celebrity gossip magazine. She swallowed a groan when she realized it was nearly eighteen months old. Well, it was better than nothing. Resting her elbow on the arm of the chair, she set her chin on her palm and flipped through the stories.

After a while, still immersed in one of the stories, Emily could've sworn she heard a familiar female voice.

"I'm looking for Leon Hughes. His wife is Diane; his son is Jake. And I'm practically family!"

Oh no. It can't be!

Emily slowly turned toward the reception desk and spotted the owner of the familiar voice.

Claire Chapman.

Emily slumped down in the seat and lifted the magazine, hoping to hide her face. But Claire's green eyes locked on hers before a devilish smile lifted her lips.

Claire waved and rushed across the waiting area toward her with her high heels clacking all the way. "Emily!" she called.

Ugh!

As if she'd just strutted off the pages of a fashion magazine, Claire sported a light green peasant top, a pair of jeans that accentuated her hourglass figure, and peep-toe pumps. As usual her makeup was perfect and set off her jade eyes, high cheekbones, and pouty lips. And her blonde hair was perfectly smooth. She'd always looked so perfect that she reminded Emily of a Barbie doll—tall and elegant, with flawless skin and curves in all the right places.

And she was sitting across from Emily, who sported a messy ponytail, an oversized gray hoodie, ripped jeans, and pink high-tops that were splattered with a rainbow of dried paint.

Could this day get any worse?

"Oh, Emily! It's so good to see you, despite the circumstances." Her eyes roved over Emily, and her fake smile widened. "You look . . ." She paused as if searching for the perfect word. "Terrific," she gushed. "Jake told me that you came back to help him with the orchard, but I didn't realize you were still in Splendid Lake."

"I sure am." Emily sat up straight and wanted to kick herself. Could she think of anything more basic to say?

Claire pressed her hand to her chest. "I couldn't believe it when I heard that Leon had fallen. How horrible! He's already been through so much with his heart attack." She stuck her lip out. "That family has just had a rough go of it. I mean, how much can poor Jakey take?"

It took everything in Emily not to roll her eyes. Claire had always called Jake "Jakey" when they were in high school, and Emily teased Jake about it. Hearing her say it now, nearly twelve years after they'd graduated, made her want to gag. But instead, Emily worked to keep a nonchalant expression on her face.

"I was here when Leon had his heart attack," Claire continued. "I sat with Jake in the ER." She pointed across the waiting area. "Right over there, and I held his hand. He was devastated, Emily. Just *devastated*."

Emily was certain every single muscle in her body tensed. So Claire had been with Jake during the heart attack. A vision filled her mind of Jake slumped over in an uncomfortable waiting room chair while Claire held his hand and whispered in his ear, promising that his father would be fine and that she'd always be there for him. Claire had been his strength, his comforter. And now she was back after his father's fall, prepared to do it all over again.

Emily felt like a fool believing that she could provide Jake all the comfort he needed. She'd never be enough for him.

And another thought hit her like a punch to the stomach: *How did Claire find out that Leon fell?*

And then the pieces fell into place. Had Jake almost kissed Emily and then called his ex-girlfriend to come to the hospital after his father's accident?

The thought sat like a lead bar in her churning stomach.

But that didn't make any sense. When would Jake have called Claire? After they arrived at the ER?

Stop it, Emily! This isn't about you. *It's about Leon and his fragile health.*

Emily gripped the hoodie's cuffs while she stared at Claire.

"Have you heard anything about Leon's condition?" Claire asked.

Emily shook her head. "I haven't seen Jake since he went back to find his parents."

Claire clicked her tongue. "I hope he's okay."

"Yeah. Me too," Emily said.

Claire recovered her phone from the depths of her Gucci purse. "I texted Jake, but he hasn't responded." She sighed. "I hope he gets back to me." Her eyes locked on Emily again, and Emily felt itchy under her stare. "How long are you staying in Splendid Lake?"

Before Emily could respond, the doors leading to the treatment area opened with a *whoosh*, and Jake and Diane headed out into the waiting room. Emily popped up to her feet.

Claire craned her neck over her shoulder and gasped as she stood. She took off toward them and hugged Diane before wrapping her arms around Jake and nearly knocking him over. He patted her back, but his eyes were focused on Emily.

Then Claire took Diane's hand and led her to a chair across from Emily before sitting down beside Diane. "Do you want something to drink?" she asked.

Diane shook her head. "No, thank you."

"I'm so sorry this happened. How is he?" Claire asked.

"His right arm is broken, and he has several bumps and bruises. He also sprained his knee and bruised his ankle."

Claire turned toward where Jake stood stoically watching them. "Jakey!" she exclaimed. "Sit." She pointed to the chair beside her.

Jake shoved his hands into his pockets and just watched her. Emily tried to read his expression. He was stressed, but was he upset about more than just his dad? She couldn't tell, and she wanted more than anything to grab his hand, yank him over to a private corner, and convince him to spill everything that was burdening his heart.

"How can I help?" Claire asked Diane, taking her hand in hers. "I can stay at the house with you."

Emily swallowed a groan. If Claire moved into Jake's parents' house, then she'd for sure head back to Charlotte soon—like, immediately!

Once again she wondered who had told Claire about Leon. Had Jake called her? But why would he call her if he was pulling away from her?

Because when the chips are down, Claire will always have his heart . . .

The thought was like a knife to Emily's soul. She sank back against the hard vinyl chair and worked to keep her raging emotions under control.

* * *

Jake brushed his hand over his mouth. He couldn't believe the scene that was playing out in front of him. Claire was holding Mom's hand and offering to stay at his folks' house to help care for his injured father. How had she found out about his father's accident, and why was she here? Was his ex stalking him, or had she suddenly contracted ESP?

He had no idea how she'd gotten here, but he knew one thing for sure—her drama was the *last* thing he needed today. His eyes flicked to Emily across from Claire and Mom. Emily had slumped back in her seat with her focus locked on the two women, and her expression was fixed in a deep frown.

Jake couldn't think of a worse case of emotional whiplash. He'd gone from the highest high—nearly kissing Emily and telling her that he cared about her—to the lowest low—realizing his father had been in an accident and he wasn't there to help his parents when they needed him most. And then he'd nearly sobbed in Emily's arms. He wanted off this nightmare roller coaster *now*!

He'd been working so hard to keep everything together at the orchard, but now it all had blown up in his face. It was his job to make sure that his parents and the business were taken care of, and he'd failed today—he'd failed *miserably*.

"Jake, stop being so stubborn and come sit with us," Claire ordered, patting the chair beside her with a hopeful expression. "You need to relax for a minute. I can see the tension in your shoulders from all the way over here."

Pursing his lips, Jake studied his ex-girlfriend. He wanted her to leave and mind her own business, and he could think of a few choice words for her. But he was too emotionally spent.

"I need some air," he mumbled before heading toward the exit.

"Jakey!" Claire cried out as her heels clicked toward him.

He gritted his teeth and kept moving forward. He despised that nickname. He could still hear Emily and the rest of his buddies mocking him mercilessly about it at school.

A hand grabbed his arm and hauled him backward. He spun and came face-to-face with Claire. "I told you, I need a few minutes alone," he repeated.

Claire rolled her eyes. "Alone time can wait. You should be with your family, Jakey."

"We're not sixteen anymore, Claire. My name is *Jake*," he said.

She blanched as if he'd struck her.

"Oh. Right. Of course." She gave an awkward little laugh. "Just come sit with us, okay? I was just telling your mom that I can come and help out. I'm back in town for a while."

Great. Just what I need, Claire hanging out and not taking a hint. As usual.

"I said I need some fresh air." He looked past her toward Emily, hoping to catch her eye and give her some sort of nonverbal clue to meet him outside. But she was busy studying her short nails and avoiding his gaze.

Why was Claire glued to his side while Emily was ignoring him? Had the world suddenly turned upside down?

Squaring his shoulders, he leveled his gaze with Claire. "I'm going outside to get some air *alone*."

"Okay. I'll stay with your mom."

"Great," he muttered before stalking out of the exit and leaving Claire standing in the waiting room.

Chapter 13

THE COOL EVENING air blew right through Jake's unbuttoned red-and-black-plaid shirt. Hunching down, he rested his fore-arms on the cold metal railing and stared across the full parking lot toward the busy highway in the distance. He tried to clear his mind and focus only on the sound of the traffic and the hum of the hospital's heating and air system, but flashes of his father moaning in pain kept playing through his mind like a horrible home movie.

Footsteps sounded behind him, and his entire body tensed.

Go away, Claire!

But the footsteps were soft, not like Claire's "Hey, look at me!" heels. So it couldn't be her. He stood to his full height and turned just as Emily approached him.

Her expression was hesitant, and her hands were stuck in the front pocket of her hoodie.

"Hey," he said with a sigh of relief.

She shifted her weight on her feet. "You okay?"

Much better now. "Yeah."

She nodded, and her gaze moved around the parking lot as if she were uncomfortable. Had he made things awkward by almost kissing her?

Oh no. The last thing he wanted to do was ruin his most precious relationship.

He spotted a bench behind her and pointed to it. "Wanna sit?"

Emily nodded.

When they sat down beside each other, she seemed to study him. "I heard your mom say your dad has a broken arm. Is that right?"

"Yeah. They're setting his arm." He grimaced. "He's in a lot of pain, but it could have been much worse." He rested his elbows on his lap and placed his chin on his palms, thoughts swirling through his mind. It was all too much. His dad was injured and now—

"None of this is your fault." Emily's words broke through his thoughts.

He lifted his gaze to meet hers, and once again the compassion in her eyes blew him away. "It's not my fault, I know that. But I need to do a better job of being in charge of things."

"What do you mean?"

He sat up straight. "I mean that I need to forget our ideas for the market. We should just keep things simple. Just the way they are."

"No."

He lifted an eyebrow. "No?"

"*No*," she repeated more emphatically. "We've done all this work, and our plans are finally starting to come together."

"But the grand opening is in a week. How on earth are we

going to pull that off?" He made a sweeping gesture toward the entrance to the hospital. "My dad is injured now. I can't take care of him *and* get the orchard ready."

"But you have me."

He shook his head. "I can't expect you to do everything."

"Why not?" She lifted her chin. "You think I can't handle it because I'm a girl?"

He snickered. "No, I know you can handle *anything*, but it's not your responsibility."

"What if I *want* the responsibility?"

He shook his head as a smile snuck onto his lips. "You're impossible."

"No, I'm stubborn, and I'm determined. And that means I can do this." She tapped her finger on the bench seat. "I have a week to bring it all together. And don't forget that Vince, Andi, and Seth are helping us too. We got this. You worry about your dad, and I'll take care of the orchard." She set her hands on his, her soft skin washing his own in a wave of comfort.

"Let's talk about this later, okay? I need to find out the extent of my dad's injuries and see what my mom and I are dealing with. Then I'll make a decision about the orchard." He tilted toward her, and once again he worried that he'd somehow fractured their friendship by almost kissing her. "For now, I think we need to talk about what happened earlier."

The emergency room doors whooshed open, and Claire stomped out. "There you are! I went to the ladies' room, and when I came out, I found Diane sitting alone."

Jake frowned at her. "What do you want?"

"We need to talk." His ex gave Emily a haughty look. "Can we have a minute, please?"

Emily's hand flew to her mother's rings, moving them back

and forth on the chain while she studied Claire with a dark expression. Jake wasn't sure if Emily was preparing to tell Claire off or ignore her request.

He started to open his mouth to protest Emily leaving but then paused. The sooner he told Claire to beat it, the better. It was time to clear the air and put her in her place.

He turned to Emily and touched her hand. "We'll talk later, okay?" he asked gently.

Emily winced. "Okay." The betrayal on her face nearly broke his heart in two, but she quickly fled back into the ER.

He would apologize to her later when they were alone. Right now, he needed to deal with Claire.

He stood. "Why are you here?"

"I got back in town earlier this afternoon. I was planning to come see you."

"But why are you *here*?" He pointed to the ground. "At the hospital?"

"What a ridiculous question," Claire began with a forced chuckle. "I'm here because I care about your family. *Our* family."

He eyed her. "How'd you find out my dad had an accident?"

She waved him off. "That's an even dumber question. Did you forget my best friend is a nurse here?"

Jessica Watson! Why hadn't he thought of her earlier? He'd spotted her in the ER, but he was so worried about his dad that he hadn't made the connection. "Isn't she breaking some privacy law by calling you every time my dad's in the hospital?"

"Well, I'm not planning to report her. I hope you're not either." She sank down onto the bench and touched the empty spot beside her. "Sit."

"I'm fine standing. Say what you need to say, and then I'm going back inside to be with my mom."

"Fine." She cleared her throat. "I'm not only here to comfort you and your family." She took a dramatic breath. "I'm here to beg you for another chance. Let's work this out." She dabbed her eyes with her fingertip, careful not to mess up her makeup. "I've lived without you for the past few weeks, and I just feel sick. All the time. I can't stand the thought of losing you after all these years."

He rubbed the back of his neck. "I don't know how else to say this since you haven't been listening." He paused. "There's nothing to work on. Our relationship is over."

"How can you give up on us so easily?" Her voice was throaty, and her eyes filled with tears.

He grimaced. *Great, the waterworks. Here we go.*

"I'm not giving up," he began. "We both need to face the fact that we're not kids anymore. We want different things, and that's okay. We've grown up and moved on."

"I haven't moved on. You're the love of my life, Jake. And I'm ready to fight for us." Tears streamed down her cheeks.

He pinched the bridge of his nose. He wasn't getting anywhere with her. She wasn't listening, and he didn't have the emotional strength to deal with her after all the events he'd endured today. "Now is not the time to have this conversation."

"But when will be?" she asked. She grabbed a tissue from her purse and gingerly dabbed her eyes and nose.

He threw his hands up. "I don't know, Claire, but it's not right now."

"This isn't over," she said, sniffing. "You're like my family."

"If I'm supposedly like family to you, then I need you to respect what I'm saying. Now isn't the time to try to talk about us. My dad is my focus, not you. So back off." He held his hands up like a traffic cop. "Just . . . just give me some space, okay?"

She nodded, but the hopeful look in her green eyes felt like a warning.

Clearly, she had no intention of backing off whatsoever.

* * *

Emily stalked over to the vending machine area and slumped against the wall while trying to swallow her heartbreak. It was bad enough to have Claire show up and then ask for a moment alone with Jake. But having Jake ask Emily to give them privacy was like a slap in the face. It was clear that he wasn't over Claire, and that knowledge nearly ripped Emily to shreds.

But Emily was here for Jake and his family, not for herself. She was being selfish, thinking about her own heart instead of Diane and Leon, who had treated her like their bonus child since she was five years old.

Squaring her shoulders, Emily pulled her wallet from her purse, purchased two bottles of water from the vending machine, and then hurried back to the waiting room, where she sat beside Diane. The woman's face was crumpled in a frown while she stared at the muted television on the wall.

Emily held out the bottle of water. "I thought you might need this."

Diane gave her a weak smile. "Thanks, sweetie." She took a long drink from the bottle and then gave Emily a glum expression. "I don't know how I'm going to tell Ally that Leon broke his arm. She'll be so upset that she's not here with us." Her lip trembled.

Emily's heart squeezed, and she touched Diane's arm. "I can call her if you want," she offered.

Diane shook her head and wiped her eyes. "Thanks, but no. I'll talk to Jake about it. He might want to call his sister."

The door opened with a *whoosh*, and Jake strode toward Emily and his mom. Emily hugged her arms to her middle while she tried to decode his dark expression.

He came to stand behind them and shoved his hands into his jeans pockets. "Any news?"

Diane shook her head and drank more water.

Emily held up her unopened bottle. "Here."

Jake wrapped his hand around the bottle, and when his fingers meshed with hers, her pulse flittered. "Thanks," he said softly before opening it and taking a long drink.

A few moments later, Claire joined him, and Emily's stomach roiled. She'd hoped that Claire had left, but she knew in her heart that her archnemesis was still there. Claire wouldn't give up a chance to be at Jake's side. Her expression was a mask of indifference, and Emily longed to know what Jake and Claire had discussed.

Had they gotten back together? Emily felt sick at that notion.

Claire sat on the other side of Diane and rubbed the woman's arm.

Jake sipped from the bottle and stared off toward the treatment rooms. When the doors opened and a nurse emerged, Jake's posture stiffened.

"The family of Leon Hughes," the middle-aged woman called.

Jake gave Emily's shoulder a light squeeze. "I'll be back."

"I'll be here," she said. She craned her neck over her shoulder just as Jake rested an arm on his mother's shoulder and guided her to the nurse and into the treatment area.

Out of the corner of her eye, Emily spotted Claire moving over one seat to sit beside her. Emily turned to face her just as the young woman gave her a smirk.

"What's that look for?" Emily asked, dreading the response.

Claire lifted her chin and eyed her. "You'll only ever be his friend."

Emily tried to mask her shock as she studied her. "What makes you think I want more than friendship from him?"

"Oh please." Claire scoffed. "I've always noticed how you look at him. You remind me of a sad little puppy. But Jake's only ever seen you as a buddy, and that's all you'll ever be."

Emily did her best to pretend that the barb didn't sting, but it did—right in the center of her heart.

* * *

Emily parked her Jeep in the driveway beside Claire's sleek Audi Q5 SUV later that evening. She kicked herself for not taking Diane's sedan to the hospital so that she could help get Leon home. But since she had taken her two-door, lifted Jeep Wrangler, Claire got to be the hero and chauffeur Diane and Leon home.

Well, good for Claire. She was, after all, perfect in every other way. Why shouldn't she also take care of Jake's parents?

Setting her jaw, Emily jumped out of her Jeep just as Jake opened one of the Audi's back doors.

"Take it easy," he instructed his father. Jake held out his hand and then gingerly lifted Leon to his feet. "Let's go through the garage so that we don't have to climb the front steps."

Claire looped her arm around Diane's shoulders and led her to the garage, where she typed in the code and then walked her inside. Of course Claire knew the garage code. She most likely still had a key to the front door of this house—and Jake's too.

"I'll help you get organized before I go home," Claire said. "I bet you're famished after that long hospital stay. Would you like me to make you something to eat?"

Emily couldn't hear Diane's response, but she imagined Claire whipping up a four-course meal in a matter of minutes. And it would be delicious to boot. She shoved away her irritation and envy to focus instead on Jake, who was holding his father up while he limped toward the door that led from the garage into the house.

She hurried ahead of them and held the door open. "Can I help?"

Leon held out his left hand, and she assisted him while Jake nearly lifted him up the two steps. The three of them found Claire and Diane in the kitchen.

"Are you sure you're not hungry?" Claire asked Jake's mom.

"Thank you, honey, but I think Leon and I need rest more than anything." She gave Claire a hug, and Emily hated herself for being jealous. "I appreciate your help."

Claire gave her a sad smile. "I'm just grateful I could be here. I'll come by tomorrow too."

"Let me sit," Leon grumbled.

Emily pulled out a chair, and Jake assisted his father as he sank down onto it.

"I'll let you all get settled. See you tomorrow." Claire gave Jake a long, lingering look, and silence drifted over the kitchen.

Jake lifted his ball cap, pushed his hand through his hair, and readjusted the cap. "'Night," he finally said.

Claire studied him, and Emily was certain she felt tension expand between them. After a few moments, Claire said, "I guess I'll walk myself out." She waited a beat and then huffed out a breath. "Good night," she said before marching out through the garage.

Diane sagged against the counter. "What a day."

Leon shook his head but remained silent.

Emily got the feeling that the family wanted to be alone, and she pointed toward the hallway. "I'll get up early and make breakfast. Good night."

"Hang on a sec, Em," Jake said quickly. "I'm going to help my dad to his room, and then I'll be right back."

She waited while Jake helped his father up to his feet and then through the doorway that led to their first-floor bedroom.

"Thanks for your help tonight," Diane told Emily. "I'm going to make some chamomile tea. Would you like some?"

"No, thank you."

Diane filled the kettle and turned on the burner. "You have a gift when it comes to Jake."

"What do you mean?" Emily asked as surprise zipped through her.

Diane gave her a knowing smile. "You may not realize it, but your presence always seems to calm him down. I noticed it when you were kids, and it's still true today."

Emily was so stunned by the compliment that she couldn't speak for a moment.

Footsteps sounded in the hallway, and Jake reappeared. "You need anything?" he asked his mother.

"No, thank you." She sighed. "But it would be helpful if you could call your sister tomorrow. I don't want to get her all upset tonight."

"Good idea." He hugged her. "It's going to be okay."

She touched his cheek. "Good night."

As he walked toward Emily, Diane winked at her.

Well, that was unexpected.

Emily played it cool and waved. "See you in the morning."

Jake took Emily's arm and led her to the stairs, where he drooped against the wall. "What a day."

She agreed but longed to rewind time back to his garage and

explore that almost kiss. But that was selfish. She should focus on Jake and his family, but she *needed* to know where she stood in his heart. Her fingers fluttered to her mother's rings on her necklace.

Jake's blue eyes filled with concern. "You okay?"

"Yeah." She considered their unfinished conversation while they sat on the bench at the ER. "You're not really going to give up on the orchard celebration, are you?" she asked. "We've already wallpapered downtown with flyers, and the barn is done."

He scrubbed his hands over his face.

"We've done the hard part. We can't give up now."

"You're right." He folded his arms over his wide chest. "I'm just worried about my folks."

"You can check on them throughout the day. I'll make sure everything is coming together."

"Okay." His expression softened. "I'm sorry about what happened at the ER."

She stiffened. "What do you mean?"

His posture drooped some more. "I shouldn't have asked you to leave me alone to talk to Claire. I just needed to try to get my point across with her."

"Oh. Okay." She hesitated, and once again she wondered if he had called Claire and asked her to come to the hospital. Of course he had. He still loved her, and the moment Emily and Jake had shared in the garage was only a fluke. He'd been caught up in the excitement of the cider and all their plans for the anniversary coming together. That was all.

Her face crumpled in a frown. "Good night." She started up the stairs.

"Whoa, whoa, whoa." He snagged her arm, and his eyebrows lifted. "What's up?"

She waved him off. "Nothing." She pulled her arm out of his grip. "It's been a long night. I think we both need some rest."

"Hold on. Do you think you can hide your feelings from me?" He pointed between them. "I know that expression. You're feeling something big. Tell me."

You'll only ever be his friend.

Claire's words played on a loop in her brain, and she tried to ignore how her throat thickened.

"Just say it. You can always be honest with me." His blue eyes pleaded with her.

She licked her lips. "Did you call Claire?"

His forehead creased. "What?"

"Did you call or text Claire and ask her to come to the hospital?"

He snorted. "No. Why would I?"

She studied him. Was he telling the truth? But why would he lie?

"Hey." He touched her hand. "You really think I called her?"

"No . . ." She hesitated. "But if you didn't, then how did she know to come to the hospital?"

"Her best friend is an ER nurse."

She grimaced. How could she forget? "Jessica Watson," she said.

"Exactly." He studied her. "You really thought I called her?"

"I mean . . . I don't know." *I hoped you didn't.*

"Come here."

He opened his arms, and she burrowed herself against his chest.

She closed her eyes and listened to his heartbeat while her mind recalled how he'd almost kissed her earlier. Had they missed their chance? Would he ever try again? Or had he realized it was a mistake to almost cross that line?

Finally, he released her, and she held her breath, hoping he might actually consider giving it another try.

But instead, he touched her shoulder. "Good night, Emily."

"Good night, Jake," she said before he turned and headed toward the garage door.

Chapter 14

THE SKY WAS bright blue on Saturday, and the September morning air was crisp as Jake's work boots crunched on the rock pathway leading from his house to his childhood home. After saying good night to Emily the night before, he fed the cat, took a long shower, and fell into bed. He was certain he was asleep before his head even hit the pillow. The stress of the day had worn him out. This morning he felt refreshed, and he planned to check on his parents before focusing on what he and Emily had to do before the orchard and market opened next week.

He'd spoken to Vince yesterday, and the seasonal workers were set to start picking the apples on Monday. Since that was taken care of, he could focus on the grand opening—as long as Mom and Dad were okay.

The sound of a car motoring up the rock driveway toward his parents' house drew his attention. He turned to see who it was—and spotted Claire's dark blue Audi.

"Can't she take a hint?" he grumbled.

He waited on the porch steps as she climbed out of the car.

Her eyes were shielded by a pair of large, expensive-looking sunglasses, and she balanced a giant tote bag on her shoulder.

"What are you doing here, Claire?"

"Good morning to you too," she simpered. "I told you I was going to help out, and I meant it."

He ran his tongue over his teeth while she strutted toward the steps. "We don't need your help."

"Could've fooled me." She pushed her sunglasses up on the top of her blonde hair. "Besides, they're like my second set of parents." She stood at the bottom step. "Are you going to move, or do I need to push you out of the way?"

He held up his hand. "Wait." He studied her for a second. "Why aren't you in Nashville?"

"Well, you would've known that if you had answered any of my calls," she snapped. "I'm home for a while."

"How long?"

"A couple weeks."

Great. He pushed off the railing and made a sweeping gesture toward the door. "After you."

"Why, thank you," she snipped before walking into the house as if she lived there.

The rich scent of coffee, mingled with eggs, bacon, and toast, wafted over Jake while he stood in the doorway. Emily set a plate of food in front of Mom. The young woman's pretty face pinched into a frown when her golden eyes focused on Jake's ex.

"Good morning," Claire sang as she waltzed into the kitchen and set her giant tote bag on the counter. "I brought bagels." She began unloading a variety of bagels and condiments.

Emily turned toward Jake. "I made eggs and bacon if you'd like some."

"Thanks. I'd love some," he told her, hoping her expression

would brighten. But Emily turned her frown toward Claire, who carried a platter of bagels and cream cheese spreads to the table.

"I wasn't sure what kind of cream cheese you'd like, so I bought one of each." Claire pointed to one of the bagels. "Would you like one, Leon?"

Dad nodded, and Claire began cutting the bagel for him.

"How are you feeling this morning?" she asked.

"Sore," he grunted.

"Well, you make sure you take your pain meds," Claire told him with a bright smile.

Emily prepared a plate for Jake and held it out to him. "Here you go."

Jake took the plate and then touched her hand while trying to transmit an unspoken "Are you okay?" with his eyes, but she spun back toward the counter. He set down his plate across from Dad and Claire and sat beside Mom, who was at the head of the table. Then he poured a cup of coffee for himself and one for Emily from the carafe on the table.

"Would you like some eggs, Claire?" Emily asked while filling another plate with eggs and bacon from the two large skillets on the stove.

"Oh no, thanks. I'm going to have one of these awesome bagels. You can have one if you'd like." Claire looked at Dad. "Did you sleep okay?"

Dad shook his head. "Couldn't get comfortable."

"I'm sorry to hear that. I'll make you a bag of ice after breakfast."

Mom beamed. "I was going to do the same thing."

"Great minds think alike." If Claire's smile were any brighter, she could've lit up the entire orchard.

Emily sat beside Jake, and her expression was grim while she chose a bagel.

"Here." He handed her his, which he'd already cut open and smothered in cream cheese.

She shook her head. "It's okay."

"Take it. I used honey-walnut cream cheese. Your favorite."

She hesitated and then complied. "Thanks."

He bent closer to her and whispered, "And I made your coffee just how you like it—lots of cream and sugar and very little coffee." He raised his eyebrows, and when she smiled, relief fluttered through him. "There's that smile."

Across the table, Jake found Claire watching him, but he ignored her and chose another bagel.

"So, Claire," Mom began, "how long are you home this time?"

Claire swallowed a bite of bagel. "A couple of weeks. I need to get back for the next staff meeting, but I wanted to check on some things at home." She speared Jake with a look before smiling at Mom. "I'm glad I can help out around here. I can handle your laundry if you'd like, or I can clean for you."

"That's so sweet of you, dear."

Jake peeked over at Emily, but she was studying her plate. He couldn't stand to see her so quiet. It wasn't like her. He needed to yank her out of her shell. "So, Em, what's the plan for today?"

"Um . . . we need to get vendors." She pushed a lock of her thick, wavy hair behind her ear. "I designed a flyer we can take to town."

"Vendors? For what?" Claire asked.

Jake summarized how they'd refurbished the old barn and set it up for their grand opening and hundredth anniversary party.

Claire scrunched her nose. "That sounds like a lot of work."

"It's actually been fun," Jake said before bumping his shoulder against Emily's, but she kept her focus on her plate.

Huh.

Was she upset with him? He'd have to find out later.

"It was all Em's idea," Jake said. "I asked for her help with figuring out the best way to drive customers from Apple Haven over here."

Mom's face filled with pride. "I can't wait to see the final product."

"Well, we only have a week left to make it happen, but we got this. Right, Em?"

Emily finally lifted her eyes from her plate. "That's the plan." She gave Mom a timid smile and then took a bite of the bagel.

After breakfast, Jake and Emily carried the dishes to the sink. While Emily began filling the dishwasher, Jake took care of the skillets and platters.

"Would you like me to make an ice pack for Leon?" Claire asked Mom.

"I can do that, but there's a load ready to go in the laundry room if you want to take care of it," Mom said, pointing toward the hallway.

"Consider it done." Claire nearly skipped toward the laundry room, and Jake managed not to roll his eyes.

"Jake," Dad called, his voice sounding ragged. "Could you help me get to my recliner?"

"Of course."

Jake guided Dad into the den, where he got his father situated in his favorite chair before turning on the television and handing him the remote.

Mom appeared with an ice pack for Dad's arm, along with ice

packs for his knee and ankle. Once Dad was settled, Mom took Jake's arm and steered him to the doorway.

"How was Dad last night?" Jake asked.

Mom frowned. "He had a hard time getting comfortable, but he finally settled down around midnight." She glanced toward the hallway and then back at him. "Things seem off between you and Claire. Is everything okay?"

Oh no.

Jake was not in the mood to discuss his breakup or get relationship advice from his mother. She had enough to deal with right now. "I told her that I need some space, but she can't seem to respect that." He swiped his hand down his plaid shirt. "Let's not waste time talking about my issues with Claire. Em and I need to work on the plans for the orchard. Are you going to be okay with Dad?"

"We'll be fine."

He held up his phone. "Call me if you need me. I promise I'll answer."

"Okay." Mom touched his shoulder. "Don't give up on Claire just yet."

Jake swallowed back his response and headed to the doorway. "Have you talked to Ally?"

She shook her head. "It would be great if you could call her."

"I'll let her know what's going on."

"Don't worry her too much. She has enough going on with her classes and internship. Tell her that we're fine and we'll see her at Thanksgiving."

"I will," he promised before returning to the kitchen, where Emily was loading the dishwasher. Grabbing a dishrag, he began wiping down the table.

"I got it. You can go outside," she told him.

He swept the crumbs into his palm and dropped them into the trash. "Is everything okay?"

She nodded and set a dishwasher pod into the compartment before closing the door.

"You've been quiet."

She started the machine and then spun to face him. "I was up late working on the flyer. I'll print it out, and we can take it to town if you want."

"Sure."

Claire walked through the kitchen and shot Jake a sugary smile before disappearing into the den. He shook his head while Emily studied him. "I didn't invite her to come today," he said softly. "I asked her to keep her distance, but she won't listen."

"I know." She moved her finger along the edge of the counter. "I'll finish up in here and then print out the flyers."

"I'll get my truck."

"See you outside."

He touched her hand. "Thanks. Really."

Her golden eyes met his. "You're welcome."

* * *

After the kitchen was clean, Emily stuck her head in the doorway leading to the den, where Leon watched an action movie involving a car chase, and Diane and Claire talked softly on the sofa.

Emily padded over to the sofa and stuck her hands in the front pocket of her hoodie. As she waited for Claire to finish bragging about how demanding her job was, Emily suddenly felt awkward, like she was back in high school and the third wheel with Jake and Claire. Even with Diane, Claire had always been the favorite, and Emily the forgotten one, even though they weren't Diane's biological children.

Claire finished her story and then turned to Emily. "Did you need something?"

Emily ignored Claire's arrogant tone and focused her attention on Diane. "I finished cleaning up the kitchen. Do you need anything else?"

"No, sweetie, but thank you," Diane told her. "Are you going to work outside?"

"Last night I designed a flyer to invite vendors to come out to the orchard. I'm going to print some out so we can take them to town."

Claire folded her hands. "That's so sweet," she gushed.

Emily wondered if Diane picked up on how passive-aggressive Claire was, but she dismissed the thought. "Call my cell if you need anything, okay?"

"I will," Diane promised.

Emily jogged upstairs and printed two dozen flyers before dashing out to the barn. Finding the building empty, she continued to Jake's house, where the garage door was open. She hurried past the refrigerator and tried in vain to banish the memory of Jake almost kissing her there less than twenty-four hours ago.

She walked into the house, where Jake was lounging on the sofa and talking on FaceTime while Dusty snoozed on the windowsill nearby. Emily set the stack of flyers on the kitchen counter before she lingered in the doorway and admired his blond scruff and his adorably messy hair under his ball cap. He turned toward her, and her cheeks flamed. Hopefully he hadn't noticed her staring.

"Hey, Em is here." He waved her over. "Come say hi to Ally."

"Ally!" Emily exclaimed as she rushed over and dropped onto the sofa beside Jake. He shifted against her and held the phone so that they both appeared on the screen, and she cherished the feeling of his whole side snuggled up to her.

"Emily!" Ally exclaimed. "It's been too long!"

That was true. It had been two years, and Ally had somehow become even lovelier. She'd always reminded Emily of Diane with her pretty blue eyes, petite nose, and angelic face. Her golden hair spilled past her shoulders and she sat on a tan sofa, which Emily imagined was in her apartment at school.

"It *has* been too long," Emily agreed. "How's school going?"

Ally made a face. "It's going." She sighed. "But now I'm worried about my dad."

"Don't worry. We're taking good care of him," Emily promised.

Jake balanced the phone with his left hand and looped his arm around Emily's shoulder. She tried to ignore how every nerve ending in her body came alive as she reveled in his cozy closeness.

"I can come home," Ally offered.

"No, no, no," her older brother insisted. "We got this. You focus on school, and we'll see you at Thanksgiving."

"Will you be there this year, Emily?" Ally asked.

Emily shrugged. "I think so."

"She will." Jake gave her a side hug, and Emily didn't want him to ever let go. "I'll make sure of it. I'm trying to convince her to move back for good."

"Yes! You need to come back," Ally chimed in.

"Are you coming back to Splendid Lake?" Emily asked her.

"I hope to. After law school, of course."

Emily grinned. "We're so proud of you."

"Yes, we are." Jake drew imaginary circles on Emily's shoulder blade, sending a flurry of chills cascading down her back. "And I can't wait for you to see what we're doing at the orchard."

Ally's pretty face brightened. "Tell me!"

While Jake filled in his younger sister on their plans, Emily's eyes scanned the room. And when they found the television stand, she could tell something was missing. It took her a moment to realize the portrait of Jake and Claire all dressed up was gone.

Had he put the photo away because he was finally letting go of Claire?

She felt her heart stutter.

"We're heading to town to find some vendors for the market," Jake told Ally, and Emily's focus returned to the phone.

"It all sounds amazing. Send me photos," Ally insisted.

Jake nodded. "We will."

A voice sounded in the background, and Ally frowned. "My study group is here. I have to go." She sighed. "You'd tell me if I should come home, right?"

"Yes," Jake told her emphatically. "But Dad is going to be fine, baby sis. I promise you."

"Okay. Tell Mom and Dad I love them and I'll call soon."

"I will," Jake promised. "Take care of yourself, Al."

She grinned. "You too. Bye, Em!"

Emily waved, and Jake disconnected the call.

Jake leaned back against the sofa. "So now what?"

"Ready to find some vendors?" she asked.

"Let's do it."

Chapter 15

THIRTY MINUTES LATER Jake and Emily walked down Main Street in Splendid Lake. It seemed as if overnight the restaurants and storefronts had been transformed into an autumn wonderland decorated with pumpkins, bales of hay, scarecrows, orange and purple twinkle lights, decorative wreaths, and *so* much orange. And adding to the ambience were the trees—boasting a dazzling display of leaves in shades of yellow, orange, red, purple, and brown.

"I love this time of year." Emily looped her arm through his. "This is the best part of living in the mountains. The days are cooler, and the air smells like fall. Even the *lake* smells like fall."

He smiled down at this adorable young woman. "I do too. So about your flyer—which is dynamite, by the way—where do you want to start distributing them?"

"Everywhere." She stopped moving. "We need to hit every store—the restaurants, the coffee shop, the ice cream shop, the bakery, the candy store, and the knickknack stores. Each one might want to have a booth. Some shops may even want to split a booth."

Jake was stunned by not only how much talent this woman possessed but also by how much she cared about the success of the market and his family's legacy. He wrapped his arm around her and hugged her body against him.

She lifted her gorgeous golden eyes to meet his. "What was that for?"

"Just 'cause." He studied her. "Is that okay?"

"Of course it is." Her smile widened. "Now let's get some vendors signed up."

They turned toward the line of stores just as someone called Jake's name.

"Hey, Jake!"

He spun, and Travis Johnson rushed over to him. Jake and Emily had gone to school with his older brother, Daniel.

"Travis!" Jake shook his hand. "The last time I saw you was at my graduation. How's Daniel doing?"

"Great. He got married a few years ago and moved to Virginia." Travis pointed to the flyers in their hands. "I heard about the hundredth anniversary you're planning for the orchard. By any chance, are you looking for a band to perform?"

Jake turned to Emily, and she grinned.

"We sure are," Emily said. "I've seen your band on social media. Carolina Dreamin', right?"

"That's us. We're a rock band."

"You're really good."

"Thanks." Travis's grin was wide. "We've mostly been doing local gigs, but we played in a music festival in Asheville back in June, and it's opened several doors for us. We're available if you need some entertainment."

Jake mulled over the idea of adding performers to the celebration.

Although it would be great, it definitely wasn't in their budget. "How much do you charge?"

"Charge you?" Travis waved him off. "For Hughes Family Orchard, it's free. Every year my mom makes the best applesauce with your apples, and when I was a kid, she took me to the orchard to help her pick them out. My band and I would be honored to be a part of your celebration."

Jake shook his hand, and his heart lifted. "Thanks, man."

They exchanged phone numbers, and Emily promised to send Travis the details about the event.

After Travis left, Jake and Emily spent the next two hours visiting each shop in Splendid Lake, sharing the news about the market's grand opening. By the time they finished, they had two vendors signed up and three that were interested.

"It's coming together. We have a couple of vendors and a band booked. Let's stop at Apple Haven on our way back," Emily suggested while Jake drove toward the orchard.

He snuck a glance her way. "Why?"

"I want to see something."

He lifted his eyebrows, but she pointed toward the road that led toward their competitor.

After parking in the nearly full lot, they climbed from the truck and headed inside. The delicious scent of apples mixed with funnel cakes and buttery popcorn filled the air, and the orchard was buzzing with patrons. Families headed toward the petting zoo area, while others moved toward the small carnival. Other folks carried their bags of apples toward the line of cashiers.

Jake pushed his ball cap down lower, scanned the crowd, and tried not to allow his competitor's success to break his spirit. How was his little market going to outdo this bustling fall festival?

Emily shook her head. "You're allowed to be here. You don't have to try to disguise yourself."

"But I feel like I'm betraying my ancestors."

She laughed, and he couldn't stop his own smile. "I promise I won't tell your folks." She threaded her fingers with his and yanked him toward the petting zoo. "Come on."

They wandered around the grounds, and the more delighted customers Jake encountered, the more despondent he became. There was no way he could ever compete with Apple Haven, and they were making a huge mistake thinking they could. He'd spent his entire savings and almost maxed out his credit card on the barn refurbishment, and now he was going to lose his business and his family's legacy.

"We can go now," Emily suddenly announced, steering him toward the exit. She had a spring in her step as she towed him toward his Dodge truck and hopped into the passenger side.

Jake took his seat beside her, pulled out his keys, and started the truck. Before putting it in gear, he glanced over at Emily and found her bouncing on the seat as if she were ready to explode. "I can tell you're dying to say something, so spill it."

"I have an idea." She turned toward him and rested back against the door. "How do you figure out what to charge for apples at your orchard?"

He eyed her suspiciously. "You don't need me to tell you that. You worked at the orchard for six years, up until we graduated from high school. You know we've always charged per pound."

"So . . . what if we didn't?" she asked, and he cocked an eyebrow. "Just listen, okay?"

"All right, I'm listening."

She held up her hand. "What if you gave out baskets, and you charged *per basket* of apples instead of per pound?"

He settled back in the driver's seat and considered it. If they charged per basket, they would lose money. Or they would make money, depending on how much they charged. But how could he convince his dad to make such a drastic change in their pricing policies? He turned toward her. "I don't know . . ."

"It could work." She bent over the console separating them. "The prices here are insane. They are way cheaper than your orchard."

He frowned. "I know."

"So if you tried this, it would make you competitive. I promise, people would come back for more of your apples." She held up her hands as another idea hit her. "You could have a special promo where they'd save two dollars if they bring back the basket! Try playing the volume game!"

He gave her a sad smile. "You know how my dad is. He's having a difficult enough time accepting the market idea. If we ask him to lower prices, he might put his foot down."

"Let me talk to your dad."

"I respect your confidence, but my dad is all about tradition. And selling apples by the pound is how his father did it, and his father before him."

She gave him a knowing look. "I got this."

Jake took in her tenacity. And her hair in a messy bun. And her face glowing with excitement. At that moment, Emily couldn't have been any more attractive to him.

His mind replayed the memory of their near kiss, and he couldn't deny the desire rushing through him. He wanted her as more than a friend.

But would kissing her be worth risking their friendship, just to find out if she felt the same way he did?

No matter the risk, his hands trembled at the idea of kissing Emily Carmichael.

Her eyes squinted. "Why are you staring at me like I'm a puzzle?"

"You *are* a puzzle. You're a woman. All women are puzzles to men."

She snorted. "No, we're not. You guys just don't pay enough attention."

"Right . . ." He shook his head and turned over the engine.

She buckled her seat belt before patting his arm. "You leave your dad to me. I can convince him to give my idea a try. I have a good track record with him."

"Don't worry. I'm happy to leave that to you." He backed out of the parking spot and motored toward the road while he contemplated when would be the perfect time to tell Emily that he cared about her—*really* cared about her.

He couldn't wait to find out if Emily would consider taking their relationship to the next level.

* * *

"We had a busy day, didn't we, Diane?" Claire carried a platter of chicken enchiladas to the table.

Jake's mom nodded while setting a bowl of rice beside the platter. "We sure did. We cooked and baked and took care of some cleaning."

Claire's smile was smug. "And it was so fun to catch up with you."

Emily bit back a frown while adding five glasses of sweet tea to the table. An irritated expression flickered across Jake's face so quickly, she was almost sure she'd imagined it. But when she did a double take, she saw the annoyance was still in his blue eyes.

Interesting. It seemed Claire got under his skin just as much as she got under Emily's.

Claire brought a bowl of refried beans to the table before sitting beside Leon. *"Bon appétit!"*

Emily took the chair next to Jake, and they all started filling their plates with the food. She hated to admit it, but Claire's enchiladas were actually pretty good. Because of course they were.

"We have freshly baked apple pie and vanilla ice cream for dessert," Claire added before waving her fork through the air with a flourish. "And what did you two do today?" she asked, dividing a look between Emily and Jake.

Emily turned to Jake, hoping he'd answer the question.

He swallowed a bite of enchilada and wiped his mouth with a paper napkin. "We went to town to round up some vendors."

"How'd it go?" Diane asked.

Jake nodded. "Pretty well. We have a band booked to help with entertainment, and we also secured two vendors, and we have three more interested."

"Two vendors?" Dad asked. "Only two?" He closed his eyes before continuing at a much higher volume. "You spent *thousands* on that barn, Jake. Two vendors are not going to give us a return on that investment. I knew this was a bad idea." His nostrils flared. "This is why I can't let you take over the orchard. You're just not ready. I knew you weren't, and this just proves me right."

Jake's posture stiffened, and his countenance darkened.

Under the table Emily rested her hand on his leg to calm him down before he said something he'd regret. "We only have two vendors so far, Leon, but we plan to go back to town tomorrow to talk to more. It's only our first try. We'll have the barn filled in a matter of days. I just know it."

Jake's dad studied her and then returned his attention to his plate.

Claire began to cut up his enchiladas for him. "I hope it works out," she said, and Emily could detect a thread of sarcasm in her voice.

"We stopped by Apple Haven on our way home," Jake added. "And Emily had a good idea for another way to stay competitive." He turned toward Emily. "I think it'll really help us a lot."

Okay. I guess we're ripping the Band-Aid off right now.

Leon studied his son. "Well, what is it?"

Jake set his fork down. "Apple Haven's prices are really competitive, and we can't possibly lower our prices and also pay our seasonal workers." He paused. "But what if we changed how we price our apples?"

"Change it how?" Leon inquired.

"Instead of charging per pound, we could charge per basket."

"What?" Leon asked. "Why on earth would we do that?"

"Just listen, Dad," Jake continued. "We could charge twenty-five dollars per basket, and if the customer brings the basket back, then we'd take off two dollars."

"Why would we want to do that?" Leon demanded, his voice rising. "What's wrong with our sacks? And where would we find the baskets? How much do the baskets cost? And where are we going to keep these silly baskets, anyway?"

Claire's green eyes rounded, and she moved her rice around on her plate.

Diane reached over and placed her hand on her husband's shoulder, but he shook it off. "You need to calm down, dear. If you get yourself into a snit, then you'll risk hurting yourself even more."

"I'm not in a snit. I'm *angry*!" Leon glowered. "Jake, you're changing everything, and it's not right. This is not how my father or grandfather did business, and I will *not* start changing it now. I refuse. I am a Hughes, and so are you, and this is Hughes Family Orchard!"

Jake slouched in his chair, his lips pressed into a harsh line.

An awkward silence expanded over the kitchen. The only sound came from their utensils scraping the plates.

Emily squeezed Jake's arm, but he kept his focus on his glass of iced tea. "Would it be all right if I explained my idea?" she asked gently.

The older man nodded. "You can, but you're wasting your breath. You won't convince me to change my mind."

Emily could feel Claire's eyes burning a hole through her skin, but she didn't care what Jake's ex thought about her. She was determined to make her point. "Jake and I walked around Apple Haven today so that I could get a sense of what they're doing. They've created an autumn festival, and there's no bones about it: Their prices are competitive. They're offering the apples at almost half the price of what we offer here." She gestured around the kitchen. "So I was trying to think of something different we could do. Then I remembered going into Mrs. Cavanaugh's little store where she sells her homemade knickknacks, and she had these really cute bushel baskets. That's when it hit me: What if we"—she paused—"I mean, *you* did something completely different from Apple Haven?"

She rested her hands on the table. "You can still offer your variety of heirloom apples, but the customers can fill a basket and pay a set price for them. Maybe twenty-five dollars, or even thirty? The price would be up to you and Jake. But if you let the customers fill the basket for a set price and then offered a discount if they bring the basket back, you'll have repeat customers. I'm sure of it. Your prices will be higher, sure. But so will your volume of customers. Plus, we can remind folks that they're patronizing a family-owned business that's been growing fresh, delicious apples that their parents and grandparents loved. That'll make them feel good about where they shop too."

Leon studied her and then looked at Jake, and several tense moments ticked by. "You think this will work?"

"Yeah, I sure do." Jake's expression warmed, and he pinched Emily's side under the table.

She tried to hide her startled surprise, but she was almost certain Claire had seen it.

Leon's blue eyes were cool as he studied Jake and then Emily. "And how much will these baskets cost us?"

"I'm not sure, but Jake and I can go see Mrs. Cavanaugh tomorrow and start pricing them out."

Leon turned to his wife. "What do you think?"

"Honestly?" Diane asked, and Leon nodded. "I think it's brilliant." She smiled at Emily. "Once again, you've come up with a magnificent idea for the orchard."

Claire looked like she was sucking lemons as she forked some more of her enchilada.

Take that, Claire! Emily almost laughed. She turned back to Leon. "Thank you. I can ask Mrs. Cavanaugh to give us a deal since we'll buy the baskets from her in bulk."

"Oh!" Jake suddenly said. "You could design a sticker that we put on the baskets to advertise the orchard."

Emily gasped. "Yes! I'm already working on a logo for the anniversary, so I can turn that into stickers."

They traded a high five, and when Emily turned toward Claire, Jake's ex glared at her.

Was Claire jealous of Emily? *Well, haven't the tables turned?*

"What do you think?" Jake asked his father.

Leon looked at his wife beside him, who nodded. "I guess we'll give it a try." He pointed at Jake with his good hand. "But if it fails, then we'll stop it immediately."

"Deal," Jake said before beaming at Emily.

* * *

Jake descended the front porch steps with Claire later that evening. They'd already cleaned up after supper, and Emily had excused herself before fleeing to her bedroom to work on a project. And now it was time for Jake to have a little one-on-one with his ex and try to get her to understand that he was done—*completely* done—with their relationship.

The sky was dark, the air was cool, and the smell of a nearby fireplace filled his nostrils. He carried Claire's enormous tote bag out to her car, and after she unlocked the doors, he tossed it onto the back seat.

"Thanks for walking me out," she told him. "I didn't expect you to."

He scratched his chin. "I appreciate how you helped my folks today. So . . . thanks."

"You're welcome." She eyed him up and down. "You look good, Jake."

Oh boy. Here we go.

He ignored the compliment. "Claire, I need you to respect me."

"I do. You know that."

"No, I actually don't. I've been asking you to back off, but you keep showing up here."

Her eyes narrowed. "First you thank me, and then you tell me to back off. Which is it, Jake? Do you want me around or not?"

"I want you to back off. I can take care of my parents."

"And run the orchard?" She scoffed. "I don't think so."

He took a few steps away from her. "What I do is my business. And since when do you even care about the orchard, anyway?" He pointed to his chest. "I can handle *my* family and *my* orchard, so I need you to stay out of it. I've already told you that I'm done. We're done." He pointed between them. "Do you understand?"

Her expression darkened. "Have you moved on to Emily now?"

He studied her. "My life isn't your business."

"I see how you two look at each other. But Jakey, she can't make you happy like I can. You're making a big mistake."

It was all he could do to keep his tone civil. "Thanks for your help today, but I've got it from now on. Please don't come back. Goodbye, Claire." Before she could respond, he jogged up the porch steps and into the house.

He made his way up to Emily's room, where she was working at the desk and drawing something. He knocked on the doorframe, and she jumped with a start before covering her project.

"Hi." She swiveled the desk chair to face him.

He sat on the corner of the bed. "Whatcha workin' on?"

"Nothing." She rested her feet on the bed beside him, showing off her magenta socks.

He grinned and grabbed her foot, causing her to yelp. "Tell me or I'll tickle your foot."

"You wouldn't dare," she hissed.

"Oh yes, I would." He grinned before he started tickling her foot.

She screeched and tried to kick him away, but he continued to tickle her while she giggled and gasped. He'd loved tickling her ever since they were kids, and it never got old.

"Okay!" she managed through her gasps. "Okay, okay! I'll show you."

He released her foot. "That's better."

She wiped her eyes with her hands before sharing a sketch of a hundredth anniversary banner. "It's not great, but I'm going to keep working on it. I thought we could hang it from the rafters in the barn."

He studied it, taking in the details on the apples and the elegant Hughes Family Orchard logo. "It's fantastic," he said, and she shook her head. "You're always your worst critic." He stood. "Put your shoes on. We're going for a walk."

She looked at him with a twinkle in her eye. "All right, I'm game for a little moonlit stroll."

Using flashlights, they walked to the dock, where they sat on the bench and looked out over the lake. The stars above them twinkled in the sky, and the lights across the lake seemed to blink in greeting.

"You have a gift with my dad," he said. "The way you convinced him to give your idea a try was phenomenal."

She shivered and hugged his jacket against her. "Thanks."

"Oh, I'm sorry, Em. I didn't even think about how it was colder out here than at the house." He pulled off his jacket and draped it across her shoulders.

"You keep it." She tried to hand the coat back to him, but he shook his head. "You must be cold."

"I'm fine. Please put it on."

"You sure?" she asked.

"Yeah, I'm positive." He blanketed her in the coat, and she hugged it close.

She stared out over the lake, and the smile he loved reappeared. "I love it here."

"Then stay here." He moved closer to her, and she reclined against him. He sighed and then rested his arm across her shoulders. This felt so, so right.

She gave him a small smile and he held his breath, waiting for her to tell him she was going to stay. But she remained silent.

"The grand opening is going to be wonderful," she finally said.

"Because of you."

She looked surprised.

"Oh please. You know it's true. I'm grateful you came to help me."

"And I'm grateful you asked."

They were quiet while they peered across the lake, and Jake tried to imagine more nights like this. In fact, he wanted to spend every night like this—for the rest of his life.

He just had to find a way to convince Emily to stay in Splendid Lake.

Chapter 16

EMILY AND JAKE climbed out of his pickup truck Sunday afternoon and walked toward Lorna Cavanaugh's Whimsical Wonders. The air smelled like rain, and the dark clouds had been threatening a downpour all morning while they ran a few errands before the orchard opened on Wednesday.

Emily smiled as they walked up to the adorable shop. Whimsical Wonders' front window was decorated with colorful leaves, a pumpkin patch, a couple of smiling scarecrows, and twinkling orange lights. Jake held the door open for Emily, and they headed toward the counter at the back of the store.

"Emily! Jake! What a nice surprise," Mrs. Cavanaugh called. She looked just as Emily remembered, with her stylish gray bob, purple cat-eye glasses, and bright red lipstick. Her store had always been one of Emily's favorites. She could spend hours browsing through the variety of tchotchkes and novelty items, from lava lamps to handmade baskets and quilts to funny little greeting cards and figurines and candy. If you were looking for an unusual gift, Whimsical Wonders was the place to visit.

"Hi, Mrs. Cavanaugh," Emily said. "We have a request that's a little unusual. We were wondering if you could sell us a couple hundred bushel baskets."

Mrs. Cavanaugh pushed her purple glasses on top of her head, and her gray eyes grew wide as saucers. "A couple hundred?"

"Yeah." Jake's heart-stopping grin appeared on his lips. "Do you have that many?"

"I have about a hundred here." She pointed toward the back of the store. "And there are plenty more at my house."

"Great!" Emily pulled her wallet from her purse. "We're here to take them off your hands." She fished out her credit card. "Name your price."

Jake cut her a look, but she ignored it. So far he hadn't allowed her to pay for anything, but that was going to change today.

"May I ask what you're going to do with them?" the store owner asked.

Jaked rested his muscular arms on the counter. "We're planning a celebration at my family's orchard. The grand opening of a brand-new market is on Wednesday, and then our hundredth anniversary is Saturday."

"Isn't that something?" Mrs. Cavanaugh's voice was wistful. "I remember going to Hughes Family Orchard with my grandmother when I was a child. It was our favorite place to get apples in the fall. In fact, it's *still* my favorite." She lowered her voice and tipped forward as if sharing a juicy secret. "I always thought your apples were better than McClains'."

Pride glowed on Jake's face, and Emily's heart squeezed.

"Thank you," he said.

"Now, about those baskets. If you're going to use them for the orchard, then I can't take your money."

Jake looked as stunned as Emily felt. "W-why not?" he stammered.

"Honey, I'd be honored if you used my baskets as part of your celebration. Your orchard is part of my family history too."

"Then what will you take in exchange for them?" Emily asked.

Mrs. Cavanaugh smiled. "How about a bag of those Carolina crisp apples?"

"I'll save you a bag of the best ones," Jake promised.

"You got yourself a deal." Mrs. Cavanaugh beckoned them to follow her to the back room.

Thirty minutes later, they had one hundred baskets loaded into the back of Jake's truck under a tarp, and they'd placed an order for another hundred.

Emily pointed down the street toward Morningside Bakery. "Let's go get a cookie to celebrate. And we can also ask Dani if she's decided about having a booth at the orchard." They started down the street, and a cool mist kissed Emily's cheeks. "I guess we're going to get that rain after all."

As they moved past an empty storefront, Jake caught her arm. "Hold up." He pointed to the glass window. "I just had a great idea. You should open a gallery here."

"What?"

"You heard me."

She studied him, searching for his signature lopsided grin, but he wasn't smiling. "You're joking, right?"

"No, I'm completely serious." He took her hands in his. "You've been searching for something to do for years—for a purpose. This could be it. How many paintings do you have in my parents' basement?"

"I have no idea."

"Guess. How many?"

"I don't know." She tried to calculate in her head. "Maybe a few dozen."

"Take all of those paintings and drawings out of my folks' basement and open a place here. In your hometown." He pointed to his chest. "*Our* hometown."

She shook her head. "Who would buy my paintings?"

"Are you kidding?" He scoffed. "Tourists come here every summer. That's why Mrs. Cavanaugh sells little signs that say *Splendid Lake*." He pointed to the shop across the street. "And Mr. and Mrs. Cox sell Splendid Lake T-shirts."

He gave her hands a squeeze. "But you've painted dozens and dozens of lake landscapes, and they're just sitting in my folks' basement collecting dust. You need to bring them here and sell them. The tourists would love them. They'd hang them above their mantels, and every time they look at one of your paintings, they'll remember the fantastic vacation they spent here in our town." The passion in his voice took her by surprise. "*This* is what you've been searching for. This is your calling: to bring the joy of our hometown to people all over. What do you think?" His eyes searched hers, and for a moment, she couldn't find her words.

"I . . . I have to think about it." She pulled her hands away and started down the sidewalk.

Just then, the heavens opened and rain began to pour down on them.

She squealed, and he took her hand before they ran through the rain, their shoes splashing through puddles. He guided her under an awning, and they both started to laugh.

"We're soaked!" she declared, taking in her wet jeans and hoodie.

When she looked up at Jake, his smile had smoothed out. His soft expression had transformed into a smolder.

She held her breath as her nerves stood on edge.

"Emily," he whispered, and his voice was husky. He gently angled her chin toward his, and when his lips met hers, her knees buckled.

Happiness blossomed in the pit of her belly as he cradled her head in his hands, and she melted against him. She closed her eyes, savoring the feel of his muscled frame leaning against her as she lost herself in his kiss.

Oh my goodness. It's happening. It's finally happening!

She'd been kissed by boyfriends over the years, but this was like nothing she'd ever experienced before. The heat, the emotions. Finally feeling Jake's lips against hers was all she'd fantasized—and more. So much more.

He trailed kisses down her jaw and her neck, and when his lips finally moved away from her skin, he whispered softly in her ear, "Emily."

Hearing him say her name—her *actual* full name—was almost too much. She was going to melt into a puddle right there on the Main Street sidewalk.

When he shifted away from her, she grasped his shoulders for balance. "I've wanted to do that for the past week," he admitted.

"Well, I've been waiting for you to do that since I was sixteen."

His brow wrinkled as his lips curved up in a smirk. "What do you mean?"

She guffawed. "Oh, Jake, please. You had to know that I've had the biggest crush on you since we were teenagers."

"Wait. For real? You have?" He had the nerve to look shocked. "Why didn't you tell me?"

"Why would I tell you that?!" She wiped her hands over her wet hair. "You only had eyes for Claire, and I didn't want to mess things up for you since you were happy. So I've spent years convincing myself that I could just be your best friend, but I've always dreamed of having more with you. I've always wanted to have you all to myself."

Finally saying those words out loud to him was like having a giant boulder lifted from her shoulders.

He winced. "Oh, Em. I'm sorry." He brushed his hand over her face. "I wish I'd paid better attention. But trust me, you have my attention now. *All* of my attention."

With that, he lowered his mouth to hers and kissed her again. And this time she looped her arms around his neck and pulled him closer. He tilted his head, the kiss suddenly becoming deeper, and the feel of his body under her fingertips, the way his muscled torso pressed up against her, made her feel as if all her cells were on fire.

When he pulled away, he rested his forehead against hers and grinned. "I'm sorry I waited so long, but I can't say I'm disappointed." His smile wobbled, and Serious Jake seemed to reappear before her eyes. "Would you consider being more than my friend?"

"What about Claire?"

He stood up straight and shook his head. "That's been over for months."

"Does *she* know that?"

"I keep telling her that I need space. We've grown up and changed. I asked her again yesterday to just back off and told her that we're done." He took Emily's hands in his. "I really would like to give us a chance. What do you say? We can take it slow so that no one interferes. We'll keep it between us so that my family, and Claire—*no one* can get in our way."

Emily was sure she was dreaming, but she wasn't. Jake was standing in front of her and asking her to be his girlfriend. And this was real life.

Her heart felt like it was going to explode.

"I'd like that," she said.

"Great." Then, dipping down, he kissed her again.

He began slowly, taking his time to explore her lips. Her hands moved to the nape of his neck, and her fingertips combed through his hair.

And the world around them fell away.

* * *

Jake steered his truck into his driveway later that afternoon. The sun was peeking through the clouds, and he couldn't stop smiling. He'd held Emily's hand the entire drive home, and all they could do was grin at each other. His heart felt so full.

But the same questions kept running through his mind. Why hadn't he noticed sooner that Emily cared about him? How had he missed the signs?

Why had they wasted the last fourteen years as friends when they could've been more?

But the past didn't matter. All that mattered was the future—which they would spend together.

He shifted the truck into Park and then turned toward her. "What do you say about the gallery? You can move back here, open it up, and I'll run the orchard. Sound like a plan?"

"One thing at a time." She held up her hand. "Let's worry about the orchard first, okay?"

He smirked. "Nope. Right now, the only thing I'm worried about is kissing you."

"If you say so." She moved closer to him and closed her eyes.

He laughed, dipped his chin, and brushed his lips over hers. He let himself get lost in the gentle swell of her lips and let all his worries dissolve. All that existed was him and Emily, along with this perfect moment.

When they parted, he touched her nose. "I guess we need to get to work."

"Yup, that would probably be good." She held up her laptop bag. "The stickers for the cider jugs should be here first thing tomorrow. I need to get working on a sticker for the baskets." She held up a finger. "Oh! And the banner for the barn. Jake, we have so much to do before Wednesday." She pushed the truck door open.

He sighed. What would he do without her?

Later, after lots of work and a little more kissing, they held hands and walked up the path to his folks' house so that Emily could grab the banner and her supplies before returning to his house.

A gray BMW SUV sat behind Mom's beige Camry in the driveway.

"Who's that?" Emily asked.

"Looks like Claire's parents."

She froze, and worry flashed across her face. "Oh."

"Hey." He pulled Emily behind his dad's pickup. "She has no power over you or me." He traced his finger over her cheek. "Don't let her get to you, okay?"

She nodded, but he found uncertainty in her beautiful golden eyes.

He brushed his lips over her forehead, and then, dipping his chin, he kissed her long and slow, allowing his mouth to explore hers. He didn't mind the lingering taste of coffee from their work session at his house. Not one bit.

A moan escaped from her throat, and he felt his blood heat.

He released her and brushed her soft hair over her shoulder. "Claire can't come between us. I promise you."

Her lips were swollen as she moved her fingertips over the stubble on his cheek. "Okay," she whispered.

He studied her face and tried to swallow back the riot of emotions tugging at his chest—elation, hope, love.

Love!

He'd fallen in love with his best friend. How lucky was he?

"Why didn't I kiss you years ago?" he asked, his voice sounding husky.

"Jake, I ask myself that question every day."

He laughed and kissed her again before taking her hand and tugging her toward the house. "Let's go inside."

"Uh . . ." She hesitated. "That's okay. We can get the banner later."

He brushed his hands through her soft ponytail. "C'mon. We'll say hello, grab the banner, and then go back to my place."

"Promise?"

"Promise."

"Okay." She allowed him to steer her up the stairs and in the front door.

The smell of Italian food—was that lasagna?—along with the sound of voices drifted from the kitchen. And when they reached the doorway, Emily dropped his hand.

Jake peeked in to see Mom, Claire, and Claire's mother, Sherry, drinking tea.

Male voices echoed from the den, where he assumed Dad and Ron, Claire's father, were visiting.

"Jake!" Sherry popped up from her chair, rushed over, and hugged him. "It's so good to see you." Then she turned to Emily. "Hi, Emily. I think it's been forever since I've seen you. How've you been, sweetie?"

Emily's smile didn't quite reach her eyes. "Fine."

"Come join us," Mom called from the table.

Jake rested his hands on Emily's shoulders. "Thanks, but we

have some work to do. The orchard opens Wednesday, and we're running out of time."

"Just give us a few minutes," Sherry insisted. "It's been so long."

Claire flashed him a smug look over her mug.

Had she deliberately dragged her parents here to force him to spend time with her? She needed to leave, and he wanted to instruct her to do it now. But he couldn't risk upsetting and embarrassing his mom. So he pressed his lips together and tried to stop his angry words from escaping.

"I'm sorry, but we're really on a deadline here." He pointed to the hallway. "We need to grab Em's art supplies and get back over to my place. It's great to see you, Sherry."

"We were waiting for Jake and Emily to get here, and they're here now." Claire pointed to the oven. "The bread and lasagna are just about done. Why don't we have supper now, Diane?" Her face clouded with a smarmy expression.

Mom stood. "That's a fabulous idea! The rain is over, and we can eat out on the deck."

"Wonderful." Sherry started for the doorway. "I'll tell Ron and Leon." Then she patted Jake's shoulder. "Have supper with us before you go back to work. Everybody's gotta eat, right?"

"Sure." Jake tried to keep his voice upbeat, but he knew he and Emily were stuck having supper with Claire and her parents.

Chapter 17

I THINK THE market's grand opening is going to be a huge success," Sherry announced while they sat out on the deck. "Don't you agree, Ron?" She lifted her glass of sweet tea as if toasting the orchard.

Jake sat beside Emily, across from Claire and her parents, while they ate the lasagna and garlic bread. If he were honest, he had to admit that the food was delicious, but he was ready to get back to his to-do list. Aside from that, he also was tired of answering Sherry's zillions of questions about the orchard while Claire eyed him from across the table.

But he was most worried about Emily. He could feel tension radiating off her while she remained mute and barely touched the food on her plate. He'd tried to catch her eye, to touch her thigh under the table to try to convey that everything was going to be okay, but she seemed to be completely inside her protective shell.

"Have you seen what the new owners have done with your family's house, Emily?"

Jake's eyes snapped to Sherry's across the table just as Emily froze.

Oh no. Sherry couldn't have chosen a worse conversation starter.

Jake reflexively covered Emily's hand with his, and Claire appeared to seethe at them across the table.

"No," Emily said, barely above a whisper.

"Oh, it's lovely," Sherry began before turning to her husband. "Don't you agree, hon?"

Claire's dad nodded before taking another bite of garlic bread.

"They've made such good use of all of that space your family had. They expanded the deck and put in a large in-ground pool. And they also added a dock for their huge boat. You should go see it. You'd just love it. I'm sure your folks would have too. We know the new owners—I'll bet they'd give us a tour so you could see everything up close. We can walk over there if you'd like."

He waited for Emily to respond, but she only stared at Sherry. That was his cue to speak up for her. "I don't think so," Jake said.

"They're such a nice family," Sherry continued. "Have you met them?"

Emily shook her head.

"I think they're both surgeons." Sherry consulted her husband, who nodded. "Yes, that's right. They both work at the hospital, and they have four kids. Of course, that place is huge, so there's plenty of room for a large family. I always thought it was a shame that your folks only had one child in that enormous house."

Jake's jaw tensed. Couldn't Sherry read the room?

Emily's lip trembled, and he moved his fingers over her hand, hoping to soothe her. But it didn't seem to help. Her leg began to bounce, brushing her jeans against Jake's. He reached under the table and set his hand on her thigh, stopping the movement.

"Ron," Mom began. "How's business at your car dealerships?"

"Busy," Claire's father said. "We purchased another one out in Asheville. We have five now."

While Ron continued detailing his successful businesses, Jake moved closer to Emily. "We'll finish here soon and get back to work, okay?" he whispered.

She nodded, but he could hardly stand the anxiety lining her features.

Jake forked more lasagna, and when his gaze tangled with Claire's, she pinned him with a glare. He brushed it off and focused on his meal.

When supper was over, Jake and Emily helped Claire, Sherry, and his mom clean up.

After the dishwasher was full, Emily touched Jake's hand. "I'm going upstairs to get my supplies and then heading back to your house to work on the banner," she whispered, out of earshot from Mom, Claire, and Sherry, who were busy discussing the weather.

"I'll be there soon," he told her before touching a lock of her hair.

She turned toward the group of women. "Thanks for supper."

"It was good seeing you," Sherry told her.

Claire's smile was so phony it reminded Jake of plastic. "See you soon."

Without a word, Emily dashed toward the doorway before her footfalls echoed on the staircase.

Jake narrowed his eyes at Claire, but she shrugged and returned to wiping down the counter.

After packing up the leftovers and stowing them in the refrigerator, Sherry hugged Mom. "This was so fun. We have to do this more often."

"Yes, we do," Mom said, reaching to hug Claire next.

Claire held on tight, and Jake rolled his eyes. "Would you like me to come over to help you tomorrow?"

Tell her no, Mom! Jake wanted to scream the words.

"You're so sweet, but that's not necessary." Mom patted her hand. "I appreciate all your help, honey."

Go, Mom!

"Okay, but if you need me, please let me know. I'm just a phone call away." Claire's eyes filled, and she sniffed. "You and Leon are like my second set of parents."

Oh please. Claire is such an actress!

Jake turned to his mom and yearned to tell her not to fall for it.

"That's so sweet, honey," Mom said.

Yup, she'd fallen for it. He rolled his eyes and folded his arms over his chest.

Mom and Jake walked Claire and her parents to the door and waved as they drove away.

He turned to his mother after they were gone. "Why were they here?"

"Your dad and I have been friends with Claire's parents since they moved here. We take care of each other in this community, and Sherry and Ron wanted to check on us."

"I'm sure it was Claire's idea," Jake added.

Mom's blue eyes searched his. "Is everything okay?"

"Yeah. I'm just stressed. The orchard is opening in three days, and I don't feel ready."

Mom cupped her hand to his cheek. "I have faith in you and Emily. It's going to work out."

His lips widened into a grin. "Thanks, Mom."

* * *

Emily's thoughts ran wild as she sat at the patio table on Jake's small deck, working on the banner. Her plan was to sketch it and then paint it in the morning.

She was certain she'd been transported to another dimension. She was finally Jake's girlfriend. *His girlfriend!* Her lips tingled as she recalled the kisses they'd shared, which were even more intoxicating than she'd ever imagined. And boy, had she imagined them often over the years.

While she drew, she considered his suggestion of opening a gallery, and she couldn't deny the thread of excitement winding through her. She imagined putting her precious paintings on display for purchase and sharing them with the world. Could her own gallery be successful? Would people want to adorn their homes with her work?

She allowed her mind to run with the idea. She envisioned working side by side with Jake while they set up the studio, holding his hand and kissing him during a ribbon-cutting ceremony. Having her own gallery would make her a true professional artist.

Her eyes stung at the thought. Would her parents be proud of her? Would they support her using their money to make that dream a reality?

Hot tears began to pool in her eyes, which she wiped away with the sleeve of her hoodie.

"Get ahold of yourself," she whispered.

It was too much to ponder right now. She needed to focus on the orchard and Jake.

Jake!

Finally, he was hers.

But . . . was he really?

Her stomach twisted as an unsettled feeling coursed through her. Everything had been perfect when she and Jake were alone. Conversation flowed easily between them as it always had. They laughed, talked, and kissed—a lot. But once they entered his folks' house, everything had changed.

She could feel Claire staring daggers at her, and Sherry's inappropriate comments about Emily's family nearly tore a hole through her. She would've burst into tears right there in front of everyone if it hadn't been for Jake, who knew just how to calm her down.

How could Jake truly be Emily's boyfriend if Claire put up roadblocks everywhere? Would Claire ever respect Jake's wishes and back off?

Why wouldn't she just go away? Was it because Jake wasn't truly over her?

She growled out a frustrated noise and then focused on her banner. She was outlining the last section when footsteps sounded on the deck stairs. She rolled her neck before turning toward Jake.

He sauntered over, looking positively delicious in a blue-and-tan-plaid shirt, along with jeans and a ball cap. And he was *her boyfriend*! She swallowed a happy screech.

"Hey," he said.

"Hey yourself."

He perched on a chair beside her, and she inhaled his enticing smell—sandalwood and Jake. *Her* Jake!

"How's the banner going?"

"Okay. I'll need to start painting it tonight. It's going to take a while." She held it up. "What do you think?"

"I love it."

And I love you. I always have.

Could he ever love her the same way she loved him?

He pushed a lock of her hair over her ear, and she slanted her head into his touch. "You okay?"

"Yeah." She dropped the banner onto the table.

"Come here." He leaned over, and when his lips brushed hers, his kiss was slow and gentle. "Wanna go for a walk?" he asked while his fingertip traced her cheek and jaw.

"Yeah."

They headed down the deck stairs toward the path leading to the orchard. Their shoes crunched along the leaves, and the air smelled like fresh apples, the windswept lake, and a woodburning fireplace. The sky above them was clear, and the sun had started to set. Jake held her hand, and she couldn't stop herself from smiling.

Emily couldn't shake the notion that they belonged together. She was with Jake, and they were in her favorite place—the orchard at Splendid Lake. Her home.

He led her down the path toward their old fort, and they picked up the pace. When they reached the tree, he turned toward her. "How about a visit to our ol' fort as our first official date?"

"I love it!" She giggled.

He made a sweeping motion toward the ladder. "Ladies first."

She climbed up onto the platform and scooted over as far as she could before he joined her. As soon as he sat down, she claimed his mouth with hers. He cradled her head in his hands and tunneled his fingers through her hair. As he deepened the kiss, she wound her arms around his neck and allowed all time and space to melt away. Nothing mattered except for her and Jake.

When they finally came up for air, she tipped her head against his shoulder and sighed.

He chuckled under his breath while he wrapped his arm around her. "You warm enough?"

Was he kidding? She was on fire! "Yeah," she managed to say. "You?"

"Yup."

Silence stretched between them, and she enjoyed the view of the trees with the lake in the distance. She turned toward him. "Okay. Confession time."

"This ought to be good," he teased.

"Do you know how many times I sat up here and wondered what it would feel like to kiss you?"

"I have no idea."

"At least a thousand."

"Huh." He rubbed his jaw.

"Let me guess. You never even thought about kissing me when we were up here, did you?"

"That's actually not true." He held up a finger. "The last time we were up here and you hugged me, that was the first time I felt the urge to kiss you."

She studied him. "The last time we were up here?" She pointed to the platform, and he nodded. "You mean like a month ago?"

"Exactly. You held on to me, and I had to stop myself from lifting your face up from my chest and kissing you until you were breathless."

His words sent a shiver racing through her. "Why didn't you?"

"Honestly, I was afraid that you didn't want the same thing. And I didn't want to risk losing you because that would kill me. I can't imagine not having you in my life."

She swallowed as emotion clogged her throat. "I feel the same way," she whispered.

He lifted her hand to his mouth and kissed it. "Knowing what I know now, I should've kissed you then, huh?" His grin was wolfish.

"Yeah, you should've." She laughed.

His expression softened. "I'm sorry about Claire and her oblivious mom."

She shrugged. "It's okay."

"No, it's not." He reclined back against the tree, and she snuggled closer to him. "I keep trying to make it clear to Claire that I want space and she needs to stay away. But she keeps inserting herself. Before she left tonight, she offered to come back over to help, but thankfully my mom told her she doesn't need her. If she comes around again, I'll make it clear that she's not welcome here anymore." He rubbed Emily's back, and she rested her head against his shoulder. "And just ignore her mom. She has no filter."

Emily glanced in the direction of her former home and tried to imagine walking over to the fence, but her insides twisted up. She couldn't do it. Her grief was still too raw and painful. Maybe someday she'd visit it again, but she doubted it would be anytime in the near future.

"So we've signed some vendors," he began. "Now we just have to get it all together. In three days." He rested his hand on her arm. "Are you certain we can do this?"

"Of course I am. We have to make sure the booths are ready, hang the banner and the lights, and go through our last-minute list. Andi texted me earlier. She and Seth will be here tomorrow."

"Good. We definitely need their help."

She snuggled closer and kissed his cheek. "Let's just enjoy a little bit of rest and relaxation before tomorrow."

That wolfish grin returned, sending tingles racing down her arms. "Good idea."

As Jake began to kiss her again, Emily was certain she was floating. And she didn't want to return to earth anytime soon.

Chapter 18

EMILY DROPPED DOWN on a stool and swiped her hand over her forehead. Every muscle in her back was screaming after spending the day sticking labels on jugs of cider and the bushel baskets. "I think we've done all we can do," she told Andi. "I think we've labeled just about everything we've got."

It was Monday night, and Emily was grateful that Seth and Andi had spent the day helping. While the guys worked in the barn, Emily and Andi had set to work on the cider and baskets.

Andi retrieved two bottles of water from the nearby refrigerator and handed one to Emily before hopping up on a stool beside her. "All right. I let it go all day, but now you need to spill it."

"Spill what?" Emily opened the bottle and took a long draw, enjoying how the cold liquid soothed her parched throat.

Her friend rolled her eyes. "Something's changed in the past few days since I've seen you and Jake. What's up?"

Uh-oh. This secret was going to be more difficult to keep than Emily had imagined. "What do you mean?"

"I feel a different vibe between you two." A grin spread over her lips. "Are you guys dating?"

Emily longed to deny it, but her flushing cheeks made that impossible.

"I knew it!" Andi hopped off the stool and hugged her. "I'm so happy for you. I always knew you and Jake would make a cute couple."

"Thanks, me too. But you can't tell anyone."

Andi returned to the stool, and her forehead furrowed. "Why?"

"Jake wants to keep it just between us for now. After we get through the orchard opening, then we'll tell the world. But right now we want to keep our stress to a minimum."

Andi's nose wrinkled. "That's odd, but, um, okay." She shrugged. "I'll keep it quiet, but I still think it's great. I can see you two getting married and raising a family together here in Splendid Lake." She held up her bottle to toast her. "Here's to you and Jake. And also, I'm very proud to say, I told you so."

"Thanks." Emily tapped her bottle against Andi's, and her heart skipped a beat as she imagined a future with Jake. Was that possible for them? Could they settle down together, have a family, and be happy?

Right now she needed to focus her attention on the orchard and not worry about her future. "How about we load up the cider and baskets in those two wagons and haul them to the barn?"

Andi took another long drink from her water bottle. "All right. Let's do it."

* * *

"Here goes nothin'." Jake plugged in the extension cord, and the inside of the barn illuminated with thousands of white fairy lights. And just as Emily had promised, it looked magical.

No, it looked *romantic*.

Jake cringed. What was wrong with him? He'd turned into a lovesick guy within the twenty-four hours since he first kissed Emily.

Maybe I've lost my mind. Or maybe I'm actually falling in love with Emily, and this is how love is supposed to feel.

He cupped his hand to his forehead. *Whoa. That's super deep.*

"You okay?" Seth appeared beside him and studied him with concern.

"Yeah." Jake pointed to where the fairy lights twinkled from the rafters. The colorful banner Emily had painted with *Happy 100th Anniversary, Hughes Family Orchard!* and decorated with bright red apples hung in the center of the barn. "It's finally done." He shook Seth's hand. "Thanks for your help, man."

"It was actually fun."

Jake snorted. "Your idea of fun and my idea of fun are way different."

Seth laughed and pivoted just as Andi and Emily appeared, each hauling a wagon filled with jugs of cider. "Here come the women." He dashed over and took the handle of Andi's wagon from her hand. "I got it."

His wife gasped as she entered the barn. "Wow, you guys. It looks great in here." She faced Emily. "You were right about the fairy lights."

Jake took the handle of Emily's wagon. "What do you think?"

She twirled around in the middle of the barn, and her smile was so bright that she could rival the sun. "It's perfect!"

You're perfect. And adorable. "It sure is."

"We did it!" Emily announced. "People are going to love it, Jake."

Jake looped his arm around her shoulder. "I think so too."

They spent the next two hours setting up the booth for the cider and then stowing the baskets for the apples by the cashier stations.

After Seth and Andi left, Jake took Emily's hand and led her toward the barn. He'd planned a surprise for her earlier in the evening, and he couldn't wait to put it into action.

"Where are we going?" she asked.

"I have a surprise for you."

"Oh?" she asked. "What is it?"

He laughed. "If I told you, then it wouldn't be a surprise." He steered her to the middle of the barn. "Now close your eyes."

She cocked an eyebrow. "Why?"

He shook his head. "You can be so frustrating sometimes. Just close your eyes."

"Okay." She sighed, closed her eyes, and folded her arms over her chest. "How long do I need to keep them closed?"

"Until I tell you that you can open them." He rushed around the barn, turning off the overhead lamps so that only the fairy lights cast a romantic glow. "Almost done," he called.

When she stuck her tongue out, he couldn't stop his chuckle. Emily always knew how to make him laugh. He set up his Bluetooth speaker and connected it to his phone.

"What's going on?" she asked.

"Hold on, Miss Impatient," Jake told her while he found the perfect song. He pressed play before locking his phone and pushing it into the back pocket of his jeans.

Then he came to stand beside her, and he leaned down and whispered in her ear, "You can open your eyes now."

She trembled at the sound of his voice, and his insides heated.

She opened her eyes, and as she scanned the barn, her pretty lips formed a perfect O. The fairy lights twinkled above them, casting the entire barn in a soft glow, while Ben E. King's "Stand by Me" came through a nearby speaker.

Jake held his hands out to her. "Will you dance with me, Emily?"

"Yeah," she whispered, her voice full of awe. "I'd love to."

Jake drew her against him and rested his hands on the small of her back while she wrapped her arms around his neck. She leaned her head against his chest, and he breathed in her flowery scent and felt her soft body press against his as they swayed to the music.

When he spun her around and dipped her, she giggled. Then he lifted her chin and kissed her velvet lips. He closed his eyes, savoring the feel of her mouth against his, and a shiver of longing vibrated through his body.

"Is this almost as good as prom?" he whispered as the song ended and then "Groovy Kind of Love" by the Mindbenders began.

"It's better, since we're dancing to the oldies instead of pop songs."

"Right." He grinned. "You and your oldies."

She sighed and rested her cheek on his shoulder. "I almost asked you to prom."

He stopped moving. Had he heard her right? "Really?"

"Yeah," she said, her eyes meeting his. "But you had asked Claire." She touched his cheek. "Actually, I wanted to ask you to homecoming, but she got to you first."

If only he could turn back time . . . "I'm sorry I didn't realize you were interested in me that way, but I wish I'd known." He held her close. "Let's pretend this is our prom."

She smiled as she lay her head against his chest. "It's perfect," she whispered, and he kissed the top of her head.

"I agree." He held her close, and they continued to sway with the music. Being this close to her was different from anything he'd ever experienced. He'd never felt so much joy with a woman—not even Claire. It was as if his heart had been brought back to life.

Oh boy. He had turned into a hopeless romantic for sure!

"There was a song that I always imagined would be our song," she suddenly said.

"What is it?"

She lifted her gaze to meet his. "That song from the early nineties by Vanessa Williams. 'Save the Best for Last.'"

"Whoa." He held up his hand. "You know a song from the nineties?" he teased.

Her eyes narrowed. "I happen to like a variety of music." She lifted her chin. "Are you going to let me finish my story?"

"Of course." He pulled her close. "Go on."

"Thank you. So the song is about two best friends who end up falling in love, and how sometimes we end up saving the best for last." Her cheeks turned bright pink, and she was even more irresistible than usual. "It's silly, but I used to imagine that we'd dance to it at our . . ." She cringed and covered her face with her hands. "Never mind. I can't believe I'm saying this to you out loud. I feel so silly right now."

"Hey, look at me."

She squinted up at him, and he chuckled.

"You're adorable when you're embarrassed, but you shouldn't be embarrassed. Tell me. Please."

"Fine, fine." She gulped. "I used to fantasize that it would be our wedding song." The words tumbled out of her mouth before she buried her face in his shirt. "I'm going to just dissolve into a puddle now." Her voice was muffled by his clothes.

"Don't worry about it." He kissed her head again. "The song sounds perfect."

They continued to move together, and he felt his entire body relax. He wanted this night to last forever.

* * *

Emily still felt like she was floating Tuesday morning. She had started her day by setting up the outdoor painting area where she planned to give lessons to customers. Then she began walking around the orchard grounds, checking on how the last-minute touches were coming for the grand opening tomorrow. She hummed "Groovy Kind of Love" and waved to the seasonal workers who were busy picking the apples. She'd fallen asleep singing the song, and she'd dreamed about her dance with Jake during the night. His impromptu barn prom had been the most romantic date she'd ever been on, and it even trumped their make-out session in their fort the night before. She'd been Jake's girlfriend for less than forty-eight hours, but she couldn't remember a time when she'd been so happy.

She continued humming while she took in the employees organizing the cashier counters, the bins full of apples, and the bushel baskets. Leon sat on a chair near the seasonal employees and pointed while giving orders, and she smiled. It was good to see him out of the house and getting involved in the orchard.

Emily began singing "Standy by Me" to herself while she made her way toward the barn. When she found Jake pacing back and forth and frowning while talking into his phone, she quickened her steps.

She approached him and touched his arm, but he continued his phone conversation.

"We can make this work, Tom," Jake said. "Just give me a chance.

The grand opening is tomorrow, and I need you here. I'm sure you'll have a lot of sales. In fact, you'll probably sell out the first day." He held his fist up to his forehead. "Please don't back out. I'm begging you." He paused for a few seconds. "Fine. I understand." He disconnected the call, and his nostrils flared.

"What's going on?" she asked.

"The pumpkin vendor just backed out." His eyes narrowed. "This is going to be a disaster."

"No, it's not." She touched his cheek.

"I've got a bad feeling. I woke up with it this morning, and it's been following me around all day long like a dark shadow."

"Jake, everything's going to work out."

He pursed his lips. "I hope you're right."

She curbed the urge to hug and kiss him, reminding herself that their relationship was supposed to be a secret. At the moment, however, all she wanted to do was console him.

"I need to go check on a few things," he told her. "I'll see you later."

As she watched him walk away, she hoped she was right: that somehow, some way, everything was going to fall right into place.

* * *

Jake stalked through the barn later that afternoon as all of his worst fears had come to fruition right before his eyes. Every single one of the vendor stalls was empty. Because every single one of the vendors had backed out, without giving him a good reason why.

And tomorrow was the opening.

"This is going to be a disaster," he whispered to himself.

"Son, I told you this was a bad idea!"

Jake pivoted toward the entrance of the barn where his father stood, leaning his good arm on a cane. Jake bit the inside of his lip to keep a disrespectful response from escaping.

Dad pointed his cane toward the ceiling. "Now we've spent all this money on the barn for nothing."

"*My* money, Dad," Jake retorted, pointing to his chest. "*I* spent *my* money on this. I didn't touch any of your money, or the orchard's."

"That's not the point, and you know it." With the help of the cane, he hobbled toward Jake. "This was just a lesson in futility, son. If you'd have just kept doing what we've always done, then we wouldn't be in this mess right now."

Jake's body shook as white-hot anger built up inside him. This was not the moment he wanted to hear an "I told you so." But he especially didn't want to face the financial consequences of taking a risk. He'd emptied his savings and maxed out his credit card. His sister's tuition was coming due. His father's medical bills were piling up, and he had the seasonal workers to pay. The responsibility was all on Jake's shoulders. He felt like throwing up.

Emily appeared in the barn doorway as if she'd heard his thoughts. "Where are the vendors?"

"They all backed out," Dad answered for him. "I told you two that this wasn't going to work, but no one listens to me." He hobbled out of the barn while mumbling about how bullheaded kids were these days.

Jake lifted his ball cap and raked his hand through his messy hair.

Emily grabbed his arm and tugged him. "We're going to town. Come on."

He remained cemented in place and studied her. "What on earth can we possibly do to fix this?"

"Do you trust me?" She lifted her chin.

He hesitated and then nodded. He'd always trusted her. That would never change. "I do. With every fiber of my being."

That comment earned him a cute smile and offered him a moment of relief from his anxiety. "Good. Let's go."

They jumped into her Jeep, and she drove the five miles to Apple Haven and parked at the back of the lot.

"Why are we here?" he asked her.

She removed her key from the ignition. "I have a hunch, and I want to see if I'm right."

They headed into the orchard, and soon they came upon a vendor area, where they found Tom, the pumpkin farmer, and the other vendors setting up booths.

So Apple Haven had stolen his customers, his employees, and *now* his fall market idea.

Well, wasn't that just peachy?

"You've got to be kidding me," Jake grumbled as he marched over to Tom. "You told me that you couldn't sell pumpkins at my orchard, but you're here at my competitor's. Why?"

Tom shrugged. "I'm sorry, Jake, but business is business."

"Just tell me why," Jake nearly begged him.

"Better deal," Tom explained. "Apple Haven is waiving the booth fee for the first few weeks, plus they're not taking a percentage of sales for the time being." He looked over at Cassie Ridgeway, who was setting up her jewelry booth beside him. "Right?"

"Yeah," the woman said. "Sorry."

Jake rubbed his eyes and tried to take deep breaths in order to stop himself from having a meltdown in the middle of Apple Haven. Wouldn't his competitor just *love* to see him fold right there on their property?

"Let's go." Emily half yanked, half dragged him out to her Jeep, where he sank down onto her bumper. "I can't stand seeing you like this."

"Sorry, babe, but I'm not sure what else I can do."

She grinned, and he stared at her.

"Why are you smiling at a time like this?"

"Because you just called me 'babe,' which means we're officially a couple."

He snorted. "I thought we became official when I kissed you, but okay." He studied her pleased expression. "Now what are we going to do?"

"First, you're going to climb into my Jeep, and then I'm going to take you to the flea market."

"The flea market?"

"Yup." She retrieved her keys, and they jingled. "We're going to round up some vendors and fill that barn before the grand opening tomorrow."

He shook his head. "It's a great idea, but I just don't know . . ." He covered his face with his hands.

"Talk to me."

"So much is riding on this." He opened his eyes and found her sitting beside him on the bumper. "You know I'm responsible for the orchard, for paying Ally's tuition, for paying all of the bills. Now my dad's hospital bills are piling up, and I have the seasonal workers to pay. How can I do that when I maxed out my credit card refurbishing the barn?"

Emily threaded her fingers with his. "Honey, we got this."

"You think so?" He hated the uncertainty he heard in his voice.

"Yes, I'm sure of it. And if you need money, I can help."

He shook his head. "I can't take your money."

"We'll argue about that later. But right now we need to get

to the flea market and round up some vendors before the day is over." She popped up to her feet. "Get it together, Hughes."

He stood, drew her to him, and kissed her. "Thank you."

"For what?"

"For believing in me. And the orchard."

"Of course I do. Now let's stop wasting time and get to the flea market."

He smiled as he climbed into the Jeep. For some crazy reason, he was sure that everything was going to be okay if he had Emily by his side.

Chapter 19

LATER THAT EVENING Emily climbed out of the shower. She was certain every muscle in her body hurt—even muscles she didn't realize she had. After leaving Apple Haven, she and Jake had driven to the Splendid Lake Flea Market and spent more than an hour talking to vendors about the grand opening at the orchard. Before they left, they had three vendors signed up and another four who were considering the offer.

She was grateful that they ended the day on a good note, with the vendors promising to arrive early tomorrow to set up. Seeing a smile on Jake's face was such a relief. All Emily wanted was for this grand opening to be successful and for Jake to be happy.

She dressed in a pair of shorts and a tank top before piling her hair on top of her head. As she made her way into her bedroom, she recalled the gallery conversation she'd had with Jake. For a moment she allowed herself to envision opening a place to showcase her work—her paintings on the walls, people wandering through, customers discussing where they'd hang her pieces in their homes or businesses. Having her own gallery would mean that she'd finally share her art with the world and possibly make a living as a real professional artist.

It all sounded wonderful—like a dream come true—but was she kidding herself? Would people *really* want her artwork on their walls? Sure, Jake and Diane had displayed her art, but they were like family. Would some random stranger also consider her work good enough to spend their hard-earned money on?

Well, she mused, *guess there's only one way to find out!*

Emily smiled as she pushed her feet into a pair of fuzzy purple slippers and then padded down the stairs, where muffled voices sounded from the suite that belonged to Jake's parents. The delicious aroma of candy apples lingered in the kitchen as Emily made her way to the door leading to the staircase that plunged down to the finished basement.

She flipped on the lights and then hurried down the stairs. A flood of memories filled her mind—the hundreds of playdates and parties Emily had attended there with Jake and their friends from the time they were in kindergarten until they graduated from high school. The basement had once served as an enormous playroom containing a humongous sectional sofa, a large television complete with video game systems, a stereo, lots of toy cars, and tools.

Now the room seemed lonely. The sofa, the games and toys, the tools—everything that used to be here was long gone, and the room had been converted into a second attic. But this attic mostly held Emily's possessions—furniture and collectibles from her childhood home, along with her paintings.

She waded past the random boxes and plastic containers until she came to the paintings leaning against the wall. She began to unwrap them and flip through them, silently criticizing her work and contemplating whether any of the pieces were good enough for a gallery.

Her gallery!

A mixture of excitement and fear rushed through her. Was she even ready for this?

Emily found four companion pieces featuring the same landscape of Splendid Lake in the four seasons, and she unwrapped them before displaying them in a row—spring, summer, fall, and winter. She pulled a couple more paintings from a plastic container and studied them, silently picking out the brushstrokes that could have been improved. *Who would pay good money for these pieces? They're definitely not perfect.*

Heavy footsteps sounded on the stairs, and Emily turned just as Jake peeked over the banister.

"Hi." She touched her messy bun and wished she'd actually dried and styled her hair.

She almost laughed out loud at herself. She'd never before worried about how she looked in front of Jake, but now that he was her boyfriend, she felt self-conscious.

He rested his arms on the banister. "I was looking all over for you. What are you doing down here?"

"Just taking a trip down memory lane. Come join me."

He jogged down the stairs and closed the distance between them. "I remember these pieces. I never understood why you didn't hang them up in your folks' house."

"My parents had their own art—real art that was worth real money."

He shook his head. "I hate how hard you are on yourself. You're *so* talented. I wish you could see what I see." He unwrapped another painting of a sunset over a beach. "This is one of my favorites."

"I forgot about that one. I painted it when I went to Coral Cove with my folks. We stayed in this awesome condo on the beach, and the sunsets were out of this world." She leaned against Jake.

"I always wanted to ask you for this one, but I never had the nerve."

She smacked her lips. "Are you kidding?" She pointed to it. "It's yours."

"Nah. This should go in your gallery. It'll be the first piece that sells."

She snorted and waved him off. "Just take it." She unwrapped another piece, which featured wild horses on the beach in the Outer Banks. "Oh, I remember this. It was the summer when I was sixteen and went to the Outer Banks. We went out to Corolla, and there were these wild horses there, and I—" She stopped speaking when she realized Jake was staring at her. She glanced down at her clothes and brushed her hands over her tank top and shorts before she focused on him. "Why are you staring at me?"

"I need to know something."

"What?"

"Why on earth did you stop painting?"

Her throat thickened, and tears stung her eyes as she tried to find the words to describe how she felt.

Moments ticked by, and he waited patiently for her to speak.

Finally, she rubbed at a spot on her shoulder and took a ragged breath. "When I lost my parents . . ." She trailed off as her parents' loving faces swam into her mind. And before she could stop them, a waterfall of tears spilled down her cheeks. "I just . . . I mean . . ." She sucked in air and tried to swallow past the knot in her throat. "S-something inside me broke apart."

Jake's eyes glistened. "I know. I'm so sorry." He hauled her against him and rubbed her back while she wrapped her arms around his waist. "I thought painting might be your way to heal. To help you express what you were—what you *are* feeling."

"I thought so too. But I lost part of me when I lost them."

He kissed the top of her head. "I know, babe. I know. I'm sorry I brought it up."

She sighed deeply and rested her face against his chest. Closing her eyes, she listened to the comforting sound of his heartbeat. "Now that they're gone, I have this hole in my heart."

He tilted her chin so that her eyes met his. "I get that. And I know that nothing will ever replace them. But I'd love to be the one to help you fill that hole."

She smiled through her tears and touched his cheek. "You already are."

His chin dipped, and her breath hitched as his lips again met hers. She wrapped her arms around his neck and drew him closer. When he opened his mouth to deepen the kiss, a fire ripped through every cell in her body. She would never get tired of kissing Jake. She'd waited a lifetime for this, and now that she finally had him all to herself, she wanted to keep him forever.

When he pulled back, she rested her head on his shoulder and closed her eyes as happiness bloomed in her heart like a flower.

"So, about that gallery . . ." he began.

She chuckled. "You're not going to let that go, are you?"

"Nope." He peered down at her. "And I'm not going to let go of you either."

"I hope not," she whispered.

He kissed her again, and she held on to him, trying to memorize the feel and taste of his lips after more than a decade of longing for them.

After he released her, they wrapped up and stored the paintings. When she spotted a small box across the room, she picked it up.

"What's that?" he asked.

"I think my old journals are in here. It might be fun to thumb through them."

He smiled at her. "Ready to go upstairs?" he asked, holding his hand out to her.

She took it before they walked up the steps. At the top, he flipped off the lights and closed the door. When they ambled through the kitchen, he said, "Go wait by the door and close your eyes."

"Why?" she asked.

"It's a surprise."

"*Another* surprise?" She folded her hands.

"Yeah. Now go to the door."

She did as she was told, and soon she heard his footsteps.

"Keep your eyes closed," he said.

"Okay . . ." She couldn't stop her smile.

"Ready?" he asked, and his voice was close to her ear, sending a shock wave of tingles rushing over her skin.

"Yeah," she said.

Then his lips claimed hers, and they were sweet and tangy, tasting almost like a mixture of caramel and apple. His kiss was slow and soft, and she basked in the warmth and deliciousness of his mouth. When he pulled away he said, "Now you can open your eyes."

"What was that?"

"A candy apple kiss." He held up the candy apple. "Did you like it?"

"Very much. And I want *more*."

He chuckled and bit into the apple before holding it out to her. "Have some."

She took a bite before he kissed her again.

"Your candy apple kisses are the best," she told him before kissing him once more.

"I'm glad you like them." He lifted his eyebrows. "And you'd better not get any from anyone else."

She grinned. "Trust me when I tell you that I only want *your* candy apple kisses."

"Good answer, Carmichael." He tossed the remaining apple in the trash.

When he cupped his hand to his mouth to cover a yawn, she touched his face. "You need to get some sleep. Tomorrow's going to be a big day."

"Yeah, it sure is." He brushed his lips over hers once again. "I'll see you tomorrow morning for the grand opening."

"Bright and early."

He wrenched the door open and then kissed her again. "Good night, babe."

"Good night." *I love you.*

She lingered in the doorway while he disappeared down the path toward his house, and she sighed. She longed to tell him that she loved him, but she feared scaring him away. When the time was right, she'd tell him. And she couldn't wait for that moment to arrive.

* * *

Jake was certain he was stuck in a nightmare. He'd seen only a handful of customers travel through the orchard since the grand opening three hours ago. Perhaps he'd missed the crowd. Maybe. Hopefully.

He walked over to the first cashier. She was eighteen years old and hard to miss, with her purple hair and her eyebrow and nose rings. "Hey, Sidney. How's it going?"

"Slow." She smacked her gum. "I've sold one basket of apples."

"Only one?" he asked.

"Yup." She turned toward the teenager at the next cash register. "Hey, Maddy. How many baskets have you sold?"

The brunette gave them a sad smile. "Only one." Then she brightened. "But it's early. I'm sure we'll have more people later today."

"Right. Thanks," Jake grumbled before heading toward the barn. Hopefully the barn was busier than the front end.

But it was empty.

Oh no. This can't be happening.

He walked into the barn and was greeted by Emily's colorful banner and the twinkling fairy lights. It felt like a lifetime ago when they were dancing under those lights. Now a black cloud seemed to hover over Jake as he glanced around the empty barn. Only two of the three vendors had shown up today—Mona Horton, selling her homemade fall decor, and Warren Lewis with his booth full of metal signs and collectibles. The third booth featured Jake's employee Brian Holmes handling Mom's candy apples and Jake's cider.

"How's business?" Jake asked.

Mona and Warren shared glum expressions.

"Slow," Warren said, and Mona nodded.

Jake massaged the back of his neck. "Hang in there. It'll get better," he promised before walking away.

"I hope so!" Warren called after him, and Jake gritted his teeth.

Crossing over to the open-air area, he spotted Emily; she sat on a stool in front of a blank easel and twiddled a paintbrush in one hand while staring at her phone in her other. She looked completely relaxed, and the mid-morning sun illuminated her beautiful face and highlighted her dark hair.

She glanced up as he approached, and a radiant smile filled her face. "Hi." Her smile flattened. "What's wrong?"

"What's wrong?" He gave a sardonic laugh. "No one's here. That's what's wrong."

She threw her arms around him and drew him closer. "It's going to be fine. I promise you." Her golden eyes searched his.

He rested his hands on the small of her back. "This is a disaster," he said, and his voice trembled. "I don't know what to do."

"I'll tell you what to do: Don't give up hope." She pushed a lock of hair away from his eyes and brushed her lips over his.

Her soft kiss warmed the cold places inside him. He wanted to believe her. He longed to hold on to the idea that the orchard was going to be a huge success, but he was grasping at his last shred of hope.

When she pulled away, she beamed up at him before something behind him caught her attention, and her happy expression dissolved into a frown.

"What?" he asked, craning his neck over his shoulder just as Claire disappeared into the barn. He scoffed. "What's she doing here?"

"I don't know, but she didn't look pleased. I think she saw me kiss you. I forgot where we were for a second. I'm sorry."

He huffed out a breath. "Don't worry about it."

"Oh!" Emily bounced on the balls of her colorful Converse. "I have a couple of customers!"

Two young women who looked to be about their age approached.

"Is this where we take the painting lesson?" one asked.

Emily clapped her hands. "It sure is. Take a seat, and I'll be right with you." She touched Jake's shoulder. "See? Everything is going to be great. Keep that cute chin up." She winked at him before joining her students. "I'm Emily, and I'm your teacher today. What are your names?"

Jake folded his arms over his chest, and he hoped the young women had a whole bunch of friends who were wandering around the orchard and ready to purchase apples and tchotchkes in the barn. If not, then he and the orchard were in big trouble.

* * *

"How have things been over here?" Andi sat on a stool in front of Emily later that evening.

Emily sighed and set down her paintbrush on her easel. "I had two customers before lunch and then none after that. I even wandered around the orchard and asked the few folks I saw if they wanted a painting lesson, and none of them were interested. I think about a half dozen customers total walked through the barn."

"Yeah." Andi rested her western boots on a rung. "Seth has been helping pick apples, and I was working up by the cashiers. If we sold six baskets of apples, that's a lot." She frowned. "I'm afraid this may be a failure."

Emily rested her arms over her waist. "I hate this for Jake and his family. I've been telling him all along that everything is going to be fine. But clearly it's not." She turned toward the barn and nibbled her lower lip. There had to be a way that she could help him, but she was coming up empty. "How can we fix this?" she asked as she faced her friend again. "We need to do more advertising. I've already posted on the orchard's socials. I'll have to keep highlighting all of the cool stuff we have going on here."

"That's a great idea. Can I help?"

"What if we took more photos of the orchard and posted them?" She pointed toward the sky. "The evening is a great time to take good photos and videos of the trees and the barn, with the lake in the background. Would you mind taking some and texting them to me?"

Andi nodded. "Sure, we can try that. I'll ask Seth to help too."

"Great." Emily felt a ribbon of hope flutter through her.

Andi turned toward the orchard entrance and then back at Emily. "I saw Claire here earlier."

"Ugh. I did too."

"She was with Diane over at the house. I'm not sure what she was up to." Andi rubbed her hands over the thighs of her jeans.

"Jake has told her more than once that it's over, but she can't seem to accept it. Earlier Jake stopped by. He was really upset about how quiet the orchard was, so I kissed him. And when I opened my eyes, Claire was watching us with a dark look on her face. She gave me a really weird vibe." She shivered at the memory. "It was like she was shooting daggers at me with her eyes."

"That can't be good." Andi hopped down from the stool. "We're going to be closing soon, so I'll go see if the cashiers need any help."

"Okay. I'm going to clean up here and then find Jake. I'll see you later." Emily stowed her art supplies and then headed toward the office.

Chapter 20

JAKE STARED DOWN at the sales sheet and hung his head in his hands. It was a disaster. No, it was a nightmare, just as he'd assumed earlier in the day. They'd sold a whopping total of eight baskets of apples. *Eight.* That wasn't enough for him to pay his employees. Heck, that was hardly enough to put a tank of gas in his truck.

He was ruined. The orchard was ruined. And thanks to him, after a hundred years, his family's name was ruined.

He groaned into his hands.

Footsteps echoed in the hallway outside the orchard office, and he ignored them. Hopefully whoever it was would just keep walking.

But they didn't. Instead, the soft footfalls entered the office, but Jake didn't move. Motion sounded beside him as the person sat down on a chair. Then arms encircled him.

Emily. His sweet Emily. Of course she'd be the first person to come encourage him.

"Hey." Her voice was soothing in his ear. "It's not that bad. We'll get through this. I'm sure of it."

She settled him against her, and he sighed and sat up straight. "The entire day was a bust. We only sold eight baskets of apples. We might as well put the orchard up for sale. The new owners of Apple Haven wanted it, so I might as well start negotiating a price."

"No, no, no." Her expression was fierce. "Come on, Jake. You can't give up that easily."

He lifted his palms in a gesture of surrender. "I'm not giving up. I'm facing facts. Apple Haven beat us. My dad can get a good chunk of change for the land and we can pay for Ally's education and have enough for my folks to retire well. I'll find a job somewhere." He snorted. "Maybe I can work for the new owners."

She studied him, and her expression darkened. "That's what you really want?"

"No, of course not, but I'm facing the truth. I appreciate your enthusiasm and your faith in me, but the orchard is bleeding money."

Emily tapped her fingertip on the desk. "I have an idea. What if we—"

"Supper's ready."

Jake and Emily spun toward the doorway, where Claire watched them with an unreadable expression on her face.

Great. As if this day couldn't get any better.

"What are you doing here?" Jake seethed.

Claire grinned at him. "Helping your mom, of course."

Emily pushed back her chair and stood, and Jake hated the pained expression that flickered over her face. "I'm going to go wash up," she muttered before pushing past Claire and hurrying out of the trailer that served as the orchard office.

Jake's chest pinched with anger. "Claire, you need to stop whatever it is you think you're doing. I believe I've made it clear that we're through. So why are you still hanging around here?"

Her face seemed to mock him. "You and Emily have gotten awfully close." She pointed toward the window. "I saw that adorable kiss you shared earlier."

His eyes narrowed.

"So you replaced me with her, huh? You said you needed space, but I guess you really needed more than that."

He shoved his phone into his pocket and stood. His hands shook with the fury surging through his veins. "What I need is none of your business."

"Please. This is just a little phase. I know she can't make you half as happy as I did."

"Listen, my life is none of your concern. And you need to accept that."

She winced as if he'd struck her, and he could almost see the gears turning in her mind.

He continued, "I don't know what you're trying to prove by sucking up to my folks, but I can see right through it."

She had the nerve to gasp and press her hand to her chest. "How can you say that? I love your family."

"Right. Sure you do." He glared at her. "Why don't you admit the truth? You're just trying to worm your way back into my life, all because you *love* sticking to your little plans. But it's not going to work. We're done. I've moved on. And you should too."

He tried to walk past her, but she blocked the doorway.

Claire gave him an arrogant smile. "I'm helping your parents while you play in the orchard. You need me. And not only do your parents need me, they *love* me."

Jake fought the urge to shout and somehow kept his voice even. "Do us all a favor and just go home."

"Well, I made supper. So I'm going to go back to the kitchen, and you and your little girlfriend can join us." Turning on her high heel, she flounced back toward the house.

Jake rubbed his eye sockets. It was going to be a long night.

* * *

"Eight baskets of apples? That's all you sold all day?" Dad's fury seemed to bounce off the cabinets.

Silence suffused the kitchen, and Jake ran his tongue over his teeth while he glanced across the table at his father. He could feel his mother and Claire staring holes into his head, but beside him, Emily was studying her plate of fried chicken, noodles, and stewed carrots. He longed to grab Emily's hand and whisk her out to their fort.

But he couldn't. Instead, he was stuck in the kitchen with his angry father, his irritating ex-girlfriend, his disappointed mother, and his sad girlfriend. And it was driving him crazy.

"What are you planning to do now?" Dad demanded. "How are you going to pay all of our bills, along with the employees and Allyson's tuition? I believe that's all in the toilet, thanks to your brilliant plan to rebrand the orchard."

Jake sat up straight. He was almost thirty. He could stand up for himself—and *his* orchard. "We got off to a bad start, but—"

"A bad start?" A sardonic bark of laughter erupted from deep in Dad's throat. "I'd call it an abysmal grand opening, not a bad start. You've been insisting that I should step down, that the orchard would be in good hands if I gave you the reins. But you did exactly what I thought you'd do—you failed."

Jake held up a trembling hand. "Please, Dad, let me speak."

He took a deep breath. "This was just the first day. We're going to try again tomorrow."

"And what makes you think anything is going to change between today and tomorrow?"

"I'm going to post on the orchard's website and social media accounts," Emily announced.

Jake's eyes snapped to hers. He'd been certain she'd given up on him, thanks to Claire's interference. But Emily's eyes were laser-focused on his father. Jake was so overwhelmed with gratitude that he touched her hand, but when she moved it away, her rejection felt like an ice pick to his heart.

"I'm not giving up, and I hope you won't either," Emily said. "I believe in the orchard." She turned toward Jake. "And I believe in your son."

A snort sounded from the far end of the table, where Claire sat.

Jake shot her a look, and she stared defiantly back at him.

Emily swallowed. "I think if we keep publicizing the orchard, then people will come. We can't throw in the towel after one bad day. The anniversary celebration is Saturday, and it's only Wednesday. We have time to promote it and get people in the door."

"I agree with Emily," Mom chimed in. She looked at her husband. "Your parents and grandparents went through hard times, dear, but they never gave up. In fact, we suffered last year when that terrible storm took out more than half of our crop. We didn't give up then, and you can't now. If you did, what would your father and grandfather say?" Her face dared him to challenge her.

Preach it, Mom!

Dad opened and closed his mouth before clearing his throat. Then he turned toward Emily. "Well, you go ahead with your posts, and we'll see what happens."

Emily sat back in her seat, a satisfied smile on her face.

Mom looked over at Claire. "This fried chicken is delicious. You'll have to give me the recipe."

"Thank you." Claire beamed. "It's my grandmother's. I'll text it to you."

While Mom and Claire prattled on about recipes, Jake leaned close to Emily.

"Thanks for saving my butt."

Her smile faded. "Sure," she said before taking a bite of chicken.

"You okay?" he asked.

She nodded, but she was avoiding his eyes. "Uh-huh."

Jake tried to ignore how his worry and guilt nipped at him during the rest of supper. When the excruciating meal was finally over, Emily excused herself and fled upstairs while Jake hefted Claire's giant tote bag and pointed to the door. "Let me walk you out," he said.

"Oh. Okay." Claire almost pranced out the front door.

He walked out to her SUV and set the tote bag down. "I've had enough. It's time for you to stop."

"Stop what?" She batted her long eyelashes at him.

"Stop *everything*," he began, his voice rising. "Stop bullying Emily."

"But I . . . I'm not bullying Emily. What do you mean?"

"Oh, come on! I heard you make a noise when Em said she believed in me at supper. I see the dirty looks you shoot her way. She's innocent in all this." He rested against her car. "Stop pretending to help my mom. Stop chasing after me. You need to go home and stay away from my family and me. We're done. *Done.* Do you understand?"

Claire's lip began to tremble, and her green eyes filled with tears.

Jake rolled his eyes. *Seriously? Not again.*

"Please, just give me a chance to explain," she whined.

"There's nothing to explain. It's time for you to go." He opened the back door and set the tote bag on the seat. "Take care."

"Wait."

He turned just as she wrapped her arms around him.

"Claire, stop," he said, and he tried to push her away, but she locked her arms around his neck. "Stop!"

"Jakey, I miss you," she whimpered before lifting up on her toes and pressing her mouth to his.

* * *

Emily stared out the bedroom window, and her stomach bottomed out.

Claire and Jake were kissing in the driveway.

Kissing!

Bile rose in her throat, and tears built up in her eyes.

She flopped down on the corner of the bed as her sobs broke free and her heart shattered.

You'll only ever be his friend.

The cruel words played on a loop in her mind.

Claire was right. Emily wasn't good enough for him and never would be.

Why would Jake want her when he could have beautiful, gorgeous, *perfect* Claire?

Covering her hands with her face, Emily fell back on the bed as sobs continued to rack her body.

* * *

Jake clamped his hands down on Claire's arms and pushed her away. "Stop!" He took several steps away from her and held up his hands while his heart hammered in his chest. "I've told you a hundred times that I'm done."

"But it can't be over," she exclaimed, tears rolling down her pink cheeks. "After all these years, how can you give up on us? What we had was special. I still love you!"

He shook his head and began walking backward away from her. "I don't love you anymore."

She gasped. "How can you say that after all we've been through together?" Her voice sounded strange, hysterical.

He scrubbed his hand over his face. What did he have to say in order to make her understand that he was over her?

"Listen to me," he began, his words measured. "I'll always care about you, but we're done. We're no longer a couple, and we never will be again. What we had is in the past. Do you hear me? It's over. *Over!*"

She stilled, and they studied each other for what felt like several moments.

Suddenly a devious smile overtook her lips. "That's what you think."

"What did you say?" he asked as a feeling of foreboding wafted over him.

But instead of answering, Claire climbed in her car, started the engine, and drove away.

* * *

The alarm clock blared next to Jake's head. He groaned and rolled over. He'd slept in fits all night long. Every time he closed his eyes, he saw Emily's hurt expression at supper and then Claire's deceptive smile.

His mind replayed Claire's kiss over and over again. When her lips touched his, he'd felt nothing—nothing at all. No spark, no excitement, and no love.

But as Claire kissed him, he also realized that he did love one person—Emily.

He loved her wholly and completely with his entire heart. And while his ex was kissing him, all he could think was that he wanted to be with Emily and only Emily. Claire had done him a favor by making him realize just how much he loved Emily.

He loved her. *Loved her.*

And he wanted Emily in his life for the rest of it. He wanted her by his side forever. He just needed to find the right moment to tell her.

In the middle of the night, he'd considered going to his parents' house and knocking on Emily's bedroom door to tell her what had happened between him and Claire and also confess all the feelings in his heart. Twice he'd gotten out of bed, gotten dressed, and started for the door. But when he realized it was three in the morning, he changed his mind. He didn't want to scare his parents or her, but he couldn't wait to tell her how he felt. No matter what happened with the orchard—whether he had to sell it or the situation turned around—he wanted Emily by his side, and he prayed she felt the same way.

After a long, hot shower, Jake shaved and dressed before jogging out to the kitchen, where Dusty wove herself between his legs, meowing and purring for her morning meal.

"Hey, Dusty," he sang while he filled her bowl with a fishy breakfast. "It's a great day, girl. You know why? Because I'm going to tell Em that I love her. Do you think she'll say she loves me too?" He set the bowl down, and the cat began inhaling the food. "Well, I'll take that as a yes. See ya later, kitty."

He grabbed his phone and headed out into the bright morning sun. The sky was blue and cloudless, but the late September air was cool. The perfect fall day.

While he walked toward his parents' house, he opened his Instagram app and immediately found a post on the orchard's page highlighting the grand opening and the anniversary celebration. He scrolled through the photos—and all of them were gorgeous views of the orchard. He smiled. Emily was the best at what she did. She was the best at everything. And she was his. He just had to make it permanent.

He checked the orchard's other social media pages, and all of them had been updated with photos and new appeals for customers to join them for the celebration.

Pocketing his phone, Jake jogged up the steps and entered his parents' house. He expected to find his parents and Emily in the kitchen, but only Mom and Dad were there. He waved to them as he entered the room.

"Morning," Mom said.

"Mornin'." Jake swiped a piece of bacon off a platter on the table. "Where's Em?"

Mom pointed toward the door. "She was up and out of the house early. She left me a note saying that she'd eaten and would see me later."

"Huh." He pulled out his phone and dialed her number. It rang once before going straight to voicemail. Strange. Maybe her ringer was off. He picked up a toasted bagel. "Can I have this?"

"Sure," Mom said.

He smothered it in cream cheese, placed it on a napkin, and then started for the door. "See ya later."

He ate the bagel on the way to the barn, where he found the

vendors setting up for the day. He waved to them. "Have you seen Emily?"

Mona shook her head. "Nope."

He asked Warren, but the man had the same answer.

Jake traipsed out to the plein air area, where he found Emily's easel and supplies set up, but no sign of his favorite artist. So odd. Where was she?

He headed over to the cashiers and spotted his girlfriend talking to Maddy and Sidney, and his heart skipped a beat. He was definitely becoming an old sap, but that realization made him grin. "Hey! I've been looking all over for you."

Emily faced him, her lips pressed into a flat line.

Uh-oh. Something was definitely wrong. He picked up the pace and tossed his napkin into a nearby trash can. "You okay?" he asked as he approached her.

"Yeah," she said, but her normally bright eyes were dull and lined with dark circles.

A thread of worry twisted through him. "Are you feeling all right?" he asked.

"I didn't sleep well last night," she said, her voice as dull as her eyes.

He reached for her face, and she took a step back.

Whoa. Something was very, very wrong.

He took her arm and led her away from his employees, who were watching them with curiosity. "Why didn't you sleep?"

She shrugged.

"What's going on?"

"Nothing." She crossed her arms over her chest and looked past him. Now she was avoiding his gaze.

"Emily," he said, and her eyes snapped to his. "What's going on?"

She shrugged again, but her eyes glistened.

He reached for her and tried to pull her against him, but she pushed him away.

"What's wrong?" he asked, but when she remained silent, he leveled his gaze with hers. "Did I do something to upset you?"

Something almost imperceptible flickered over her face.

"What did I do? Please tell me," he begged her. "No matter what it is, I'll make it right, okay? I care for you—*deeply*—and I don't want to mess this up. You're too important to me."

She took three steps back. "I think I'm getting a cold, and I don't want to get you sick. We have the anniversary celebration in two days and—"

"Jake!"

He pivoted just as Vince rushed over.

"I need you," Vince called, beckoning him. "We have an issue in the orchard."

"Can it wait?" Jake called as frustration filled his voice.

"Sorry, Boss, but no. I need you now."

Ugh! Perfect timing. "All right." Jake faced Emily. "We'll talk later, okay?"

She pursed her lips and nodded, but he could see the pain in her eyes. She wasn't getting sick. No, she was upset with him, and he wanted to fix it now. He'd have to bury his worry for now and focus on work.

But later he'd get her alone, and they would hash it out. Jake would find a way to fix it because the idea of losing Emily made it hard to breathe.

Chapter 21

EMILY MANAGED TO stay busy all day and avoid being alone with Jake. She swept the plein air area, took more photos of the orchard and posted them, and taught two painting classes—each including only two students. She spotted a grand total of ten customers in the orchard all day long, which wasn't much of an improvement. Still, she was grateful some more people had decided to come.

Yet Emily had spent the entire day on the verge of tears. She couldn't wipe the vision of Jake and Claire kissing in the driveway out of her mind and fought the urge to pack up her things, climb into her Jeep, and drive to Charlotte. That way she could leave Jake, his family, the orchard, and Splendid Lake in her rearview mirror for good. But she'd promised to help with the orchard. She couldn't back away now, especially when so many vendors had done that themselves. So she stayed cemented in place despite her agony.

She'd hoped that she could unload all of her burdens on Andi, but Andi had texted her earlier in the day to say that she and

Seth had to sort out some issues with their lawn care business. Her friend promised that they'd be back at the orchard as soon as everything was settled. It couldn't be soon enough. Emily needed a friend's shoulder to cry on, but for now, she'd stay strong and keep her tears at bay.

Emily was closing up the plein air painting area when Diane approached her.

"Pack up, sweetheart. We have plans tonight."

After stowing her paints, she pushed her thick ponytail over her shoulder. "What plans?"

"Claire's mother called me, and we're all invited to their house for supper. Sherry was very excited and said that it's going to be fun."

Claire Chapman and her unfiltered mother were the last people on the planet Emily wanted to see. Emily worked to keep her expression blank despite the irritation nipping at her. "Oh, no thanks. You all go and have fun. I'm pretty tired, so I just want to—"

"Nonsense," Diane declared. "Claire wants you to come too."

She does, huh? That can't be good. "I appreciate it, but I'm happy to just rest tonight. This is a family thing."

Diane rubbed Emily's arm. "You *are* family. You're my second daughter."

Oh boy! Now Emily had to work extra hard to hold back the tears building in her eyes. If Diane started talking about how much Emily meant to her, then she'd really lose it. Leaving Splendid Lake was going to be even more difficult than she imagined, since she'd have to leave Diane and Leon behind. They were the only surrogate parents she had left.

Emily had to come up with an excuse to avoid the supper before she burst into tears and wound up telling Diane that her son had completely annihilated her heart.

"You go on without me. I have so much to do before the anniversary celebration on Saturday. We're running out of time, so I really need to be here, but you have fun. And if there's cake, save me a piece, okay? You know I'm a cake fiend." Emily tried to laugh, but it came out as a squeak.

Diane shook her head. "I'm not gonna hear it. You deserve a break from all the work you've done. We're leaving at six, so be ready."

While Diane headed back to the house, Emily sagged against her stool and rubbed her forehead. Now she was forced into going to supper with Claire and her parents—the day after she realized Jake was cheating with Claire. Could this day get any worse?

"Emily!" Jake called as he darted over to her. "I've been trying to get you alone all day."

Yup. Unfortunately it can *get worse.*

Squaring her shoulders, Emily faced him. "Jake, I don't feel like talking. Just—just leave me alone." She shouldered her bag of painting supplies, and he took it in his hands.

"Let me carry this for you."

Ugh. Why is he always so nice?

They started down the path side by side toward his parents' house, and the sound of their feet seemed to echo off the trees. Emily couldn't remember a time when she and Jake had run out of words, and the silence between them tore at her soul.

When they reached the driveway, he spun, facing her. "Why are you ghosting me in person?" His striking blue eyes seemed to beg her. "What did I do? Tell me so I can fix it. It's killing me, babe."

Her lip trembled. *Oh no. Keep it together, Em!*

She swallowed back her threatening tears. "Things have come into clear focus in my mind."

"What does that mean?" he asked.

"It means I understand how things stand, and it's okay." She hated the vibration in her voice, and she fought to keep her emotions under control.

He studied her. "Are you talking about us?" He motioned between them.

"I'm talking about a lot of things."

"Emily . . ." He drew out her name.

Diane appeared on the porch. "We have to leave in ten minutes, so you need to get ready now. Chop-chop!" she sang before disappearing into the house.

Emily reached for her bag, and he captured her hands in his. "Promise me that we'll talk later."

"If I promise you, will you give me my bag?" she asked.

He nodded, and the pain in his expression sent a knife slicing through her chest. She couldn't stand hurting him, but hadn't he done the same to her when he kissed Claire?

Her eyes snapped to his lips, and she recalled how he'd tasted like those delicious candy apples. That had been the most romantic, intimate, exhilarating experience of her life. Had those candy apple kisses meant *anything* to him?

The lump in her throat doubled in size, and tears filled her eyes.

Stay strong, Emily. He cheated on you! He deserves your silence.

"Please," he said, his words rasping from his throat. "I can't take this. We need to talk later. It's tearing me apart."

"Fine. Sure. Whatever." She tried to sound like she didn't care, but she cared so much that she was ripping apart at the seams.

Jake released her hands, and his Adam's apple bobbed. "Don't give up on me. Promise me."

She grabbed her bag and ran up the porch steps as her tears broke free and raced down her cheeks.

* * *

Jake gripped the wheel of his mother's Camry while he drove his parents to the Chapmans' house. His mother's discussions about the weather and the orchard were background noise while he steered down the road.

He peeked in the rearview mirror and spotted Emily following in her Jeep. He'd tried to convince her to ride with them, but once again, she'd given him the cold shoulder and muttered something about having to get back to the house to prepare for Saturday. He had no clue what she had to do, and when he'd asked, she'd ignored him and climbed into her vehicle. She was still ghosting him in person—completely blowing him off—and the pain in her eyes was slowly chipping away at his heart.

His world had been turned upside down, and he wasn't sure which end was up anymore. He'd gone from wanting to confess his love to Emily to begging her to talk to him. He couldn't figure out how everything had gone sideways in the past twenty-four hours.

And this is why you shouldn't have ever kissed her. All you did was ruin your friendship!

Jake tried to convince his mother that it wasn't a good night for them to go to supper, but his mother wouldn't concede. No matter what he said, Mom insisted that they had to go. He was determined to get it over with and get out of there as quickly as possible.

At a red light, he studied the reflection in his rearview mirror. Emily's face was masked by her sunglasses, but her mouth was fixed in that same glower he'd seen since that morning. He tried to rack his brain and analyze what he'd done to hurt her, but he came up empty.

"Did you hear what I said, Jake?"

"Huh?" He shifted to face his mother in the back seat. "I'm sorry. What did you say?"

Mom's expression turned worried. "Are you okay, sweetie? You've been acting strange all day." She tapped her chin. "Come to think of it, so has Emily. Did you two have an argument?"

Jake hesitated. "We have some things we need to discuss." He paused. "That's why I didn't want to go to the Chapmans' tonight."

"Oh. Well, I'm sure you two will work it out later. You always do." She brightened. "Sherry sounded so excited when she called and invited us. She said she has some news. I can't wait to find out what it is. Do you have any idea?"

He shook his head and turned his attention back to the windshield. He had no clue what Sherry had planned, but he was certain he knew who was behind it.

The light turned green, and Jake continued the short journey to the Chapmans' sprawling brick colonial on the other side of Splendid Lake. He parked in the driveway behind their BMW SUV and then helped his father out of the passenger seat and up the stairs.

As soon as they reached the top step, the door opened and Sherry greeted them. "Come on in!" She beckoned them into her fancy foyer, which ended at a sweeping open staircase that Jake knew led up to a gallery of expansive bedrooms. "We're ready for you in the dining room." She pointed toward the hallway.

Dad waved off Jake's help, and Mom took his arm and guided him toward the dining room.

Jake lingered in the foyer and shoved his hands in his pockets. Emily finally emerged through the front door, and she stopped short of him. "You can't avoid me forever."

Her golden eyes challenged him.

"My goal is to get us out of here early, and then you and I can go to my place and talk. Deal?"

Her hand flew to her neck, and her fingers began absently moving her mother's rings back and forth on her necklace while she stared at him.

"Em, say something to me, *please*."

"I hope you two are hungry."

Jake turned toward the end of the hallway, where Claire stood dressed to the nines in a little black dress, silver high heels, and more makeup than he'd ever seen her wear. Her blonde hair was done up in a fancy-looking twist, and she posed as if she were a model awaiting her turn to strut down a runway.

His eyes flitted to Emily beside him. She wore a pair of jeans and a purple hoodie. Her face was makeup free, and her hair was arranged in a long thick braid. At that moment, he was certain she was the most beautiful woman he'd ever seen.

Why had it taken him so many years to appreciate her as more than a friend?

"Well?" Claire asked, dramatically tapping her foot. "Are you coming to the dining room or what?"

Jake held his hand out to Emily. "Take my hand."

She stared at it, and he sucked in a breath as the moments ticked by.

Please, Em. Whatever I did, please just forgive me.

Finally, her eyes met his, and she hesitated before doing as he asked.

Some of the tension slid out of his body as he threaded his fingers with hers. "Thank you," he whispered before guiding her down the hallway.

They reached the enormous dining room, and the long table was set with the fancy china Jake had seen only during holidays and special events. The scent of steak and freshly baked rolls wafted out of the nearby kitchen.

Claire pointed to an empty chair beside Jake's mom. "You can sit there, Emily."

Emily released Jake's hand and sat where she was told.

Jake felt a muscle jump in his jaw as he looked at Claire. "What's going on?"

"You'll see," she sang before she began distributing champagne flutes.

When she gave one to Jake, he studied her. "Tell me *now*."

Her smile was coy, and his blood began to boil.

"Stop playing games," he grumbled. "I want to know why we're here."

His ex pointed to her mother. "You're about to find out."

Just then Sherry tapped her fork against her glass. "I'm so glad you're all here tonight." She beamed in the direction of her daughter. "Now, I believe Claire and Jake have an announcement."

At that very moment, Jake noticed a sparkle of light glinting off a large antique diamond ring on Claire's finger—*that* finger.

Huh?

Claire rested her left hand on Jake's arm, and his eyes widened.

"Last night Jake and I did some soul-searching, and we realized that it was time to move on to the next stage of our relationship." She looked up at him and gave him the phoniest adoring smile he'd ever seen in his life.

Wait. What?

Then she took a deep breath and angled her left hand toward the group of people at the table. "He proposed! We're getting married in Nashville on New Year's Eve!"

The world stopped, and everything seemed to move in slow motion as Claire's words registered in Jake's brain.

Proposed? Getting married?

What on earth?

And then Jake's head began to spin.

Mom gasped. "Oh my goodness! My prayers have been answered!"

"Isn't this wonderful?" Sherry asked Mom. "We knew it would happen eventually."

The two mothers began talking at once while the walls slowly closed in on Jake. He tried to make sense of it all, but nothing made sense at that moment.

Jake glared at Claire. "What are you talking about?" he demanded. "I *never* asked you to marry me!"

But his words were lost in the chaos.

The two mothers' voices grew louder—discussing plans, what they would wear, where they would stay, and how many guests they would invite to their children's wedding.

His mother was so happy—stunningly so.

Jake turned to Emily. Her eyes were rounder than two saucers, and her mouth hung wide open in shock.

Panic built in his chest. He couldn't allow Claire to hurt Emily like this. He opened his mouth to protest, but Claire cut him off.

"Emily!" Claire called, and the room instantly went silent. "You can be Jake's best man. You could wear a dress—or even a tux." She sneered. "What do you think?"

"What a great idea," Sherry exclaimed. "Oh, that would be so cute!"

Emily looked physically ill. She pushed back from the table as tears collected in her eyes.

Jake's stomach twisted. "Emily! Wait!" he called, but she had already fled the room. "No! I didn't—!"

He started after her, but Claire blocked the exit.

He glared at Claire. "How could you do this?"

Claire was too busy staring at her ring to respond to him. "Jake knows I've always adored my great-grandmother's ring, so there was no need to buy me one." She leaned over the table, and Mom began to examine it. "Isn't it lovely?"

"Oh yes, sweetheart. It's perfect!" Mom popped up from her chair and pulled Claire in for a hug. "I've been waiting for this day. This is just what we need after Leon's health troubles. Tell me you'll make us grandparents soon."

Sherry started clapping. "I can't wait to be a grandmother. Children are the best blessing there is."

Mom moved over to Jake and swept him into a hug. "Why didn't you tell me you were going to propose? No wonder you've been acting so strange all day. How did you manage to keep this a secret?"

"Mom, I didn't—" he began, but his words were cut off when Sherry hauled him in for a hug.

"Oh, Jake," Sherry gushed. "You've made us so happy!"

Jake peeked out the dining room window toward the driveway, hoping for a glimpse of Emily, but her Jeep was already gone. He had to go after her and tell her that this was all a horrible lie. He couldn't let her believe that he was actually going to marry Claire. He moved toward the door, but Claire and her mother pulled him into a corner while they continued to discuss plans for their imaginary wedding.

Chapter 22

TEARS POURED FROM Emily's eyes while she steered her Jeep away from Claire's house. She pulled over to the side of the road, shifted into Park, powered off her cell phone, and covered her face with her hands while sobs racked her body.

Jake had proposed to *Claire*. He was going to marry *Claire*.

How could Emily have been so foolish to think that Jake would actually pick her?

She couldn't shake the woman's haughty grin from her mind's eye. She could still hear her saying:

Last night Jake and I did some soul-searching, and we realized that it was time to move on to the next stage of our relationship.

You can be Jake's best man.

Hugging her arms to her middle, Emily tried to calm herself, but her sobs continued to pour from deep in her soul. This all seemed like some terrible nightmare. How could Jake go from dancing with her in the barn and giving her candy apple kisses to cheating on her and proposing to Claire?

It just didn't make any sense.

When her tears finally subsided, she wiped her eyes and nose with a tissue and then collapsed onto her steering wheel. She had no idea where to go or what to do. She considered driving over to Andi's house, but she didn't want to burden her friend.

Instead, she started her engine and drove. She had no idea where she was going, but she couldn't stay still any longer. She continued around the lake while memories of the past week flashed through her mind—kissing Jake in the rain, kissing Jake in their fort, kissing Jake in the barn, kissing Jake in his parents' basement.

Her body began to tremble again. What had gone wrong between them? Had it all been some cruel joke? Jake and his friends, including Claire, had loved to pull pranks in high school. The night before senior year started, they had broken into the school and covered the principal's office with toilet paper. And after prom, they'd filled the main hallways with balloons.

Had Jake pulled the ultimate prank when he found out that Emily had always been in love with him? Did he just pretend to care for her before pulling the rug out from under her?

But she'd known Jake nearly her entire life, and he'd never been callous or cruel. The pranks he'd pulled had been harmless, not hateful. Plus, he'd stood up to bullies on the playground to defend the smaller kids. She'd never once known him to deliberately hurt anyone.

So then why would he have lied to Emily and convinced her he cared about her? Had their fake relationship been part of a bigger plot? Perhaps Jake used Emily to make Claire jealous? She wiped away more tears, continued driving, and mulled it over.

But that didn't make sense! If he'd only used her, then why had he planned their romantic evenings together in the barn, by the lake, and in the fort? If he'd only wanted to get Claire's attention, then he wouldn't have actually acted like Emily's boyfriend. He wouldn't have asked Emily to stay in Splendid Lake and encouraged her to open a gallery in town.

But if Jake truly cared for Emily . . . then why had he proposed to Claire?

Emily hit the brakes and glanced around the street. Her plan had been to drive aimlessly, but she suddenly realized that she'd driven to her childhood home.

Her body began to vibrate. She'd been avoiding this place since she arrived in Splendid Lake, but she'd accidentally driven there.

Had it been an accident? Or had she subconsciously craved the love and protection of her childhood, her home, and her beloved parents?

She bit her lower lip, parked her Jeep in the driveway, and stared down the long, winding driveway toward the large colonial. Did she have the courage to face this house after she'd lost the man who was most precious to her?

Her eyes filled again, and she pushed herself out of her Jeep before walking halfway up the driveway. Slowly she scanned the enormous front yard and the large house that had once been her sanctuary.

Warm lights glowed in the windows while memories rolled through her mind like old movies. She recalled the Christmas tree that had once adorned the picture window at the front of the house. She smelled the fresh pine and envisioned the piles of colorful packages there. She could still hear her parents' laughter while they opened gifts and sang Christmas carols in front of a roaring fire in the fireplace.

She remembered the Thanksgivings gathered around the dining room table, talking, laughing, and eating with her parents and grandparents. And the days spent out in their boat—enjoying the beloved lake and their wonderful family.

But then there were the memories of Jake.

Jake.

The hundreds—no, thousands—of times she and Jake had watched movies in the den, talked for hours on the deck, listened to oldies music in her bedroom, and sat out on the dock and dreamed about their futures. And all the while, Emily had been fantasizing that he would pick her as his life partner.

Just recently she'd believed her dream had come true. She had loved and lost her parents, but she thought she finally had Jake all to herself—until he changed his mind.

Now she had no one. She was all alone.

Her chest felt as if had been cracked open, and her world crumbled around her.

All of the grief that Emily had kept locked inside her heart since her parents died erupted like a volcano, and she dropped to her knees as more tears overcame her.

She'd lost everything—*everything*! Without Jake she was a boat without its rudder, lost at sea.

Emily sat on the ground and took deep, shuddering breaths until she regained control of herself. Then she picked herself up and threw herself into her Jeep.

She drove the short distance to Jake's parents' house, ran up to her room, and grabbed the box she'd found in the basement, along with a battery-powered lantern, her sketch pad, and colored pencils. Then she drove to the far side of the orchard and left her Jeep under a tree canopy before trudging through the trees.

She stopped at the entrance to the path that led to her former home. She paused and took a deep breath. For a moment she considered walking down the path that led to her old backyard.

But the memories felt too painful, still too raw for her to face them.

But she had to. She had to work through that grief, or she'd never move past it. She lifted her chin and drew up all of the courage she could muster deep inside herself.

I can do this.

With her heart thudding in her chest, she ambled down the path, and her eyes focused on a piece of her childhood—the swing her father had hung from a tree overlooking the lake shortly after they'd moved into the house. She'd spent countless hours out there pumping her legs and pretending to swing all the way up to the sky, floating up high enough to touch the fluffy clouds. She smiled as the memories of childhood overtook her mind once again. Life was so easy then. Her home was filled with love and laughter, and she never imagined that she would have to bury her parents when she was only twenty-five.

She faced her former house again, and the light in the window had dimmed. Instead, outdoor lights glowed on the corners of the house and over the large deck that the new owners had renovated. Lights also illuminated the in-ground pool surrounded by a concrete patio and a cabana. Nearby was an impressive dock where a boat—a yacht, really—was moored.

It wasn't the same yard where she'd run around flying kites, playing tag, or drawing. The new owners had definitely made good use of the land, as Claire's mother had so graciously pointed out. Emily tried to ignore the sadness crowding her chest. The home she'd known since she was five was gone, and she'd lost Jake to Claire. It was too much to process at once.

She studied the swing and it called to her, beckoned her to revisit what it was like to be a carefree child, pretending she could float up to the sky without a care in the world.

Emily studied the house for a moment. Would the new owners spot her sitting on their swing and call the police?

But the house was dark. Surely they wouldn't even notice her.

Emily padded through the grass and leaves to the swing and gripped one of its cold chains. She lowered herself onto the cool metal seat. She looked out over the beautiful lake and drank in the colorful sky as the sun began to sink below the horizon. The sound of the tiny waves lapping against the shore was a soothing melody for her fractured soul. Moving the swing back and forth, she tried to lose herself in the sights, sounds, and smells of the lake she loved so much.

After several moments, she opened the box and sifted through it. She spotted an envelope featuring her mother's handwriting, and when she opened it, she found a birthday card addressed to *Our Daughter* with drawings of flowers on it.

Inside was a poem about the specialness of daughters, along with a handwritten note:

> Emily,
>
> We are in awe of all you've accomplished this year—straight A's in your classes, and you even went out of your comfort zone and joined some extracurricular activities that weren't art related. We're so impressed by how you've blossomed. You're becoming such a lovely young woman.
>
> Don't ever forget that we're proud of you. You can accomplish anything you try. Reach for the stars, Emily!
>
> Love,
> Mom and Dad

Emily swallowed back more tears while she sifted through the letters and notes until she found an envelope with her name written in her father's slanted script. When she opened it, she found a card featuring a Christmas tree surrounded by gifts. She opened it and read the note:

> Emmy-bug,
>
> Merry Christmas! I can't believe how fast the year has gone and how much you've grown. I can't wait to see what new things you discover. It's hard to believe you're ten now. Mommy and I hope you like the art set that Santa brought you. It's so fun watching you create colorful pictures. Your mom is hoping that you become a doctor or lawyer. But honestly? We'd be happy knowing that you chose to follow your heart, whatever you decide to do. Just find something that brings you joy.
>
> Love you, Emmy-bug!
> Daddy

Emily read the card over and over again. Her father had given it to her when she was ten, but it wasn't familiar. Had she ever read it before? Maybe her dad had stuck it in her Christmas stocking, and she'd overlooked it in favor of her new art supplies from Santa.

But the words, those precious words, swirled through her mind as if on repeat:

Your mom is hoping that you become a doctor or lawyer. But honestly? We'd be happy knowing that you chose to follow your heart, whatever you decide to do. Just find something that brings you joy.

She read the lines again. And then she read them another time. She couldn't remember one time when her parents had encouraged her to follow her dreams, but her father had told her to do just that.

They wanted her to find joy, and she knew that art brought her joy. Creating something that came from her soul and brought happiness to others was what she'd always wanted to do.

Could she do that after losing her parents and then losing the love of her life?

Emily closed her eyes as another wave of grief crested in her heart.

She sucked in a breath and hoped that the ache working its way from her heart to her extremities would fade.

But then something unlocked deep inside her soul.

Her eyes flew open, and she studied the rainbow of colors as the sunset reflected on the lake, and an idea gripped her: a drawing that she yearned to create. Something deep, personal, and inspiring overtook her mind, and her fingers began to tingle with the need to draw it.

Now.

Her pulse began to pound. And she realized that her muse had finally reawakened after nearly four long years.

Emily flipped open her sketch pad to a fresh page and started drawing.

* * *

Jake was certain steam was spouting out of his ears. He was so furious that his entire body was shuddering. He followed Claire into the kitchen. He was going to get her alone and give her a piece of his mind.

"Have you completely lost your mind?" he demanded. "I've made it crystal clear that it's over between us."

She smirked and waved him off. "Nah. You just needed a little push."

"A little *push*?" His voice rose. "I told you I was done! What part of 'done' do you not understand? Do you think we can really build a life based on whatever sham this is? I will *not* go along with this."

She pointed toward the doorway, where beyond it he heard their parents talking and laughing. "See how happy our parents are? Isn't that what you want for them after all your folks have been through?"

"No. This is not what I want, and you know that. I will not allow you to manipulate me or my parents. This stops now!"

She shook her head. "You know as well as I do that we're meant to be together. The sooner you realize it, the better." She shoved a chocolate cake into his hands. "Take this out to the table, please."

He slammed the cake down on the counter. "Are you completely delusional? I'm *not* going to marry you. I'll admit, it's the ultimate prank, Claire, but *you're* going to be the one to tell our parents that you lied."

"No, I won't. Because they believe we're getting married. You're going to have to be the one to ruin their happiness."

He stared after her. He'd always known that Claire craved attention and loved to pull pranks, but this was taking it too far—even for her.

He couldn't stop thinking about Emily. More than anything, he wanted to talk to her alone and tell her that this was all a ruse—a cruel and painful one.

Just then, Sherry entered the kitchen and threw her arms around Jake. "I'm just so happy. I'm finally going to be able to call you my son." She clicked her tongue. "This is just so wonderful! We'll have to start making plans right away. New Year's will be here before you know it." Sherry picked up the cake and headed out of the kitchen. "Let's have dessert."

A hand latched onto his bicep. "Just go with it. You'll be glad you did." Claire kissed his cheek, and he shifted away from her.

He followed Claire out to the dining room, where Sherry was serving pieces of chocolate cake.

"I always knew they'd get married," Sherry said as she set a piece in front of his mother.

Mom dabbed her eyes with a paper napkin. "I'm just so thankful. A wedding is just what we need right now."

Jake's stomach twisted, and he was certain he was going to be sick. "Excuse me," he grumbled before he slipped down the hallway and into the half bath, where he locked the door. Then he slumped against the sink and dialed Emily's number.

When it went directly to voicemail, he rested his free hand on his forehead and waited for her voicemail to pick up.

"Em," he began, "please call me. Please. I had no idea Claire was going to pull this charade tonight. I had nothing to do with it. You have to believe me. I *never* proposed to Claire. She made the whole thing up." He closed his eyes. "I know this sounds crazy, but I'm telling you the truth. You're the only woman in my life and the only one I want in my life. *Please* call me. Let's work this out." His voice sounded tight. "I'll be home soon, and we'll talk, okay? Please. Call me back or text me."

He disconnected the call, sagged against the sink, and tried to think of a way out of this ridiculous mess.

* * *

"We only have three months to plan this wedding," Mom announced during the ride home. "Claire and Sherry are going to reserve the church and the reception hall, so we need to think about a rehearsal dinner, Leon." She leaned forward in the back seat and tapped Jake's arm. "Are you going to ask Emily to be your best—uh—attendant, or do you think you'll ask Seth? I noticed you and Emily have been spending a lot of time with Andi and Seth."

Jake only half listened to Mom while she continued babbling about the wedding that was never going to happen. He'd spent the entire evening staring at the tabletop and trying to figure out the best way to break the news to his hopeful mother that this wedding was a farce. The engagement was a farce. In fact, his entire relationship with Claire was a farce.

As much as he wanted to tell his mother the truth, the guilt of disappointing her was also weighing heavily on him. And then there was the issue of Emily. He'd tried to call her repeatedly during the evening. He'd excused himself each time and retreated to the bathroom or the hallway and dialed her over and over again. Each time he left her a voicemail, begging her to call him. He'd also texted her to no avail, and his body vibrated with anxiety. He hoped she was waiting at his parents' house, but he feared she had left town.

He steered into his parents' driveway and found only his father's truck sitting there. Emily wasn't home.

He rubbed his forehead. Hopefully she'd gone for a ride and would be back soon, but he had a feeling he was wrong. A pit expanded in his stomach.

"Does that sound good, Jake?"

"What's that?" he asked, turning to face his mother.

Mom harrumphed. "You've been quiet all evening, sweetheart. What's wrong?"

"I have a lot on my mind."

"Well, you're going to be a married man soon." She patted his shoulder. "I'm so happy for you, honey. I've prayed for this day for so long." She wagged a finger. "I had a feeling it would happen soon."

He set his jaw. "Let's get inside."

Jake helped his father into the house, finding all of the lights off. Taking a chance, he jogged upstairs and knocked on her closed door. "Em, are you in there?" When he didn't receive a response, he rapped again. "We need to talk."

He waited a few moments before pushing the door open and finding her room empty. His stomach fell, but when he glimpsed her enormous suitcase in the corner and a stack of art supplies stashed around the room, his mood lifted—slightly. She wasn't at his parents' house, but she had to be close. Now he just had to find her.

Jake hurried down the stairs and pulled his truck keys from his pocket. Before he hit the front door, his mother called his name.

He spun to face her concerned expression.

Oh no.

He didn't have time for a heart-to-heart right now. If he told his mom that the wedding was off, she'd have a million questions, and he needed to find his real girlfriend—if he still even had a girlfriend.

"Honey, what's going on?" she asked.

He rubbed his hand over the back of his neck. "I need to find Emily."

"Tell me why you're upset."

He held his hands up. "I promise I'll explain everything soon, but right now I need to find her." He wrenched open the door. "I'll see you tomorrow."

"Be careful," she called after him.

Jake sprinted back to his house. And as he climbed into his truck, he knew it was going to be a long night.

Chapter 23

JAKE JOGGED UP his parents' steps the following morning. He'd hoped to find Emily's Jeep in their driveway, but it wasn't there. His shoulders sagged with more disappointment.

Throughout the night, he'd searched for Emily while trying to call and text her. He drove past Seth and Andi's house, but when he didn't find her Jeep there, he kept going. He checked the park and their favorite restaurants, and he even went to the mini-golf course they loved when they were kids, but Emily was nowhere to be found.

After running out of places to visit, Jake finally retreated to his house after midnight, where he tossed and turned in bed. He'd slept in short spurts, during which he dreamed about finding Emily, explaining everything, and sealing his love for her with a kiss.

Every time he woke, he checked his phone, hoping he'd missed a call or text, but he hadn't heard a peep from her.

Jake was running out of options. All that was left to do was wait, but his worry was getting the best of him. He feared she'd been in an accident and was lying injured in a ditch or under an overpass.

Now your imagination is getting the best of you!

With a sigh, he wrenched open the door and hurried into the kitchen, where his mother was washing dishes. "Have you seen or heard from Emily?" he asked.

"She was here earlier." Mom swiveled to face him. "I told her that you were worried about her last night."

His pulse jumped, and he leaned on the back of a kitchen chair. "What'd she say?"

"She said she got in late and she had to run because she had a lot to do today."

"Like what?"

Mom shrugged. "I don't know, but I assumed it had to do with the orchard."

"Was she carrying her suitcase?"

"No, but she had that big bag she always uses for her art supplies."

Well, that seemed like a good sign. Maybe she was working in the orchard.

"Thanks." He turned to go.

"Hold on a minute. You're not leaving until you tell me what's going on." Mom tossed the dish towel on the counter and made a beeline toward him. She touched his arm. "Talk to me."

Jake rubbed his collarbone. It was time to tell her the truth, no matter how painful it might be for her. He took in a deep breath. "There isn't going to be a wedding. I never proposed to Claire."

"What are you talking about?"

"It's complicated, but Claire made it all up as a way to trap me into staying with her. I broke up with her more than a month ago, but she can't seem to accept it."

Mom's mouth opened and then closed, and he waited for her to burst into tears.

Instead, she just looked sad, but it tore him up just the same. "Why didn't you say something last night?"

"I tried to. But every time I attempted to talk, my words were cut off." He moved his fingers over the doorframe. "Plus, you seemed so excited, and you kept saying that this was what you and Dad needed. I didn't know how to tell you the whole thing was fake. Not right then."

He hesitated. "I'm sorry I didn't admit the truth last night, but I was overwhelmed. I was furious with Claire, and I was worried sick about Emily. She hurried out of there, and when I tried to stop her, Claire blocked me, and I didn't want to make a scene. I tried to call and text Emily all evening, but she never responded," he said. "And I wanted to wait until the right time to explain what was going on. Claire was determined to keep her lie going, and it ended up getting out of control. I figured it was best to tell you the truth in private and deal with her later."

Mom searched his eyes. "You should know that you can tell me anything," she said. "I mean that. Always."

He ran his hands down his face. He *needed* to tell her everything. His mom deserved the whole truth. "I've been seeing Emily. We've been keeping it private for now, but after what happened last night, I think I may have lost her."

"You and Emily?"

Mom cupped her hands to her mouth as he nodded.

"That's . . . Oh, I can't believe it. That's so sweet. You two grew up together." She clicked her tongue and smiled. "How romantic."

"I'm not sure how romantic it is when she won't return my calls or texts."

"She hasn't left town, and Splendid Lake is only so big. You'll find her." Mom touched his arm. "I've known that she was in love with you for a long time."

"You have?" He could hear the thread of hope in his voice.

"Yeah, it's obvious." She pointed toward the door. "Now, go find her and tell her how you feel."

"Thanks. I will." He hugged his mother while his chest swelled with hope. Then he rushed out the door and down the path toward the barn.

"Jake!" Vince sprinted over to him. "I've been looking all over for you. Have you seen the mural?"

"What mural?"

Vince pointed to the barn. "On the barn. You've got to see it. She's amazing."

"She?" Jake asked as he picked up the pace.

"Yeah, Emily. Who else?" Vince grinned.

Emily!

Jake took off running down the path and stopped short when he spotted Emily perched up on scaffolding.

His breath caught as he found the most magnificent mural he'd ever seen coming to life on the side of the barn facing the road.

The details weren't completely colored in, but he could tell it featured his family's orchard logo at the top. She'd sketched out the lake, the orchard, and the barn itself. Across the top stretched the words *100th Anniversary Celebration.* Then the bottom featured a message that read: *Serving the Community for 100 Years.*

It was Emily's masterpiece, and she was displaying it in Jake's orchard. She was finally sharing her talent, her gift, with the world. A mixture of pride, love, and appreciation roared through him.

Cupping his hands around his mouth he called, "Emily!"

She turned toward him, and her gray hoodie, jeans, shoes, and face were all dotted with paint. She had never looked more beautiful.

And at that moment he felt it again: He was madly in love with her. He yearned to fix things between them—*now*.

She studied him with an unreadable expression. "What?"

"We need to talk."

"I'm busy." She pointed toward the mural and then turned her attention back to her project.

Jake sighed and shook his head. She could be so stubborn sometimes!

"Seriously, we need to talk!" he called. He waited a few moments before he growled out an impatient noise. "Fine," he muttered. "If you won't talk to me, then I'll come up there and talk to you."

He climbed the scaffolding, but she only glanced at him before she continued painting details of the lake.

"Are you really going to ignore me while I'm standing right here?" he asked.

"I told you I'm busy." She swiped her hand over her temples and then continued.

He watched her work, taking in her pinched forehead and serious expression.

"The mural is fantastic. Your best work yet."

"Thanks," she muttered.

He waited for her to speak, but only silence stretched between them. When he turned toward the ground, he spotted a group of orchard employees watching them, along with some curious folks who had stopped along the side of the road. "You have an audience," he said, but she remained silent.

Emily Carmichael sure knew how to hold a grudge. It was up

to him to get her talking, and the only way to do that was for him to start.

"Did you get any of my messages?" he asked. "I must have left you at least two dozen last night."

"I got them." She dipped her brush in blue and applied it to the lake.

"And . . . ?"

She kept her back to him.

He was ready to yell his frustration. "*Please* talk to me, Em. I'm begging you." He folded his hands as if he were saying a prayer.

She spun to face him. "What's there to talk about?" she demanded. Her face was all business, but her hands were shaking.

He reached for her, and she took a step back from him. He pulled his arms back, not wanting her to lose her balance on the scaffolding. "I'm sorry about last night, but you should know I had nothing to do with it."

Her eyes narrowed.

"Seriously. I'm not marrying her."

"Could've fooled me," she muttered.

"What do you mean by that?"

She sighed. "I don't have time for this."

He groaned. "Look, I was just as blindsided as you were. I never proposed to Claire. That was all a setup. She's been determined to get me back ever since I told her we were done. Then she figured out that I was seeing you, and she was even more persistent. That's why she did it. I honestly had no idea why her parents invited us over."

She continued painting with her back to him.

"I don't love her."

She froze.

"Emily, I want *you*, not her. My greatest fear is losing you. I drove around for hours last night looking for you." His voice sounded thin and reedy. "I woke up at least once every hour during the night, hoping you'd called or texted me. I was so frantic. I worried that something had happened to you. You have to believe me."

Emily finally turned toward him, and her golden eyes locked on his. "Then why did you kiss her?"

His heart froze. "What are you talking about?"

She set down the paintbrush. "I saw you kiss her Wednesday night."

"When? Where?"

She pursed her lips and picked up the brush. "Forget it."

Placing his hands on her shoulders, he gently turned her toward him. "I can't stand this distance between us. What are you talking about?" And then his mind clicked into place. "You mean Wednesday night in the driveway."

She sniffed. "It doesn't matter." She spun back to the mural.

"No, it *does* matter. And I didn't kiss her. *She* kissed *me*, and I pushed her away. I told her it was over, and she said, 'That's what you think.' I didn't know what she meant, but that must've been when she cooked up her stupid idea to tell our parents we were engaged." He touched her shoulder. "You have to believe me. I'm telling you the truth."

She shook her head. "Look, forget it. We were kidding ourselves when we thought we could make this work. You clearly belong with Claire, and I'm okay with that." Her voice sounded thick.

"But I'm *not* okay with that, because I disagree." He touched her shoulder again. "Please look at me."

She turned, and they stared at each other. A heavy silence settled between them, but so much was left unsaid. Everything was falling apart before his eyes, and he needed to find a way to fix it.

He had to find the right words to get through to her. Why couldn't they communicate like they used to? How had things gotten so complicated so quickly?

"I wish you both all the happiness in the world." Her words faltered, and she swiped the back of her hand over her eyes.

He swallowed, and his eyes pricked with threatening tears. "I know you don't mean that. I can see it in your eyes and hear it in your voice. I don't want Claire. I don't want to date her or marry her. I never proposed to her. I'm telling you the truth."

She wiped away a few tears. "It doesn't make sense that Claire would cook up such an insane scheme. Why would her parents and your parents believe a lie like that? And who in their right mind would even try that? Why would she make that up? Was this just another one of the crazy pranks you all played in high school?"

"I don't know what that was. But I think she did it because she can't let me go." He took a shuddering breath. "She's maniacal enough to try that. You know she's pulled some crazy things over the years. Don't you remember when she told the entire junior class that her father was running for mayor, and it wasn't even true?"

She nodded. "Yeah."

"Claire craves attention. She's always wanted all eyes in the room to be focused on her. I don't even think she loved me. She only loves herself and the life she thinks she should have."

Silence stretched between them once again. For a moment, he thought he might've won her back, but then her brow puckered again.

"But you didn't deny it last night." She wiped away more tears.

"You didn't tell them that you wanted to be with me or that Claire was a liar. You went along with it."

"I was completely blindsided. I was so shocked by her announcement, and then her mom and my mom started to talk all at once, and I couldn't get a word in. And I'll admit it: I worried so much about hurting my mom in that moment. I didn't know how to make everyone happy. And goodness knows I didn't make *anyone* happy. Least of all you." He reached for her hand, but she pulled it out of his reach. "I tried to stop you from leaving, but you ran out the door so fast."

"Did you really expect me to sit there and listen to Claire discuss your wedding?" She shook her head. "She deliberately invited me to hurt me. You know that, right?"

He nodded. "Yeah, I do, and I'm sorry. If I had known what she was going to do, I would've stopped it." He searched her face, hoping to find the right words to convince her to forgive him. "I'm sorry for everything she did to hurt you, and I'm so sorry I didn't make it right in the moment. I've been sick over this. You can't give up on me. On us. We can make this work."

She swallowed, and her eyes filled with fresh tears. "No, Jake. I don't think we can."

Her words crushed him, and he tried to swallow against his dry throat. "Why not?"

"Because I'm not supposed to be your girlfriend or anything else. I'm your buddy, your friend, your *best man*." She gave him a sardonic smile, but he could see the pain in her eyes. "And that's okay. That's why we never dated."

"No, you're wrong. We never dated because I was too stupidly distracted by Claire to notice you had feelings for me. If I had been more observant, then we could've moved to the next level. But I can't do anything about the past. I'm here *now*, begging you to forgive me for not acting sooner. Let's give this another chance. Please."

She sniffed and his heart twisted.

"I've waited most of my life for you to choose me," she said. "You once asked me why none of my relationships worked out. The truth is that I measured every man I dated against you, and none of them lived up to the image I'd built of you in my head. None of them were kind enough, loyal enough, thoughtful enough, funny enough, or handsome enough. I held on to this childish dream that someday you'd realize I was the woman you needed in your life, and we'd date, and get married, and raise a family here in Splendid Lake."

"We can still do that." His voice sounded raspy. "Just give me a chance. Please."

She shook her head. "No. I've grown up, and I've accepted that you'll never choose me. That's why you wanted to date in secret. You were too embarrassed to be seen with me. You liked the idea of dating me. Of kissing me. But it was never real." She eyed him with suspicion. "Did you use me to make her jealous?"

"What? No!" Her words were like a knife to his soul. "No, that's not—"

"Just forget it. It doesn't matter anymore."

"It does to me." He tried to touch her, but she snatched her arm back as if he'd stung her.

"I'm going to finish helping you with the anniversary celebration and then I'm leaving. I'm going to go back to Charlotte to rebuild my life there. I don't belong here."

These were the words he'd dreaded the most. "No. Please don't leave. You broke my heart when you sold the house and left. Please don't leave again."

"*I* broke your heart?" She touched her chest. "Do you want to know why I left?"

He nodded.

"I left because *you* broke *my* heart." Her voice was laced with agony. "I realized it was time for me to wake up and face the truth—that you'd *never* choose me. The idea of staying here and watching you build a life with Claire was too painful. That's also why I didn't come for the holidays last year. Watching you and Claire flirt, hold hands, whisper to each other, and kiss was too much for me. And that's why I need to go. You and Claire will be happier without me."

"Em, you're not listening to me." His words were measured. "I'm begging you. Stay here with me. Let's build a life together—just you and me."

Tears streamed down her cheeks, and he longed to brush them away and then kiss her until she was breathless.

"I don't belong here," she whispered.

"Yes, you do. This is your home." He took a deep breath. "Don't leave me. Let's work this out."

"Jake! Hey, Jake!"

For goodness' sake, not now!

He turned just as Vince came to the bottom of the scaffolding, and the rest of their seasonal employees were gathered behind him.

Oh no.

Had everyone heard their conversation?

Great. Just great.

Vince held up his phone. "Smile."

"What?" Jake asked.

"Smile, Boss. I'm going to take a photo and share it on the orchard's social media pages." He waved his phone.

Jake turned to Emily, who watched him with a hesitant expression. "Should we pose together?"

"Um . . . I don't think so."

She wiped her eyes, then moved her fingers over her paintbrush. She slipped over to the other side of the mural before she peered down at Vince, a half smile on her lips.

Vince held up the phone and then dropped it into his pocket. "This is great. It's just what we need to get people out here." Then he rubbed his hands together. "We need to talk through the plan for the events."

"You'd better go," Emily said. "The big day is tomorrow, and Vince needs you."

He hesitated. His relationship with Emily was more important than the orchard or anything else. He wanted to fix this *now*.

"Go," she repeated, pointing to Vince.

"I'm going, but I'm not going to give up on this. On us." He pointed between them. "Will you talk to me later?"

She shrugged, as if a conversation about their future meant nothing to her, but her hands were still trembling.

He climbed down the scaffolding and approached Vince, but his mind and his heart were still focused on saving his relationship.

Chapter 24

THE MID-AFTERNOON SUN was warm on her back as Emily kept painting. The inspiration for the mural had hit her like a bolt of lightning last night while she sat on her childhood swing, and once she started sketching the piece, she couldn't stop. She'd finished the draft after midnight and then sneaked into Jake's folks' house to grab a few hours of sleep. She'd spent most of the night crying and replaying the horrible scene at Claire's parents' house, and she'd decided then that she would paint the mural and then leave for Charlotte to try to rebuild her shattered life without Jake.

She'd dragged herself out of bed at dawn, eaten a piece of toast, and then hurried out to the barn, where she'd managed to assemble the scaffolding they'd used to paint the barn and then climbed up and started drawing. She'd poured all of her heartache and grief into the mural, and she had to agree with Jake—it was the best piece she'd ever painted.

While she worked, she noticed a parade of visitors walk past the barn and also slow down on the street to watch her. Finally, the orchard was busy. She was thankful that Jake and his family were getting the traffic they'd hoped for.

Her throat thickened as her thoughts shifted to Jake and the heartfelt words he'd spoken to her earlier in the day. While she was starting to believe that Claire had set up the dinner both to hurt Emily and to somehow trap Jake into a life of wedded bliss (*What planet is she from?* Emily thought), she still couldn't understand why he hadn't immediately called out Claire for her lie. And why couldn't Jake stand up for Emily? Why was he so embarrassed to tell the world that they were together? How could Emily believe Jake might love her if he didn't have the courage to declare his feelings to his own parents?

All that made sense was that she still wasn't good enough for him, and that truth ripped her to shreds. Tears began to spring from her eyes for what felt like the millionth time that day.

Hold on, Em. Just a little bit longer. You're almost done.

"Excuse me!"

Emily kept painting and ignored the voice. Surely the person wasn't calling her.

"Um, hello up there! Are you Emily Carmichael?"

She stilled and then turned toward the ground, where a woman stood holding a fancy camera. "Yes?"

"I'm with the *Splendid Lake Times*, and I'd like to get a photo of you with the mural. Would you mind smiling for me?"

"Oh." Emily touched her hair, which she'd styled in a messy braid. "Why would you want to take my picture?"

The woman gestured around the orchard. "You haven't noticed? Your talent has drawn a huge crowd today. The mural went viral on social media, and now traffic's bumper-to-bumper out on the highway—people want to get a good look for themselves. I was just talking to the orchard owner, Jake Hughes, and he said the phone has been ringing off the hook all day long. A news station was pulling in when I got here. I think you're going to wind up on the news all over the state, if not around the nation."

"Really?" Emily asked, and her stomach pitched.

"Yeah, really." She grinned. "Now, would you mind smiling?"

Emily stood beside the mural and gave her cheesiest smile, and the camera clicked before the photographer gave her a thumbs-up.

"The mural is really fantastic. It shows what makes this community so special. Thank you for sharing your talent with the world," the photographer said before ambling down the path.

Emily stared after the woman.

Thank you for sharing your talent with the world.

The words played through Emily's mind on a loop as she recalled Jake begging her to open a gallery.

Maybe he was right. Maybe she should sell her paintings.

And maybe he really loves you, Emily, but you pushed him away before he got a chance to tell you.

She swallowed back a ball of grief rising in her throat.

She couldn't allow her emotions to derail her. She had a job to do, which was finishing the mural.

"Emily?"

She peeked down as a man she recognized from the evening news hurried toward the barn, with another man holding a camera following close behind.

Am I living in an alternate universe right now?

"Hi! I'm Chuck Miller from Channel Four News, and I heard about this incredible mural you've painted for the orchard's hundredth anniversary. It's the talk of the town. I'd like to get some shots for our evening broadcast. What do you say?"

"Uh. Sure?" Emily shrugged.

"Great. So tell me, how long have you been painting?"

She leaned on the scaffolding. "All my life."

"Are you a professional artist?" Chuck asked.

"I'd like to be."

The man pointed toward the mural. "From what I can see here, you certainly should be. What was your inspiration for this mural?"

"Well." Her hand flew to her mother's rings on her necklace, and she began moving the rings back and forth. "Honestly, my love of Splendid Lake and this orchard. It's my home." Her words quivered, and she cleared her throat.

"That's beautiful," he said. "Well, thank you for your time. You can go back to painting, and we're going to take some video. Just pretend we're not here."

Emily turned her focus back to the mural, and while she worked, she considered what she'd told the reporter.

Splendid Lake *was* her home. She loved the orchard, the lake, and Jake more than anything in the world. She knew to the depth of her bones that she wanted to make things work with Jake. But could she trust him?

All Emily knew for sure was that she'd be shattered if she had to leave him again. She just didn't know how to convince her heart and her head to let go of her doubts.

* * *

Jake rested his chin on his palm while he spoke to another reporter on the phone. He hadn't been able to leave his office in more than three hours. Thanks to Emily's mural, which had gone viral on social media after Vince had snapped a photo of it, the phone had been ringing off the hook. He'd heard from vendors who called begging to move their business to the orchard, reporters who wanted to interview him and Emily, and folks who wanted to double-check the times for the celebration tomorrow.

The anniversary celebration was going to be a success because of Emily.

Emily.

He needed to figure out how to win her back, but he didn't have a moment to think about it with the constant phone calls.

After answering the last round of questions, he hung up the phone and rubbed his eyes.

The phone rang again, and he growled. When was it going to end?

"Hughes Family Orchard, this is Jake," he said into the phone.

"I'm Melissa Gomez, and I'm calling from Mayor Fairmount's office."

Jake sat up straight. "How can I help you?"

"The mayor heard about a mural that one of your employees is painting, and he asked me to research what's going on there at your orchard. I checked out your website and Instagram page and saw that you're having a hundredth anniversary celebration tomorrow."

"That's—that's true."

"Well, you may already be aware that Mayor Fairmount likes to be involved in community events, and he wants to participate in your anniversary celebration. Would that be possible?"

Jake was speechless for a moment, and then he found his words. "That would be fantastic. I'm planning a ceremony." He pulled out the event schedule and ran through it with Melissa. "Would it work for the mayor to say a few words at the beginning?"

"Absolutely. Your orchard is important to our community, and he would love to be there to share how much it has meant to him and his family."

Jake shook his head. He had to be dreaming. "I can't tell you how much that means to *my* family and me."

"We'll see you tomorrow," Melissa said before she hung up.

Jake disconnected the call and stared at the phone. Jake had never imagined that the mayor of Splendid Lake would invite himself to the Hughes Family Orchard's anniversary celebration. He had to be dreaming!

A knock sounded on the office door. "Come in," he called.

"That mural," Mom gushed as she and Dad entered the office. "It's stupendous!"

Mom and Dad each sat on a chair in front of his desk.

"And the orchard is so busy," Dad added, shaking his head. "I haven't seen a crowd like this in years. The barn was packed with vendors and customers when we walked by too."

Jake reclined in the chair. "The phone hasn't stopped ringing all day. The mayor invited himself to participate in the ceremony tomorrow."

Mom and Dad shared surprised expressions.

Dad leaned over and tapped the desk. "Jake, you were right. This was a grand idea." He paused for a moment. "I'm sorry for not believing in you." He took a deep breath. "I was wrong. You've more than proven yourself during these past few months. And I never should have said that your ideas were harebrained. They're brilliant and innovative. And I'm grateful for everything you've done to keep our family's legacy alive. It's obvious that you're putting your heart and soul into this place. You deserve your chance to run things, and I'm ready to let go and let you."

Jake swore he could hear his dad's breath catch.

"So, please, son. Forgive me for the terrible things I've said. I'm truly proud of you."

Jake nodded, and his eyes felt wet.

Mom rubbed Dad's shoulder. "We're *both* so very proud of you."

Jake cleared his throat and tried to keep his emotions at bay. "Thanks."

"Did Emily tell you she was going to paint that mural?" Dad asked.

Jake shook his head and focused on Mom. "Did you tell Dad the truth?"

"About you and Claire?" she asked, and Jake nodded. "I did. He said he had a feeling it wasn't true."

Jake's gaze whipped to his father's. "You did?"

Dad gave him a knowing smile. "The shock was apparent on your face. I could tell you hadn't proposed." He paused for a moment. "Truth be told, I've always thought Claire was full of herself and you could do better."

Jake couldn't stop his laughter from bursting from his throat. "You were right."

His father eyed him. "I also got the feeling that something was going on between you and Emily."

"You could tell?" Jake asked.

"Yeah." He pointed toward the window. "She's one talented young lady, and she's smart too. And she has a good heart."

"Yeah, she does. You're not dreaming; there was something going on. But I messed it up."

Mom shook her head. "I doubt that. She's been devoted to you since you were kids. I doubt she'd give up on you so easily."

"But I didn't defend her last night." He sighed. "I shouldn't have stayed quiet while Claire was going on and on about our fake engagement. I just . . . I knew how much you guys wanted a wedding, and I didn't want to hurt you. I had no idea what to say in that moment. But my inaction . . . I think that's what hurt Emily the most."

Jake turned toward the window and spotted the barn in the distance. An idea overtook his mind, and he steepled his fingers.

He was going to find a way to get Emily to talk to him, but first he needed to take care of another issue.

Claire.

* * *

Later that evening Jake pushed open the door at the Coffee Bean and breathed in the aroma of freshly roasted coffee and buttery pastries. He nodded at familiar faces on his way to a booth in the back corner. He adjusted his ball cap on his head and glanced down at his phone. He'd been grateful when Claire agreed to meet with him, and his plan was to keep this conversation short and sweet. He'd make his point and then get out of there as fast as possible.

Jake had attempted again to talk to Emily, but by the time he'd made it to the barn, she was gone. The mural was done—and it was breathtaking—but she was nowhere to be found. He'd tried again to call and text her, but both had gone unanswered. He hoped that his plan for tomorrow would come together and they could put this awful fight in the books before they moved toward a future together.

He checked his phone for the hundredth time today to see if Emily had responded to his messages. Finding no response, he sighed and glanced toward the front of the coffee shop just as Claire pushed through the doors. She caught his eye and waved before strutting toward the booth.

When she reached the table, she gave him a confused expression. "You're in a coffee shop, but you're not drinking coffee."

"I'm not planning to stay long."

She pointed toward the counter. "What would you like?"

"Nothing."

She harrumphed. "Then what's the point of meeting at the Coffee Bean?"

"Just sit down so we can get this over with," he seethed, working to keep his flaring temper in check.

She studied him and then did as she was told. "Okay. Go ahead and get it over with." Her tone mocked him, but he ignored it. She folded her hands on the table and sat up straight. "I'm ready."

"Good." He paused for a moment. "I'm not sure what you were trying to prove by staging a fake engagement party last night. Maybe it was your idea of the ultimate prank, but you're not going to get away with it. I told my parents the truth, and now it's time for you to tell your parents. We're not engaged, Claire. I'm not going to marry you. I'm not going to get back together with you. It's over. You need to accept it because that is never going to change."

She stared at him for a moment, and her expression remained blank. "Your mother was so excited last night that she was in tears. I guess you told her and broke her heart?"

"Actually, she understood completely. I should've done it last night. That's on me." He leaned forward and tapped his finger on the table. "Now, I need you to listen to me. I'm done. Don't call me. Don't text me. Pretend I don't exist, because I'm over you and I've already blocked your number. So move on. I sure have."

"With Emily?" She scrunched her nose as if she smelled something foul.

"Yes." He leveled his gaze with hers. "Yes, with Emily. I'm crazy about her, and you're not going to change that."

She snorted.

"I really don't care what you think." Jake pushed himself out of the booth. "Have a nice life." And as he walked toward the exit, he felt as if a thousand-pound boulder had been lifted off his shoulders.

Now he just needed to convince Emily that he was ready to begin forever with her.

* * *

Emily sat across from Andi at the Splendid Kitchen and pushed a piece of meatloaf around on her plate. She'd managed to avoid Jake the remainder of the day and then texted Andi to ask if she could meet for supper. Emily shared the events that had happened at Claire's house and then told Andi about the mural before their server brought their meal.

"Wow," Andi said. "I never liked Claire that much, but I didn't imagine she would ever stoop so low as to throw herself a fake engagement party."

Emily sagged in the booth. "Yeah. Jake begged me to take him back this morning, but I was so hurt and angry that I couldn't do it."

"I believe that Claire arranged it all. I don't think Jake would use you like that."

"I know." She sighed and summarized what he'd said to her. "I think he meant it."

Andi reached across the table and touched her hand. "I do too. I truly believe that you two are meant to be together. If he was begging you to talk to him, then he really cares. Jake's a genuine guy. He's one of the few good ones."

"Emily Carmichael?"

She turned as a middle-aged man stopped by the table. "Yes?"

"I'm sorry to interrupt, but I drove by the Hughes Family

Orchard today and checked out your mural. It's really a sight to see," he exclaimed. "I'm going to take my family to the anniversary celebration tomorrow, and I told my neighbors about it. You're really, really talented."

Emily was stunned silent for a moment. "Thanks," she managed to say.

"I only speak the truth." The man nodded at Andi. "Enjoy your meal."

Emily stared after him.

"That was incredible!" Andi said. "Seth drove by the mural today, and he told me about it. I can't wait to see it tomorrow. He said the orchard was crazy busy because of it, that all kinds of people wanted to get their photo in front of it. You're a viral artist now." Her smile dissolved. "Are you okay?" She touched Emily's hand.

"I feel like I'm at this crossroads. I can try to work things out with Jake or go back to Charlotte. And I don't know what to do."

"What's your heart telling you to do?"

Emily met Andi's sympathetic gaze. "Give Jake a chance."

"Then that's your answer."

Emily nodded. She agreed with her friend. She just had to find the right time to talk to him.

* * *

Emily steered her Jeep toward Jake's house. She parked in his empty driveway and spotted Dusty sleeping in his front window. She drummed her fingers on the steering wheel and then pulled out her cell phone. She'd listened to all of Jake's voicemail messages and read all of the texts he'd sent, and they basically said the same thing. They begged her to forgive him and talk to him.

Guilt weighed heavily on her shoulders as she recalled the pain in his voice. She should've talked to him earlier in the day, but she was still working through her own heartache. Now she was finally ready to talk, but he wasn't home.

Maybe it serves me right.

Turning toward the orchard and the barn, she smiled as her heart began to put itself back together. "This is home. Jake is home. I can't let go. I love him too much."

At that moment Emily knew she was going to fight for him, no matter what it took.

She unlocked her phone and then stilled. This wasn't a conversation she should have on the phone. Instead, she wanted to talk to him in person.

Jake was hers, and she was going to tell him tomorrow. She stuck her phone in her pocket and then drove toward his parents' house as a plan came together in her mind.

Chapter 25

YOU'RE NOT GOING to believe this." Maddy, one of Jake's employees, hurried over to him the following morning. "We're out of candied apples *and* your cider."

Jake glanced around the orchard and shook his head. The place was buzzing with people. They were moving in and out of the barn and lining up to buy bushel baskets of apples. This kind of crowd was more than he could've dreamed of—because of Emily's genius and talent. His heart turned over in his chest.

He'd missed Emily at his parents' house again this morning, but his mom said she'd left smiling, which was a good sign—he hoped. She'd told his mom that she'd see her later, which was another good sign that she wasn't leaving town today.

"Jake."

He turned as Vince approached him.

"The mayor is here," Vince said. "It's almost time to start."

"Right." Jake wrung his hands and scanned the area. "Have you seen Emily today?"

Vince shook his head. "Not since early this morning."

Andi and Seth emerged from the barn, and Jake rushed over to them. "Have you seen Emily?"

A strange expression flickered over Andi's face. "I know where she is."

"Where?" Jake asked.

Andi and Seth shared a look before she faced Jake again. "Don't worry. I'll get her."

Jake pointed to the stage, where Carolina Dreamin' had just wrapped up their first set of the day. "I need her here before the presentation starts. I have a surprise for her, but please don't tell her," he said. "Can you get her?"

"No problem," Andi said before she headed toward the orchard.

Seth patted Jake's shoulder. "Don't worry. My wife will handle it."

Jake hoped so as he headed toward the mayor. "Mayor Fairmount," he called. "Good morning."

* * *

A rustling noise sounded from the nearby bushes.

"Em!" Andi called. "It's almost time for the presentation."

Emily checked the time on her phone and gasped. "Oh no. I didn't realize how late it was." She stood up from behind the easel and checked the drawing. It wasn't done. "I need to finish this. I'll be there in a little while."

"No," Andi insisted. "I need you to come *now*." She hurried down the dock toward her.

Emily studied her friend. "Why?"

Andi huffed at her. "Just come, okay?" she said.

Emily studied her drawing. She'd wanted to paint it, but she'd run out of time. She had to settle for a drawing, but if Jake liked it, and she hoped he did, then she'd paint another version of it later. She moved her fingers over the edges, and her pulse skipped while she imagined presenting it to him and telling him that she loved him. Saying those words out loud after all these years would be—

"Hey!" Andi touched her arm. "Get out of your head and come with me."

"What's the rush?"

"We gotta go. Jake's looking for you." She groaned. "Please don't ask me any more questions, okay?"

Was Jake planning something for her just like she was planning something for him?

She looked at the drawing again. Well, she'd done all that she could. She'd have to finish it after she gave it to Jake. She set it in a box and then tied it with twine.

She thought her heart might beat out of her chest as she picked up the box. Everything needed to be perfect. "Do I look okay?"

Andi smiled. "You look beautiful." She touched Emily's French braid and glanced down at her colorful dress. "I love that dress—especially with the high-tops."

"You know I love my Converse."

Andi grabbed her hand and tugged her. "Come on."

Emily followed Andi off the dock, down the path, and into the grove of trees. The voices of customers milling around the orchard drifted over her. When they reached the barn, she found a knot of people gathered around it, and she smiled. She was so grateful that the anniversary celebration had attracted the crowd that Jake and his parents had hoped for.

Jake stood on the stage with his parents and the mayor. Emily's gaze roved over Jake. He had never looked more handsome. His chiseled jaw was clean-shaven, and he wore a pair of khaki trousers, a blue-and-gray-plaid shirt, and black shoes. His signature ball cap was missing, and his sandy-blond hair was wavy and perfectly styled. His blue eyes scanned the audience, and she wondered if they were searching for her.

Mayor Fairmount, a middle-aged man with gray hair, dark eyes, and thick horn-rimmed glasses, approached the podium. "Good morning. I'm George Fairmount, the mayor of Splendid Lake, and I'm honored to be part of this special celebration. Some of my favorite childhood memories are of coming to the Hughes Family Orchard in the fall with my parents and siblings to buy apples. This orchard has been a part of our town's history for a century now, and I'm so grateful that the Hughes family has kept this tradition alive."

He lifted a framed document and slipped reading glasses on his nose. "In honor of the orchard's one hundredth anniversary, I'd like to declare today Hughes Day." He turned toward Jake and his family. "I'd like the Hughes family to come here and accept this."

The audience clapped as the mayor handed the declaration to Leon. A few hoots and whistles sounded.

Leon and Diane made their way to the microphone, and the mayor took a seat on one of the chairs on the stage.

Leon cleared his throat. "Thank you, Mayor. It's an honor to share this stage with you. I'm Leon Hughes. My grandfather started this orchard many, many years ago. Well. . . I guess it was a hundred years ago," he said. "When I was a boy, I never imagined I'd be standing on this stage celebrating a hundred years of the orchard, but here we are." He paused. "This orchard is more than a place; it's my home, my heart. It's where I grew up, where I brought my beautiful bride." He glanced over at Diane. "And where we raised our two children." He smiled at Jake, and Emily's heart swelled.

Then he returned his focus to the crowd. "I've seen many ups and downs here. We've had good years and bad years with the crop, but one thing has always been constant, and that's my love for this orchard." He cleared his throat. "This year, my son insisted we make some changes and modernize things. I was against it. I was focused on tradition, but my son made me realize that you can honor tradition while also changing with the times and with the community, and he was right. I'm proud of this orchard and all of the changes." He looked at Jake again. "And I'm so proud of you, son. Thank you for loving the orchard as much as I do. I know I'm leaving it in good hands."

Jake nodded and mouthed, "Thank you" to his father, and Emily wiped her eyes.

Leon glanced around at the audience. "Thank you all for coming today. This orchard has been my family's legacy, and it means the world to us that you all continue to come here and allow us to share our home with you. We hope you enjoy your time here today and that you'll come back again. It's our honor to grow apples for our friends and neighbors. We hope we can do it for many years to come."

The crowd clapped enthusiastically, and then Leon made a sweeping gesture toward Jake. "Now here's my son," he said before he and Diane sat down in the chairs lining the stage.

Jake crossed to the podium, pulled a piece of paper from his pocket, unfolded it, and smoothed it out.

"Good morning," he said. "I'm Jake Hughes. My dad and I have managed the orchard together for years, but this year he wanted me to take over. When I said I wanted to plan a celebration, Dad wasn't too keen on it. You know how it can be between fathers and sons." He grinned over at his father, and a ripple of laughter spread across the audience. "I wanted to do something special, so I knew I needed someone to help me. And that's why I called my best friend. Well, I texted her, and I begged her to come home."

He paused and rubbed his chin. "This celebration never would've happened without her help, and she's really special to me." His eyes once again raked over the crowd, and when they found Emily, a small smile lifted the corners of his lips, and his stiff posture relaxed.

She took in his gorgeous face, and a thousand butterflies fluttered in her chest.

"I'm thankful she's here today." He took a deep breath. "She not only came up with the idea of turning the old barn into a market, but she also painted that incredible mural." He pointed to the barn behind him. "She's the reason why you're all here today, and she's the reason why I'm the man I am today."

Jake's bright blue eyes focused on her. "Emily, you came into my life like a whirlwind when we were only five years old. You showed up in my orchard, introduced yourself, and informed me that I was going to be your best friend whether I liked it or not." A grin overtook his handsome face as more laughter drifted over the audience. "Truer words have never been spoken. Get up here, because I have something I need to say to you, and I want this crowd to be my witnesses."

Emily hesitated and scanned the enormous crowd. Was Jake crazy? He expected her to walk up onto that stage in front of all of those people?

"Emily," Jake said. "Come on."

She shook her head.

"Oh, *now* you're shy?" He chuckled and then addressed the crowd. "Everyone, give it up for Emily Carmichael. Show her how much you appreciate that mural."

Claps, hoots, and whistles erupted, and Emily was certain her face would spontaneously combust.

"Go on." Andi gave her a gentle nudge. "Get up there."

Emily spun toward her. "You knew about this?"

Andi rolled her eyes. "Stop being so stubborn and get your rear end up there."

Emily headed toward the stairs, and the clapping increased.

Jake held his hand out to her and guided her up the stairs, and she set the box down on an empty chair. Then he continued over to the podium, where he cleared his throat, and the clapping subsided. "Emily Carmichael, you're my best friend. You're the one who has always believed in me and encouraged me to follow my dreams. You never tried to change me or make me into someone I wasn't."

She didn't care a whit for the goofy grin spreading across her face. *Is this real life?*

"I didn't realize until recently that you stole my heart years ago," he continued, taking her hand in his. "You're not my buddy or my pal. You're my heart. I'm sorry for not realizing sooner how much I need you. And I'm sorry for not telling you how much you mean to me." His voice sounded thin. "The truth is that I love you. And I choose *you* and only you. Tell me that you'll give us a chance."

The crowd began to cheer.

One woman yelled, "Tell him yes, Emily! He's super-hot!"

Another called, "Kiss him!"

"If you don't kiss him, honey, I will!" another woman bellowed, and laughter circulated throughout the crowd.

Jake's face pleaded with her. "What do you say? Will you give me another chance?"

She nodded as the tears welling in her eyes broke free, and he brushed them away with a featherlike touch that left shivers in its wake. She stared up at him as her heart cracked open. "I've loved you since I was five years old. How could I ever give up on you?"

"I'm so grateful to hear you say that," he whispered, and his blue eyes sparkled.

"I'm sorry I shut down on you."

He shook his head. "No, I'm sorry for everything. Let's start over, okay?"

"Absolutely." She took his hand in hers, and he leaned down and kissed her. She enjoyed the feel of his lips, even as she was aware of the crowd watching and cheering for them.

When he pulled away, Emily's cheeks flamed as Jake waved to the crowd.

"Thank you all for coming today. Please enjoy the orchard," he said before wrapping his arm around her waist and kissing her head. "Let's go somewhere and talk."

"In private?" she asked.

He chuckled. "Yeah, in private." He tilted her chin up and kissed her again. "I love you."

Emily grinned. "I love you too."

She picked up the box, then waved to his parents and the mayor before they hurried off to his office, where he closed the door, shutting out the audience.

He sat on the edge of the desk, took her hands, and pulled him toward her. "Listen, I'm so sorry about Claire and everything."

"Shh." She placed her finger on his lips, and he kissed it. "Let me talk, okay?"

He pushed his hair back from his forehead. "Okay."

She handed him the box. "I drew this for you. I wanted to paint it, but I ran out of time."

He untied the string, opened the box, and gasped. "Em, this . . . this is unreal." He lifted the drawing of their fort overlooking the lake at sunset. Two small silhouettes sat in the fort, and the sky was a kaleidoscope of penciled-in pinks, oranges, purples, reds, and yellows of the sunset stretched across the sky and reflected in the lake.

While he studied the picture, she memorized the handsome face of the man she wanted by her side for the rest of her life.

"I . . . I don't know what to say," he whispered, searching her eyes.

"That's where our friendship began," she said. "It's where I fell for you."

"I love this. And I love you. I have for a while, but I was too afraid of losing your friendship to admit it to myself." He paused. "The truth is that I can't just be your friend. I want to be your everything. And I want you by my side forever."

"I was just thinking the same thing." She took a shuddering breath. "When I left Claire's Thursday night, I drove around and wound up by my old house."

"You did?" His eyes widened.

"Yeah. I stood in the driveway and just allowed my grief to consume me. Then I went to your folks' house to pick up the box I found in the basement, and I drove out to the other side of the orchard. I walked to my old backyard, and I sat on the swing for a while."

She took a deep breath before she continued. "When I opened the box, I found a card from my dad, and he'd written a note saying he and my mom would be happy if I followed my heart to a profession that brought me joy." Tears tracked down her cheeks. "I realized that my parents were proud of me even though I wanted to be a professional artist."

"Of course they were, babe." He set the drawing on his desk before wiping away her tears. "And I've always been proud of you too."

She smiled softly. "After reading the card, I just let all of the grief pour out of me. I stopped fighting it. I mourned them, and I mourned losing you."

He shook his head. "You never lost me."

"Let me finish," she insisted. "And that was when my muse came back to life, and I started sketching the mural. It was like something released deep inside of me, and I was able to create again. I hardly slept. I was up at dawn, and I started on the mural, pouring all of my grief into it."

She threaded her fingers with his. "I'm sorry I pushed you away. I did exactly what you told me not to—I let Claire get in my head and mess with my confidence. I was so insecure that I started to believe that Claire deserved you because she's prettier, more sophisticated, and more deserving than I am."

He shook his head and touched her cheek. "You got that backward."

She smiled. "And then last night I realized that I had to fight for you. You've had my heart for most of my life, and I couldn't allow Claire to take you away from me."

"She never stole me away. I'm just so sorry it took me almost twenty-five years to realize that my soulmate was beside me the whole time."

She grinned up at him. "But now that I've got you, I'm not going to let you go."

"Promise?"

"Oh yeah, I promise."

"Good." His grin was wolfish as he pulled a candied apple out from behind his desk. "I saved one before they sold out." He held it up. "How about a candy apple kiss?"

Her smile widened. "That's the best kind."

He took a bite of the apple and swallowed it. Then Jake's eyes seemed to smolder, and he tilted forward and touched her cheek before he brushed his lips over hers.

Heat roared through her veins as she lost herself in the feel of his lips caressing hers. She wrapped her arms around his neck and pulled him close. And as Jake's lips parted to deepen the kiss, she lost track of everything. Her fingers moved up and up on his neck until she was running her fingertips through his soft hair.

When he broke the kiss, she held on to his broad shoulders, working to slow her heartbeat to a normal rate.

"I love you," he whispered.

She smiled as her heart danced. "I love you too."

As Jake leaned down to kiss her again, Emily closed her eyes and imagined her future side by side with the love of her life.

Epilogue

Thanksgiving

EMILY GRINNED WHILE Ally shared a story about school, and as she glanced around the table in the Hughes family's dining room, her heart felt full. She loved dinners with the Hughes family, but today was even more special. It was Thanksgiving, and Ally had brought her boyfriend, Ryan, home with her for the long weekend. They'd stuffed themselves nearly as full as the Thanksgiving turkey had been, feeling deliciously sated after their dessert of pumpkin and apple pies.

A hand brushed her thigh, and she turned to Jake beside her. He was handsome, dressed in a pair of khakis and a blue button-down that complemented his gorgeous eyes. He'd shaved, and his wavy blond hair was brushed back. When he took her hand in his, lifted it, and kissed it, her heart sang.

The past two months had seemed to fly by at lightning speed. After the anniversary celebration, the orchard had stayed busy for the remainder of the season. They'd not only sold out of their full crop of apples, but the vendors who had participated had asked if they'd consider hosting a Christmas market. Jake and Emily agreed, and they were going to open tomorrow for Black Friday.

Emily had found a house to rent in Splendid Lake, just until she found a home where she'd want to put down roots, and she had opened her gallery in town last month. So far she'd sold six pieces, and she was painting more to add to the collection. She was also setting up a space in her gallery to feature works by local artists. She hoped to have that collection ready for sale before Christmas.

She split her time working in the gallery and at the orchard, and she'd been brainstorming new ideas for both. She was grateful that Jake had finally agreed to allow her to invest her money in the orchard. In the spring they planned to add a playground, as well as expand the market by adding more buildings and areas for local vendors to set up their wares. They were already scheduling hayrides and a corn maze next fall. She was so excited to open the orchard for more months out of the year, with activities for families to enjoy in the spring and summer as well.

"This pie was fantastic," Leon said. "Both pies."

Diane smiled at her husband. Leon's health had improved tremendously during the past couple of months. He'd gone from taking short strolls around the orchard to walking more than an hour along the lakeshore. He also frequently complimented Jake for his work on the orchard, which was a relief to both Jake and Emily.

Ally popped up from the table. "Ryan and I will take care of the dishes."

"We will?" Ryan teased her, and she playfully smacked his arm.

"They remind me of us," Jake whispered in Emily's ear, and a tingle danced down her spine.

"I agree," she said.

Jake took her hand. "Let's go for a walk."

"Now?"

"Yeah, now, Carmichael. Let's go."

They pulled on their jackets and ambled out into the orchard. The late-November air was crisp, and they could see their breath.

"I think I smell snow," Jake said, taking her hand in his.

She grinned. "Let's hope so."

He steered her down the path toward their fort.

"Are we going to sit in the fort and freeze?" she asked.

"Not exactly." He guided her to their special tree, then stopped and took a deep breath. A strange expression flashed over his features.

"You okay?" she asked.

"Yeah. Just hold on." He pulled a small cordless speaker from his pocket, hit the button to turn it on, and set it on the ground. Then he fished his phone out of his other pocket and began pushing buttons.

"What are you doing?" she asked.

"I'll never forget the day I met you." Jake turned toward her family's home. "You came running down that path, found me, and said, 'Hi. I'm Emily Carmichael. I just moved here from Raleigh, and you're going to be my best friend.'"

She laughed. "I remember that." She pointed to the lake. "I'd seen you and your dad out by the water, and I told my mom I wanted you to be my friend. So I came over and told you as much."

"That conversation was burned into my memory because you were right. You became my best friend and then you became so much more." He paused and licked his lips. "You told me about a song that reminds you of us. I listened to it the other day and found the lyrics online, and you're right. It's perfect for us and our story."

She shook her head. "Which song?"

He hit a button on his phone and the opening chords of Vanessa Williams's "Save the Best for Last" began to play through the speaker.

Emily cupped her hand to her mouth.

Jake put the phone on top of the speaker and held his hands out to her. "Will you dance with me?"

She beamed. "I'd be honored."

Emily wound her arms around his neck as he pulled her close and rested his hands on the small of her back. She closed her eyes and concentrated on the words, and she softly sang along. As they swayed with the music, she felt as if all her dreams had come true. She and Jake were dancing to her favorite song!

"You're right," he whispered into her ear.

"About what?"

"This should be our wedding song."

She stilled. Had she heard him right? Did he mention a *wedding*?

"Did you hear me?" he asked.

She nodded, unable to speak.

He stopped moving, and his eyes focused on her. "You said you always imagined this would be our wedding song. I think it would be perfect."

Her heart began to pound. "Jake, what . . . what are you saying?"

"I'm saying that I regret that it took me twenty-five years to figure out that the love of my life has been by my side this entire time." He paused and swallowed as his expression became more intense than she'd ever seen. "I love you, and I want to spend the rest of my life with you." He reached into the pocket of his khakis and pulled out a jewelry box.

She stilled and was certain she was dreaming. *This can't be real.*

"Emily Grace Carmichael, will you marry me?" he asked, his words soft and unsure. He opened the box, revealing a sparkling solitaire diamond resting in a white gold setting filled with smaller diamonds.

She stared at the ring, and tears stung her eyes.

She wasn't dreaming. No, her dreams had come true!

"Yes, yes, I will!" she exclaimed before pulling him toward her, wrapping her arms around him and kissing him. "Let's get married here at the orchard since it's where our friendship began."

"I love that idea. And I love you." Jake slipped the ring onto her finger, and it was the perfect fit. Then he kissed her again.

Emily closed her eyes and cherished the feeling of her fiancé's lips against hers. Jake had been her best friend, her boyfriend, and now her fiancé. She couldn't wait for him to become her husband.

They certainly had saved the best for last.

Discussion Questions

1. At the beginning of the novel, Jake is focused on running the orchard and isn't even thinking about dating. What do you think causes Jake to change his opinion about finding love throughout the story?

2. Emily is heartbroken when Claire announces her engagement to Jake. She believes that Jake used her to make Claire jealous. Have you ever been hurt by someone close to you? If so, how did you cope?

3. By the end of the story, Emily finally believes she's good enough for Jake and their friendship can actually become a romance that will stand the test of time. What do you think causes that change?

4. Although Jake has made it clear to Claire that their relationship is over and it's time to move on, Claire refuses to give up on him. She frequently shows up at his parents' house and then she throws a fake engagement party for her and Jake. She not only hurts Jake, but she also breaks Emily's heart. Do you think Claire has a right to be forgiven by Jake? Also, what would you do if you were in Jake's shoes?

5. Emily lost her parents in a plane crash and still struggles with grief after four years. Have you ever lost a beloved family member? If so, how did you cope?

6. Emily loves to draw and paint, and making art has been her favorite hobby since she was a child. She dreams of someday becoming a professional artist. Do you have a favorite hobby or pastime that you've enjoyed since you were a child? If so, what is it, and why is it special to you?

7. Leon, Jake's father, struggles with Jake's plans to modernize the orchard and change some of his family's traditions. He believes that his father and grandfather would want the orchard to remain the way that it has always been. Do you have any family traditions that you've kept alive in memory of your relatives? If so, what are they, and why are they important to you?

8. What has Jake learned about himself by the end of the novel? How does that influence his thoughts about a future with Emily?

9. By the end of the story, Emily decides to stay in Splendid Lake and build a life there with Jake. Have you ever experienced an overwhelming change in your life? If so, how did you adapt to that change?

10. Have you ever visited a small mountain town like Splendid Lake? If you could go anywhere for vacation this weekend, where would you choose to go?

Acknowledgments

AS ALWAYS, I'M thankful for my loving family, including my mother, Lola Goebelbecker; my husband, Joe; my sons, Zac and Matt; my lovely daughter-in-law; and our five spoiled indoor cats and two outdoor cats. I'm blessed to have such an awesome, amazing, supportive, and purring family.

I'm so grateful to my wonderful church family at Morning Star Lutheran in Matthews, North Carolina, for your encouragement, prayers, love, and friendship. You all mean so much to my family and me.

Thank you, Zac Weikal, for your help with my social media plans, my website, my online bookstore, and all of the other amazing things you do to help with marketing. I would be lost without you!

To my agent, Natasha Kern—I can't thank you enough for your guidance, advice, and friendship. You are a tremendous blessing in my life. I hope you enjoy your retirement with your family—especially your precious grandsons.

I would also like to thank my new literary agent, Nalini Akolekar, for her guidance and advice. Nalini, I look forward to working with you on future projects.

Thank you to my wonderful editor, Laura Wheeler, for your friendship. I appreciate how you've pushed me and inspired me to dig deeper to improve both my writing and this book. I'm a better writer because of you.

I'm grateful to editor Amy Kerr, who helped me polish and refine the story. Amy, you are a master at connecting the dots and filling in the gaps. I'm so thankful that we could work together on this book.

I'm grateful to every person at HarperCollins Christian Publishing who helped make this book a reality.

To my readers—thank you for choosing my novels. My books are a blessing in my life for many reasons, including the special friendships I've formed with my readers. Thank you for your emails and social media messages and letters.

Thank you most of all to God—for giving me the inspiration and the words to glorify You. I'm grateful and humbled You've chosen this path for me.

About the Author

Dan Davis Photography

AMY CLIPSTON is an award-winning bestselling author and has been writing for as long as she can remember. She's sold more than one million books, and her fiction writing "career" began in elementary school when she and a close friend wrote and shared silly stories. She has a degree in communications from Virginia Wesleyan University and is a member of the Authors Guild, American Christian Fiction Writers, and Romance Writers of America. Amy works full-time for the City of Charlotte, North Carolina, and lives in North Carolina with her husband, two sons, mother, and seven spoiled rotten cats.

* * *

Visit her online at AmyClipston.com
Facebook: @AmyClipstonBooks
Instagram: @amy_clipston
BookBub: @AmyClipston
TikTok: @amyclipstonofficial